Lord Phillip's Folly

Susan M. Baganz

Publishing History
White Rose Edition, 2017
Electronic Edition ISBN 978-1-5223-9767-0
Paperback Edition ISBN 978-15223-9769-4
Published in the United States of America

Dedication

To Elizabeth Grace Herman
You were the first person to ever read and edit my
novels and encourage me on my writing path.
Thank you for all the ways you've invested in me.

BOOKS BY SUSAN M. BAGANZ

Black Diamond Regency Romantic Suspense
The Baron's Blunder (Prequel) novella
The Virtuous Viscount (Book 1)
Lord Phillip's Folly (Book 2)
Sir Michael's Mayhem (coming soon)
Lord Harrow's Heart (coming soon)
The Captain's Conquest (coming soon)

Orchard Hill Contemporary Romances
Pesto & Potholes
Salsa & Speed Bumps
Feta & Freeways
Root Beer & Roadblocks
Bratwurst & Bridges…
and others coming soon!

Historical Christmas Novella
Fragile Blessings
Gabriel's Gift

Short Story Compilation
Little Bits O' Love

Author's Note

During the tempestuous years between 1800-1820, or the more specific "Regency" years of 1811 to 1820, it was common for the upper classes, especially the men, to drink various forms of alcohol as part of their daily life. The men often savored a glass of port wine after the evening meal. French brandy was considered superior and highly coveted even though England was at war with France. In these stories, my characters do at times drink, and sometimes even to excess with serious consequences for their overindulgence. This is not in any way a recommendation on the part of the author or Pelican Book Group to advocate the drinking of alcohol or to abuse any substance. Laudanum is actually an opiate that was often prescribed medicinally (although many did become addicted to the drug). The use of these in the story are merely an attempt to use this period in history and its notorious excesses as a backdrop where appropriate.

Lord, protect me from foolish men.
The Honorable Elizabeth Follett

<u>Folly</u>:
Greek αʹρέτη anoia an'-oy-ah
Stupidity; by implication rage
- folly, madness.
(Strong's Exhaustive Concordance)

But they shall proceed no further:
for their folly shall be manifest unto all men,
as theirs also was.
1 Peter 1:5 *(KJV)*

Prologue

London

Across the misty sky flew a dark figure with wings flapping silently amidst the noise of the city of London where the elite of the *ton* prepared for this night's entertainments. As the black bird swooped and dipped amongst the chimneys, he found what he searched for. Make that "whom" he searched for. He spied her on the balcony gazing up at the sky awaiting him. He dove from his height only spreading his wings within a few feet to slow descent and land lightly on her outstretched arm.

"Duke," the young woman whispered. "You're back. I've been waiting for you."

His head bobbed but he refrained from speaking. His mistress frowned. He longed to see her smile. He tilted his head to the right, straightened it, and reached his neck forward to put his long dark beak to her cheek and rub gently.

Tears dangled at the edge of her eyelashes. "Tonight is the night, Duke. I cannot go through with what Papa plans. I must escape. All these years... I cannot endure any longer."

Duke was silent, listening. He bobbed his head.

She continued. "Lord Wolton has to be sixty, if not older and has the most nauseating odor. He is creepy and I'm certain he has some evil hold over Papa. But I cannot. I will not allow myself to pay the price for Papa's salvation. He's acted foolishly, and I love him, but I won't..." She glanced up at the sky. "Why would God allow this to happen?" She shivered, although the mid-April evening was warm. "Why couldn't I simply be loved for who I am? Why all this unrelenting... evil?"

Duke ruffled his feathers and shook them, once again rubbing his beak against her cheek.

"Watch over me tonight. I've no clue how I'll escape, but I don't want to lose you when I do. Wait outside in the garden and follow wherever I go. Can you do that, sweetheart?" Her intense golden-green eyes gazed into his.

"I love you," Duke squawked, nodding and making a kissing sound. He'd do anything for her.

"I love you too, Duke. What would I have done this past year without you?"

Movement from the dressing room alerted him to danger. Duke flapped his wings and took off, circling twice above her before settling on a nearby tree. She blew him a kiss.

He bobbed his head in acknowledgment as she turned to step back off the narrow balcony and close the doors to the bedroom behind her.

He would protect his mistress.

1

Spring 1810
Manchester

Despicable town. Infuriating family. Frustrating obligations. In spite of all that Lord Phillip Westcombe had returned to London. He enjoyed hibernating in the North Country the past few months. Peace and solitude had become a comfortable companion since his friend, Lord Marcus Remington, married Miss Josephine Storm at Christmas. Their happiness was something he did not begrudge them, but he found it difficult to be around. It pointed to a gaping hole in his own heart.

Instead, he spent the time studiously applying himself to his estate, and enjoyed managing the property. He was happy for Marcus and Josie, but the process of falling in love tended to be messy and complicated if their path to the altar was any indication. He did not want that in his life.

Yet here he was, back in London for the season.

If it hadn't been for his mother's pleas, his father's command, and his little sister's enthusiastic encouragement, he would still be at Stanton Hall. Avoiding the matchmaking mammas and the cloying attempts of young debutantes trying to trap him into the parson's mousetrap was one of his least favorite pastimes. At five and twenty he had spent the last few years gaining some town polish along with experience in how to avoid the snares of the marriage mart.

It was primarily his adoration for his sister, Penelope, that brought him here. He hoped she would find a man worthy of her hand. As one of her family, he owed her the courtesy of squiring her through the season, keeping a careful watch on the court of admirers she was sure to develop.

As Fenway, his valet, stepped away from tying his cravat into a spectacular waterfall, Phillip looked in the mirror. His blond hair carefully combed off of his face—every hair in its place. His ice-blue eyes scanned the image before him as he attached a ruby pin into the folds of the linen and smiled. Perfect white teeth set in a long face with a strong jaw and aristocratic nose and full lips. His new black coat fit like a glove. Perfection was an art. With the help of his tailor and valet, he was a master.

It was time to do his duty to his sister, please his parents, and dance with the wallflowers. With a final tug to his jacket, he nodded to Fenway. "Don't bother waiting up for me." He left his chambers determined to make the best of the evening.

~*~

The Earl of Manchester and his wife of thirty-two years stood ahead of him in the receiving line. They had asked only that Phillip, their second son, remain by the side of his sister Penelope for her come-out ball. He was the last person to greet people before they entered the ballroom.

Faces swam past him in a blur of color and stench. Why some in the upper ten-thousand refused to bathe perplexed him. He greeted each gentleman with a bow of his head and every woman with a lift of their gloved hands within an inch of his lips. His sister simpered next to him, giddy that this evening was in her honor and likely to be a 'crush,' to propel his mother into rapturous delight.

Waiting for an escape, he discovered an unknown face presented to him.

"I'm Lord Follett." The older man gave him a bow. Phillip could see the balding head, and the odor of alcohol on his breath warned him the man was already in his cups. "This is my daughter, the Honorable Elizabeth Follett."

Phillip sucked in a breath at the vision before him. Her soft red hair was pulled up and held in place by small white flowers. Her dress did not do her coloring justice. But it was the eyes, those green eyes that drew him. They spoke a message to him he couldn't quite decipher. It wasn't one of desire or seduction as he so often saw. More of abject terror.

Because of him?

He held her hand. "Welcome to Manchester Hall, Miss Follett." He allowed his lips to touch the glove and a shock traveled through him as she gasped. He straightened as one corner of his lips rose. *Ah, she'd felt it too.* Instead of terror, there was curiosity, and, as those lashes lowered, he sensed a mystery.

"You are too kind, my lord." Her husky voice whispered as the crowd pushed her forward toward the ballroom. He watched her go, the sway of her hips barely discernable beneath her gown.

"Phillip?" His sister nudged him.

"Yes, Penny?"

"Will you escort me in? Father said he would lead me out for the first dance. Anthony is to dance with me next and then you. You won't forget, will you?" Her brown eyes held an eagerness he knew would someday turn to *ennui* as the years marched on and she was subjected to these now exciting activities over and over again.

"How could I ever forget? You are by far the most beautiful woman in the room and I would be honored to dance with you."

She slapped him with her fan and giggled. "I'm glad you came home, Phillip. I've missed you."

He tapped a finger on her nose and lifted his elbow. She placed her hand on his forearm and he escorted her into the ballroom. Handing her off to his father he skirted the room, periodically shaking hands with people he knew but not stopping to chat. He wasn't in the mood for talk. His eyes scanned the mass of bodies. The Earl of Manchester determined it was late enough to begin the ball.

Phillip hated these events. When he was younger, he didn't mind attending and flirting with the available misses, but now it wore thin. Was he getting old or growing up? Managing the estate left to him by his maternal aunt, Martha, upon her removal to the here-after two years hence had been a better use of his time and energy. He'd encountered success in turning a modest inheritance into profitable investments after Lord Remington took him aside and encouraged him that even as a second son, he could be prosperous and productive.

Phillip failed in his attempt to share his successes with his family. They persisted in the belief he was a ne'er-do-well, frolicking around aimlessly, gambling, and wenching his way through his monthly allowance and inheritance. As if he were still a callow youth fresh on the town.

Before Lord Remington's warnings and direction, that might have been true.

Yet his family considered him to be a wastrel, doomed to destruction if he didn't settle down with a wife soon. His father even suspected he was hiding in the north with a mistress. As if he'd waste money on such as that? He was long over his dalliances with ladies of the night. It irked him that his father would hold such a low opinion of him.

Phillip was fully cognizant that although his family loved him, he was far from the perfection of his older brother. He glanced around the ballroom and spied Anthony, only two years older than himself. Anthony tended towards portliness and while he pretended adoration toward his wife, Phillip knew that Anthony's excesses far surpassed his own when he was younger. He feared his father was misled in the belief that his heir was honorable and trustworthy to inherit the earldom someday. Phillip shrugged. Since Anthony's wife had presented him with two sons already, the title would never pass to Phillip. He found contentment in establishing his own path, and a wife was not integral to his success.

If his mother and sisters were any indication, women usually spent money, which did not help much in increasing wealth. Marcus's bride might be the exception, but it was really too early to tell on that account as they were fairly new to marriage. They had come in earlier and were on the dance floor, besotted with one another.

The orchestra finished playing the first dance. Phillip sought out his mother to lead her into the next one.

~*~

The Honorable Elizabeth Follett escaped the first dance with an excuse to check her hem but now she couldn't avoid the inevitable as she was led to the floor by Lord Wolton.

His face quickly grew red. He started wheezing with the execution of the steps of the dance. At over three times her own age, he was a prosperous landowner and neighbor. He possessed small dark eyes, bushy eyebrows, and very little hair on top of his head, which perspired terribly. His long sideburns only served to emphasize his jowls. His hands were plump and clammy to the touch.

A shiver of distaste overtook Lizzy every time his reached for hers as required by the movements of the dance, and even more at the lascivious look in his eyes as he would scan her body. His smile, crooked with a few darker teeth accompanied by his foul breath, made her fight against the bile threatening to rise inside when they drew close.

The only highlight of the exercise was the sight of the golden god dancing two couples down. Occasionally his eyes met hers in the course of the dance and she only hoped he could read her desperation. Ah, but beautiful sons of earls were not known to rescue the daughters of barons were they?

Led back to her father after the dance, she nodded her head and murmured a soft thanks to Lord Wolton.

Lord Follett had no real repute in the *ton* and felt his position keenly. He nudged his daughter and urged her, "Smile, Lizzy, for heaven's sake. Lord Wolton desires your hand, the least you could do is encourage him a little."

Lizzy once again tried to suppress a cold shiver at the very thought of any more interaction with Lord Wolton. Her father blustered and yelled when she stated her objection to the match. There would be no rescue for her from that quarter. She closed her eyes and took a deep breath, clenching her hands tightly together silently praying to a God she wasn't quite sure even existed, for a way out of the hell destined for her.

Opening her eyes, she glanced across the room to observe Lord Phillip Westcombe leading his sister out in the country dance. She could not take her gaze off of him. His kindly manner as he interacted with his sister was charming. And that smile. Would she even be able to breathe if he ever smiled at her like that? He was the stuff dreams were made of. She felt hope surge through her. Maybe, just maybe...

~*~

The evening dragged on with one dance after another. After supper, Phillip returned his young partner to her chaperone with an elegant bow. He found his attention captivated by the young woman who'd haunted him since her introduction earlier. She was difficult to miss with her red hair, although red was a bit strong to describe its softer hue. Hair that once curled around her face hung straight. She was pale, standing alone near a potted plant by the doors leading to the gardens below, as though she were hiding. She glanced his way and their gaze held. He read a silent plea and began to move in her direction.

He wove through the crowd surrounding the ballroom, stopping for brief handshakes and pats on the back as he maneuvered to that side of the room. He kept an eye on the young woman. She tracked his progress at times furtively searching the crowd. His curiosity was aroused.

"Miss Follett." Lord Phillip bowed over her hand and spoke softly so as not to be overheard in the noise of the ballroom. "May I be of assistance?"

"Lord Westcombe..." Elizabeth sighed. "Yes...I wonder..." Her eyes once again held a silent entreaty.

"Would you perhaps like to stroll in the garden?" Phillip extended his arm, and nodding, she wound her hand around it and walked outside into the fresh, cool evening air. Heat radiated up his arm at her touch. With every step, he was more aware of the woman by his side than any he'd ever known. It puzzled him. They stepped down into the garden lit with lanterns. Her lack of chatter perplexed him. Most women he met attempted to talk their way into a proposal. Few couples were in the gardens this early in the evening although lamps had been lit. He knew all the best places to engage in less than gentlemanly behavior due to his wayward youth. He led her down a path to an area by a small pond. Open and exposed. He would not compromise this young woman.

Phillip assisted Miss Follett to the bench, leaned against the tree next to it, and waited. She clenched her hands in her lap, took a deep breath, and began. "I need to escape. My father is forcing me into a marriage I do not want." Cautiously, she raised her eyes to meet his and he noted the tears at the edges.

He reached for his handkerchief and extended it to her as he came to sit beside her. "Is there no other way out of this marriage? Surely, they cannot force you to the altar. We do live in a civilized society."

"Civilized?" A short bark of laughter escaped the

young woman. "My life has never been civilized. You'd be truly horrified if I told you the things I've endured." She turned slightly to look him in the eye and reached forward to put her hand on his arm. "Truly, if I do not escape tonight I have no other hope except—"

Phillip's eyes narrowed as she considered her words. Was she being overly dramatic? Was this a manipulation? Miss Follett wasn't trying to trap him into marriage herself, was she? From what he understood, she came with a healthy dowry, something he certainly didn't need. She was far from unattractive and given time during the season her own court of admirers would vie for her favors. Yet he sensed truth in what she claimed and that before him sat a desperate woman. The knight-errant in him fought its way to the surface disturbing the peaceful waters he tried hard to maintain. "What is it you require?"

"To disappear. Somewhere, anywhere they cannot find me."

"And then what? You re-appear elsewhere? How would that be explained? The scandal-mongers would have a feast that could destroy any hope you would have of making a respectable match. What about your future? Where might you live and how would you marry if you are cut off from your father and your inheritance?"

"You fully understand the complexities of my circumstances, Lord Westcombe. To me this matter is of life and death. My life. My certain death. If I am forced to marry, I guarantee I will be dead within the year. So, my only hope is to escape. Will you assist me?"

Phillip stared at her, considering, as the silence stretched taut between them. He tended to be a good judge of people and this woman told the truth. Finally, he came to a decision and nodded to her. "Can you remain here for a few minutes? Will you be all right?"

"You won't fetch my father?"

"No, merely a discreet friend who might assist. Trust me. I am a man of my word."

"I'll be fine. I'm not alone." Her face relaxed as she looked up past the tree to the stars twinkling in the sky.

Phillip wondered at her odd statement. There were other couples in the garden, but none near here. Giving her a short bow he surreptitiously returned to the ballroom. Once he entered he searched until he spied Lord Marcus Remington finishing up a dance with his bride. Phillip wove his way through the crowd to Marcus's side and whispered in his ear, "I require your assistance."

Marcus raised one eyebrow, nodded, and together all three made their way to the hallway and a private room. Phillip shut the door behind them.

"Well, Phillip, what is it?" Marcus relaxed one hand on his wife's waist as he stood beside her.

"I need shelter for a young woman in desperate need." *Now* who sounded melodramatic?

Marcus and Josie exchanged looks before staring at him.

"Phillip? Why does this woman need immediate shelter?" asked Lady Remington.

"I've done nothing wrong or to be ashamed of. She came to me for help."

"What do you want?" asked Marcus.

His wife nodded her head in agreement.

"I must spirit her away immediately. Could you depart and have your carriage go down to the corner alley? I'll bring her there unnoticed. After we arrive at your home, you can hear her story for yourselves."

Marcus nodded and escorted Josie out of the room.

"Dearest, I'm feeling tired and would like to go home now," Josie simpered as she fanned herself.

"Certainly dear. You look fatigued." Marcus's strong deep voice would suggest they were leaving for that reason alone.

Phillip slipped out the door of the library and wandered back to the garden, avoiding the few partygoers there. He accidentally came upon a few couples engaged in flirtation before he found his way back to Miss Elizabeth Follett. "Come," he whispered as he gave her his hand to help her stand.

"Where...?"

"You ask for my help yet now you resist? Trust me. I shan't harm you."

"I never doubted that for a minute." She rushed alongside him as they slipped through a spot in the hedge and made their way down the alley. Staying in the shadows they waited silently for the Remington coach to pull up. The rise and fall of her chest as she caught her breath was distracting.

He forced himself to focus elsewhere.

The carriage arrived and Lord Phillip assisted Elizabeth inside, entering behind her and closing the door. Marcus tapped on the roof to signal for them to start and they headed for the Remington home.

"Lord and Lady Remington, may I present the Honorable Elizabeth Follett to you?" Lord Westcombe intoned.

"Miss Follett, it is our honor to meet and assist you

this evening." Josie reached across the carriage to squeeze the newcomer's hand. "You shall be safe with us."

"Thank you," Miss Follett whispered.

Phillip leaned back against the squabs and willed his pulse to slow. What had he done? He had acted on her behalf but belatedly wondered how this would reflect on him. Where was his neat, orderly life now?

2

Lizzy leaned forward to look out the window as they pulled up to the Remington house. Her awareness of the man sitting next to her caused her stomach to flutter. *Silly girl!* He was a kind soul helping a damsel in distress. Nothing more. Lord Phillip assisted her from the carriage and they followed Marcus and Josie to the entrance of the building. Leading her to the drawing room, Josie requested tea be brought. As Lizzy paced in front of the unlit hearth, Lord Remington moved past her to put the kindling in and strike the match to get a fire started. Phillip had gone to the sideboard for a glass of brandy and brought one for his friend.

Silence hung in the air until the tea tray arrived and the servants departed, closing the door behind them.

"I cannot stay long, my parents will miss me if I am not back before the end of the ball," said Phillip.

Lizzy stopped pacing as her heart raced. "What?"

Lord Remington went to her side to escort her to the settee next to his wife who handed her a cup of tea after quietly inquiring how she preferred hers.

"Phillip, you cannot rescue her and then abandon her here," Lady Remington protested.

"I will return once the ball is finished."

"But what is to become of me?" Lizzy whispered.

Phillip looked at Marcus. "Her father is forcing her

to marry Lord Wolton against her will."

Lord Remington's eyebrows rose. He nodded. "You were kind to help her escape such a fate. But why would your father do that?"

A shudder shook Lizzy and she placed her cup and saucer on the table lest she spill it. "Wolton has some kind of hold over my father." She pulled off her gloves revealing red wrists with the marks of fingers on her pale skin.

Phillip growled. "Your father did this to you?"

Lizzy nodded.

Josie reached over to touch her arm gently above the injured area. "I'm eager to hear your story, but in due time. You may spend the night here until we can figure out how to best assist you." She glanced over at her husband who nodded in agreement.

"Phillip, I hope you realize what you're doing. We don't want to be caught interfering between a young woman and her legal guardian."

Lizzy piped up, "I am of age. I possess my own inheritance."

Phillip looked surprised. "Given that, how can your father force you to marry someone you dislike?"

Elizabeth wouldn't meet his gaze, looking down into her teacup as tears started to flow. "Trust me, he will."

Josie looked at Phillip with pleading eyes. "We shall figure this out in due time."

Lizzy pulled his handkerchief out of her reticule and used it to dab her eyes.

Lord Westcombe moved over to stand in front of her and she looked up at him. "I'm sorry I must leave. I promise you, I will return in a few hours. I could leave you in no better hands than Lord and Lady

Remington's. You'll be safe here." He bowed to her and with a brief good night, he left the room to return to the Manchester ball.

~*~

Twice in one evening he had abandoned Miss Follett. It went against the grain of gentlemanly behavior. Being seen at the dance, however, would absolve him of any participation in the matter. In the end, it could possibly save her reputation and keep him from the parson's mousetrap.

The dancing was winding down and he took to the floor with another debutante. After the dance concluded he returned her to her chaperone's side and sought out his mother. Lady Manchester was short but retained her youthful figure. In spite of a few grey streaks in her light brown hair, she was still considered a beauty. Phillip tended to take after his father in looks and temperament.

"Oh, Phillip, there you are. I wondered where you had disappeared to." She tapped his arm with her fan. "Found someone you simply couldn't resist, did you? I heard the gardens were busy this evening." She giggled.

Phillip grew warm at the suggestion he'd been carrying on with a guest on his parents' property. It saddened him that she would believe something like that of him. Sometimes a past was a hard thing to live down. "You were searching for me, Mother? What can I do for you?"

"Lord Wolton was agitated earlier as the young woman he was pledged to dance with disappeared. Lord Follett, the young lady's father, was unable to locate her. We had the withdrawing room checked and surreptitiously asked around but nobody remembers seeing her. It's as if she has vanished into thin air. I do not need to tell you that this is not the kind of notoriety we want associated with your sister's come out." She gave him a coy wink. His mother enjoyed the fact that along with being a squeeze her ball would be remembered for the disappearance of the Follett woman.

"What do you think has happened to her?" he asked, schooling his features to impassiveness.

She leaned toward him and was forced to look up as she whispered. "She is worth a fortune and has sole control of the money as of yesterday when she turned one and twenty. Rumor has it that Lord Wolton intended to marry her by Special License tomorrow." She paused and gave a shiver of disgust. "Personally, Phillip, I think the girl ran away and I couldn't blame her. I'd do the same if Wolton were my intended groom."

"If they were eager for her to wed him, why wait until she gained her majority? She no longer needs his permission for her marriage. I'm praying she is safe from that sorry end. But where would she go? Does she have relatives in town who might shelter and protect her?"

"None that I'm aware of. It troubles me. A young woman alone in this town is destined for only one thing and already her reputation is ruined by this event." Lady Remington shook her head sadly. "It's too bad, really, as she seemed to be a sweet girl and was passably pretty." Of course, she probably thought no one could ever be as beautiful as her own daughter.

Phillip listened to his mother and remained silent

as he scanned the room for Lord Follett or Lord Wolton. He failed to locate them. "Where is her father and the potential bridegroom now?"

"I believe they left for the evening in an attempt to keep things quiet so when they find her they can whisk her away to the church and prevent a scandal."

"What if they fail to locate her?"

"I pray for that, Phillip, and I hope she is safe. At some point, however, she will need to access her fortune which will expose her to discovery."

"You are far too wise, Mother. Is there anything you need from me for the rest of this evening? I wouldn't mind calling it a night myself."

"Really? Phillip, you seriously cannot be thinking of going to your club or any of those other places tonight."

"No. However, I do plan to meet a friend."

"Fine. You may leave, Phillip, but remember, I expect you to accompany us to some of the balls this season to help keep an eye on a potential suitor for your sister's hand. I am counting on your support. I will send a list of entertainments I expect you to attend."

"I'll do my best, Mother." Phillip bent and gave her a kiss on the cheek. "Good night." He strode out the door and took a brisk walk to the Remington house. He wondered if Miss Follett was yet awake. He wouldn't mind seeing her again.

~*~

"Come, Elsa will help you change. You are a little taller than me but I'm sure I have a gown that will suit you for sleeping," Josie urged.

Elizabeth sank into the chair by the cheerful fireplace. "It's hopeless. There is no way out of this."

"Miss Follett…"

"Elizabeth please, or Lizzy."

"Elizabeth it is, then. A name that speaks of dignity, determination, and grace."

Lizzy looked up at that, startled. "Thank you."

"You may call me Josie. Now, what is concerning you?"

Elsa began pulling the pins out of Lizzy's hair and letting the heavy locks fall down around her shoulders. "My father has evil friends. He told me I needed to marry Wolton. I had no choice. But I'm tired of being a victim of men's schemes and debauchery."

"What *are* you talking about?"

Lizzy rose as the abigail put the pins on the dressing table and left to get a nightgown. She turned to Josie. "Maybe I can show you. Would you undo my dress?" Elizabeth turned around.

Josie rose to undo the fasteners going down the back of Elizabeth's gown. Letting it fall to the floor she pulled up the back of her chemise to reveal her back.

Josie's gasp echoed around the room.

Elizabeth walked behind a screen and finished dressing. She suspected her face was now the color of her hair.

Josie sat, mouth agape. "I'm so sorry, Elizabeth. I suspect there is much more you are not telling me."

"Yes, m'lady." Lizzy sat across from her with her head bent, awaiting condemnation from the Viscountess.

"Elizabeth, what you have endured was not your fault. It is a crime this can be done to a young woman with no one to protect her. God loves you, and Lord

Remington and myself will do all in our power to protect you from further harm."

"You won't force me to leave? I am unworthy of your kindness."

"You are more than worthy. You are a precious young woman who has suffered evil. I suspect your battle will not be only one with your father and disappointed groom, but that a spiritual dimension underlies this."

"I don't understand." Lizzy folded and unfolded the handkerchief she still held, her thumb unconsciously tracing the initials embroidered in the corner.

"You've been subjected to great evil. More I'm sure than you've shared thus far. These things are not normal or in any way condoned by God. Like you, I don't understand what hold Lord Wolton has over your father that would force him to sell you in this manner. If your suspicions are correct you are destined for more of the same. I will need to share some of this with my husband, and possibly Lord Westcombe, so they can make discreet inquiries."

Lizzy panicked. "Must you?"

"I believe it is necessary if we are to protect you and give you freedom from the terror you've experienced." Josie leaned forward, put her arm on Elizabeth's, and looked her in the eye. "I want you to be free of the prison you find yourself in. Free to select a husband of your choice. Free to be all God has created you to be as a woman, a wife, and a mother someday."

"I never dared to dream that far." She hugged herself.

"I understand," said Josie kindly. "I believe it

would be good for you to get some rest now. We will talk more in the morning when we can consider this with a fresh perspective as to what's to be done. By then Phillip might be able to give us information on what happened at the ball when they discovered you missing. I'm sure there was an uproar over that and his mother is relishing the notoriety it is giving her daughter's come out."

"Oh, I've ruined it for them, haven't I?"

"No. She will be in alt. Never fear. Phillip won't fail in keeping your secret. He has too much to lose by confessing anything."

"What do you mean?"

"A marriageable man kidnapping a young woman from his parents' ball? The only way he'd ever live that down would be to marry you himself."

Lizzy's heart sank. "I could never dream so high as to seek someone as fine as him for a husband."

"He is quite a figure of manhood is he not? A man of honor, as well. You can trust him. Now get some rest."

"May I keep the fire burning?"

"That's fine. I'll instruct Elsa." She rang the bell and the maid appeared.

"You've been all kindness, m'lady."

"Josie."

"Thank you, Josie."

"It is our pleasure. Sleep well and have pleasant dreams." Josie departed after giving discreet instructions to the maid.

Lizzy blew out the candles and strode to the window. She lifted the pane. Duke came to sit on the sill. "I'm well, Duke. Thank you. I'll see you on the morrow."

Duke nodded and flew off.

The windows were closed and the drapes were drawn. She settled into a chair by the fire, the vision of blue eyes and a strong chin were better dreamt of awake. *I'm in a safe place, I'll be fine.* She'd abandoned everything for safety. But in doing so she courted scandal. There was no way to save face after this. Even under the auspices of the Viscount and his wife, there was little cachet to be had as a runaway daughter of a baron. Even if she could gain her fortune, she'd expose her location. How would she live? Where would she go? Wearily she sought her bed and drifted into an uneasy sleep.

She ran away from one nightmare straight into unknown darkness with few options.

~*~

Duke flew to the top of the tree and settled in to sleep. The noise of the city made that hard. The gas lamps encroached on the darkness he was accustomed to in the country. His mistress was well. He spied the man who brought his mistress here, return. Duke bobbed his head. He'd do. Lizzy went with him willingly. She was safe and the terror he'd seen in her the past few days was momentarily gone. He could rest and wait to find out what would happen next. She wasn't clear of all danger yet. Evil lurked in the darkness and he would do anything to protect her.

~*~

Weariness weighed Phillip down as he stepped back into the Remington home. He strode into the parlour where Marcus awaited with Josie.

"You've returned." Josie sat down next to Marcus, snuggling against him. "I only just got Elizabeth to relax enough to go to bed."

Phillip picked up the glass he'd abandoned earlier. He took a sip and savored the heat as it burned its way down his throat. "Well?"

"She needs our help. This is an evil enemy we've engaged by assisting her. It scares me."

"That bad?" Marcus gave her a squeeze.

"Truly, worse than I could imagine."

"How is she? Did she tell you anything?" Phillip sat and stretched his legs out in front of him.

"Along with the marks on her wrists, there are scars on her back. I suspect there are deeper wounds she's not had the courage to share."

Marcus hugged Josie tight and kissed her hair.

Phillip experienced a twinge of jealousy at the love the two shared. He shook it off. He did not need a wife. He doubted he would ever find someone as perfect for him as Josie was for Marcus. He held great affection for them both.

Josie spoke again. "This woman has been tortured. Unspeakably abused, and has sole control of her fortune, an inheritance from an aunt. For some reason, her father is insisting she marry Lord Wolton as soon as possible, and she believes this man will destroy her. I sense in my spirit that she speaks the truth. She needs protection. Regardless, I doubt this evil will go away." She paused. "Lord Follett and Lord Wolton should be investigated. This poor woman is a pawn in a bigger game. Perhaps we could call on Nigel Neville to assist us."

"Are you serious, Josie?" asked Marcus.

She nodded.

"When I returned to the ball, I discovered Lord Wolton had a Special License and if he finds her he will tie her to himself as quickly as possible. What I have heard of him in the past is not favorable." Phillip sipped his drink. The warmth only provided temporary relief from the unease within.

"I'll reach out to Neville to make discreet inquiries," offered Marcus.

"Do you think her father might call for Bow Street to investigate?" she asked.

"I doubt it, however, it is not safe to keep her in town. What do you suggest, Josie?" Marcus inquired.

"I need to make a trip to Rose Hill. Give it about that I am increasing. The season was too much for me and I returned to the country. We can take Elizabeth with us, dressing her up as a maid so she is not discovered *en route* in case someone is searching for her."

Phillip blinked several times. "Is it true? My good man, are you soon to be a father?"

Marcus beamed. "So my bride informs me."

Josie blushed.

"Congratulations, to both of you." Phillip digested the news. A child. An heir. Of course, he didn't feel any need or urge in that direction. In spite of that, a deep sense of loss sliced through him. Life went on and circumstances changed. But his relationship with Marcus would once again alter. He shook off the melancholy that suddenly cloaked him.

"Back to our subject, getting Miss Follett out of the city might be wise. We can keep her safe while we set inquiries in motion," Josie said as she rose to her feet motioning for her husband to stay seated.

Marcus agreed. "I'll inform Barkley we are departing in the morning. The rest of our things may be packed up and sent later."

Josie leaned forward to plant a kiss on her husband's cheek. "Thank you, Marcus." She turned to leave. "I am fatigued. Phillip, will you be joining us at Rose Hill? Your room is always kept ready for you."

"I'll discover what I can in town first. Marcus, will you travel with them?"

"Yes, I'll accompany the ladies. I find I dislike being separated from Josie for any length of time. I'll send a note off to Mr. Neville to attend me at Rose Hill."

"I may need to stay in town for a day or two, play the dutiful son, and squire my sister to a few events. I'll listen to any gossip that comes up over Miss Follet's disappearance. After that, I will join you in the country."

"Excellent plan," said Marcus as he rose.

"Good night, Phillip. I'm proud of you for helping Miss Follett." Josie came forward to give him a hug.

"I felt compelled to act."

Josie wiggled her eyebrows and grinned. "That sounds promising." She left the room.

Phillip turned. "What did she mean by that?"

Marcus only shrugged. "No clue. Women are a delightful mystery. I pray someday you find one of your own to puzzle and enchant you."

Phillip shook his head. "Please don't pray for that." He rose and set his glass on the table.

Marcus walked him to the front door. "I will pray as I see fit, and there's nothing you can do to stop me." He patted his friend on the back.

Phillip put his hat on. "I suppose not. I'll visit you

at Rose Hill."

The door closed behind him as Phillip skipped down the stairs and hailed a hackney to take him to his rented rooms. Normally he'd be playing cards and drinking but his future held some obligations that required a sharp mind and rest was essential. As he rode, the image of green eyes and soft red hair haunted him. Well, if he had to rescue someone at least she was pretty.

3

Elizabeth stretched. A moment of disorientation as she gazed around the beautiful room soon reminded her of the events of the night before. It wasn't all a nightmare. It wouldn't be long before her father found her and any hope would be extinguished.

A knock came to the door.

"Yes?" Lizzy called.

"It's Josie. May I enter?"

"Certainly." Elizabeth rose as the door opened and Josie slipped in.

"You may sit. I won't be long. This morning we'll dress you as a maid, do something to cover that glorious hair, and spirit you away to our estate in the country. Phillip will stay in town for a few days to listen to the scuttlebutt. I detest that kind of thing but in this instance, it could prove useful."

"We're leaving London? This morning?"

"It seemed the best option for keeping you safe and I'm delighted that I shall have company when the time comes for Lord Remington to return to Parliament."

"I didn't mean to keep you from your entertainments."

"'Tis no bother. I'm increasing and find the endless round of social calls and balls to be tiring. I'd rather be home and comfortable. Country girl at heart, I guess."

"I will be bringing a companion with me."

"A companion?" Josie frowned as her brows scrunched.

"I have a pet crow named Duke. He'll fly or sit on top of the carriage. He won't be a bother."

"Unusual. I don't think Lord Remington would want him in the house."

"Oh, no. He loves the outdoors and finds his own food. He's no trouble."

"That should be fine. We leave in an hour." Josie rose and left the room.

Lizzy needed to make sure Duke followed her. She went to the window, drew back the drapes and opened it. Giving a low whistle, she stood and waited. Soon a black figure emerged, landed on the sill, and looked about with curiosity.

"Duke, I've found shelter."

Duke glanced up at her and tilted his head, waiting.

"We depart in a carriage very soon, but I'll be dressed as a servant. I will whistle so you will know when I leave. I understand it is a full day's journey to Rose Hill."

She set her hand out sideways below Duke's chest and he stepped up from the sill. Bringing him up to her face she leaned forward to kiss his beak. Duke made a purring sound which caused her to giggle. "You most certainly are a silly crow, and I am grateful you are with me for this journey. I won't feel so alone with these people who are strangers." She reached up with her other hand to pet the crow and crooned softly to him. He leaned happily into her hand. She gained comfort and strength from the presence of her special pet.

Eventually, Duke took off to a tree near the house

to await departure.

Lizzy closed the window and with a little wave to Duke, drew the drapes.

~*~

Phillip slept through the night but was startled to awareness of all that happened the previous evening. He rose, allowed his valet to help him prepare for the day, and ate a light breakfast. He glanced out the window as he sipped his coffee. The weather was favorable for travel. He shook his head in wonder at how quickly things had changed in the past twelve hours. He was now embroiled in the affairs of a young woman he had helped run away from a disastrous marriage. Setting down his empty cup, he grabbed his hat to leave only to be stopped by a messenger who arrived moments before. He accepted the packet from Fenway and sat back down to read the letter.

Phillip,

We're departing now and I've hired Bow Street to look into Wolton and Follett. Keep an ear open here in town. We anticipate your visit to Rose Hill as soon as you are able to join us.

I do not regret taking leave at this point in the season. Josie prefers the country and to be honest, right now I do as well.

M.R.

He sensed the unspoken pride Marcus had over becoming a father by Christmas. Phillip was happy for them. He sat the letter down and glanced around his apartments. He rented rooms in town to save the money of setting up a more permanent establishment with all the expenses and staff such a property would require. As a single man, his needs were fairly minimal and his valet was more than willing to make do with their limited environs. Someday, when he stepped into the parson's mousetrap, he'd consider purchasing a home in town. But not yet. For the nonce, he would save his money.

He stood up with a start. Did he just think *when*? There was no need to marry. Ever. He was content with his life as a bachelor and entertained no qualms about seeking his pleasure where he may when the need arose. A wife was unnecessary for his overall happiness. He did not need to secure the family line as his brother already accomplished that feat. He cherished his freedom. Marriage was fine for Marcus, but not for him. No, right now he only needed to meet his own desires and whims without the burden of trying to satisfy a wife.

Other than the Remington's, there were very few marriages in the *beau monde* that inspired any desire to take such a risk with his happiness. He could think of nothing that might tempt him to wrap that particular noose around his neck.

The image of Elizabeth's face rose in his mind. He had a job to do this morning and for that he was grateful. The idle life of a young man in town began to pall years ago. He picked up his hat and left his rooms to saunter down the street towards White's. He would listen for any word of Lord Follett or Lord Wolton's actions, and the disappearance of a certain young woman whose green eyes and soft red hair were hard to dismiss from his thoughts.

~*~

White's was a gentlemen's club of distinction. No women were allowed to enter the hallowed portal. Membership was only to the *crème de la crème* in society and men couldn't join without being vouched for by another of the elite.

Phillip entered the club and handed off his hat before sauntering into the main room. He settled down in a comfortable chair and picked up the morning's paper. The scandal sheets echoed whispers he'd overheard the previous evening. Any chance of keeping Beth out of the papers and her situation hushed up was moot. *Beth? Since when did he start thinking of her as Beth?* He grinned at his own foolishness and continued to read while listening to the talk of others around him.

Lord Theodore Harrow entered, hailed Phillip from across the room, and came to sit with him. "Good morrow, Phillip, I received a little note from Marcus stating you might be needing an extra pair of ears, but he neglected to give me any details. Is there trouble afoot?"

Phillip set down his paper and considered his friend. Slightly older by a few years, Lord Harrow almost seemed like a Papa Bear in their group. Affable, serious, and compassionate, he still had a good left hook in a fight when necessary. If there was a man he would want in his corner for his ability to think through a problem, this man was it. Phillip looked at him. "What have the gossipmongers been saying regarding my sister's come out ball?"

With a bit of flair, Theo moved his hand in a grand gesture and began to speak. "It was the event of the season. Your sister is a pearl beyond compare and is probably drowning in floral tributes as we speak."

Theodore paused and rubbed his chin with his left hand. His voice lowered. "Hmmm, my valet did say something this morning. What was it? Yes. Something about a young woman disappearing at the ball." His voice dropped to a whisper as he leaned in toward Phillip. "The Honorable Elizabeth Follett, was it? I remember dancing with her earlier in the evening. She's a delightful young woman and not difficult to look at," Theodore winked at Phillip, "if you know what I mean. Her red hair gives a man something to dream about."

"I'm sure it does, Theo. I've met Miss Follett and she is undeniably an attractive young woman. What is being said regarding her disappearance?"

Lord Harrow shrugged. "Your guess is as good as mine. She's disappeared without a trace and her father is fit to be tied. Apparently, she was to marry Lord Wolton, although forgive me for saying it, I cannot figure out why she'd choose such a despicable man for a husband. She is newly out, beautiful, and would likely suffer offers galore from men more suited to her in age and temperament."

Phillip was taken aback by his friend's vehement opposition to anyone. The man must be truly as bad as he said for Theo to speak ill of Wolton. "But he is a wealthy marquess whereas her father is only a mere baron."

"True. Yet if she is not under her father's guardianship in terms of her fortune, why would she make such an otherwise obvious misalliance?"

"How do you even know that? Has there been a public disclosure of her inheritance, provided she has one?" Phillip asked.

"A pertinent question. I'm only repeating what

little I know."

"I wonder what is going on between Lord Follett and Lord Wolton? It behooves us to keep listening carefully as we go about town."

"I can do that, but what of the young lady herself? Where could she have gone? I hope she is not wandering our city, as there is only one place I imagine her ending up. It is not befitting her station to be reduced to those kinds of circumstances when she is independently wealthy."

"I sincerely doubt she has entered a brothel to hide, Theodore. Miss Follett struck me as an intelligent woman, quite able to figure out a way to escape her difficulties without ruining herself."

"If she doesn't appear soon, her reputation will be in tatters and she will lose any hope of obtaining a decent match. I would go so far as to say her season is probably over, unless she has found another beau to marry or has escaped to the Continent with a chaperone. Otherwise, her chances of returning to town with her reputation intact are nil."

Phillip frowned.

Theodore sat back and watched his friend. "What, by any chance, has this to do with you anyway? Did you have an interest in that quarter and now regret your missed opportunity?"

"What?" Phillip gaped. "I am not in the market for a wife regardless of my mother's fondest dreams. Miss Follett disappeared at my parents' home and I'm concerned. She seemed like a sweet young lady and it bothers me that any woman would feel led to act in such an extreme way."

"Perhaps she didn't run away. Is there a possibility she was kidnapped? Maybe she is being held for ransom? Or what if she had a beau her father was unaware of? Could she have found a way to run off to Scotland to marry across the border?"

"No, and no. You're out there, Theodore."

"Really?" The older man's eyes squinted. He smiled and leaned forward, whispering to Phillip. "You know where she is, don't you?"

Phillip avoided meeting his friend's gaze and Theo sat back nodding in satisfaction. "Well, sounds like a mystery. I'm glad she's safe. What do you need from me?"

"Keep our ears open for word of Follett or Wolton. Something seems fishy about them."

"At your service." Lord Harrow rose to leave. "How long are you staying on town?"

"Only a day or two more, to appease Mother."

"Then off to Rose Hill?"

Phillip nodded in resignation at how easily his friend figured things out. "Yes. I'm expected at Rose Hill."

Theodore smiled. "Caught at last, huh, Phillip? Well, couldn't happen to a better man, if I say so myself." He walked away, whistling a jaunty tune as he gathered his hat at the door and stepped out into the sunshine.

Phillip would have blustered a defense but his brain seemed muddled and slow of a sudden. He inwardly shook himself. He hadn't been out drinking the night before, so why was he off balance? Theo's words shouldn't be shaking him. He needed to solve the puzzle. Once that was done he could return to his estate and books.

What would happen to Beth? He settled back with the newspaper up in front of his face again, but his eyes failed to read the page. Instead, he thought of those haunted green eyes that somehow had drawn him across a crowded ballroom. His fingers itched to touch her hair. And those lips. He shook the paper, folded it, and set it aside. This was getting him nowhere. Standing up, he sought his own hat and headed off to his parents' home.

~*~

The Remington carriage departed London with a crow perched on top. Lizzy rested well the previous night yet now she was awake and again plagued by fear. She left behind her father, a few personal belongings and her future. Not a future she would miss. To prevent being recognized, especially with her distinctive looks, she had donned the attire of a maid, with her hair pulled back severely, braided and tucked under a cap covering every inch of the red. She dressed as an abigail and sat in the carriage with Lady Remington while Lord Remington rode astride.

Josie confided she recently discovered she was expecting a baby in late November. She shared that mornings were difficult for her but all Lizzy observed was a serene and beautiful young Viscountess who extended her more kindness than she'd ever experienced in her life. She didn't know what would happen when they got to the Remington estate. In spite of her anxieties, she grew at ease with her companion, and grateful this couple had so readily assisted Lord Westcombe in spiriting her out of town.

Lord Westcombe. Now there was a man of which fairy tale dreams were made. She leaned back in the squabs and closed her eyes to think about her rescuer.

Tall, fit, and painstakingly gorgeous, with his blond hair and shimmering blue eyes. Almost like an angel. He'd listened so intently to her and didn't argue or debate. He'd believed her and cared about her plight.

She smiled a little at remembering her hopelessness last night at the ball and how, when she spied him across the room, she hadn't been able to tear her gaze away. He was highly sought after and she didn't doubt his caution in dealing with her was due to the various wiles used against him. For some reason, in spite of that, he'd come to her after she'd issued a silent plea for help.

Maybe God was listening to her after all. Her smile disappeared when she remembered who she was—a woman with a past, whom no man would want to have anything to do with—in spite of her fortune or appearance. She couldn't bring her purity and innocence to the marriage bed. Chains of darkness held her locked in a place between heaven and hell. No amount of money could purchase her freedom from those invisible bonds.

She glanced over at Lady Remington, who stared out the window, following the figure of her handsome husband. *Why, Lizzy?* Why would she embroil these lovely people in her problems? She shook her head sadly, surely nothing good could come of any of this. Despair settled over her like a dark woolen cloak, threatening to suffocate her. It would've been better for her to simply kill herself. She feared, however, that even in death she would not be free of the darkness surrounding her.

Could Lady Remington be a friend to her? And why should she? Why would she embroil herself in the affairs of one such as her? Lizzy observed the brown-eyed young woman sitting across from her. Something inside her told her this lady was acquainted with heartache, pain, and would understand. She hadn't expected an ally in her flight.

"Why?" asked Lizzy out loud.

"Hmmm?" Josie asked as she turned her gaze to Elizabeth.

"Why are you helping me?"

Josie reached over and touched Lizzy's arm. "Dear Elizabeth, you are a lovely young woman and for some reason the Lord has seen fit to bring you into our path to provide assistance. Should I deny God when He calls me to care for someone?"

"But I'm taking you away from London at the height of the season."

Josie smiled. "I'm not concerned about that. I'm sad Lord Remington will need to travel more to present speeches in Parliament, however, his need for a political hostess comes secondary to his need to cater to his wife and expected child." Josie smiled dreamily. "There is something wonderful about being in love with a man who cares deeply. I pray someday you will experience that kind of joy."

"I'm happy for you, m'lady—however, given what I've already shared, it would be virtually impossible to find a husband for myself, especially one who might love me in spite of my history."

"Elizabeth, I wish I could say everything will be all right, but I cannot. However, with God, anything can be possible. Even finding someone to love you as you deserve."

Lizzy glanced out the window. "How could God even love me? With all the darkness surrounding my life and my heart, I doubt He would look kindly on my soul. I confess the thought of Him intrigues me."

"Elizabeth, God created you, loves you, and obviously, He brought you to our door for more than the rescue of your physical person, but also for the peace you're longing for in your heart. He is real. A person, Jesus. He suffered on a cross, died, and rose again so you could have a relationship with Him now and for eternity."

"It sounds like a fairy tale made up for children."

"It's not. It is history and it is only by His grace any of us can be saved. Your past is no worse than mine in the eyes of a holy God."

"Grace?"

"Undeserved, extravagant love."

"That sounds nice, but I still don't understand..."

"I'll pray God will reveal Himself to you so you can know the peace and joy I've found, even when life has been dark and painful."

"You had dark times?"

"Certainly. When my mother died. And after I was paralyzed and blind from a carriage accident. When I thought I'd lost the love of my life." With that, she glanced out toward Marcus. "I feared he might die and I would never be able to tell him I still loved him and believed in him." Josie sniffled a little bit at the memory and brushed a tear away.

"You went through all of that?"

"Just last year. Although my mother had died a few years before that."

"I'm sorry. I didn't know. I assumed that you had been blessed. I envied you."

"Everyone experiences pain and struggle in this sinful world, Elizabeth, and I'm no exception. The biggest of those blessings has been God walking with me through all of the challenges. I doubt I would have emerged as you see me today if I didn't have Him to cling to."

"You have given me much to think about."

"If God has brought you here to us, we will help and assist as He allows."

"Thank you."

~*~

Phillip entered the Manchester mansion and handed his hat to Fredricks. He showed himself up to the drawing room, only to discover it crowded with young sprigs fresh on the town, along with giddy debutantes. Flower bouquets littered every surface. He smiled as he came forward to bend over his sister's hand. "Penelope, you have taken the *beau monde* by storm. Bravo!" He turned and bent to give his mother a kiss on the cheek before wandering over to the window to watch, wait, and listen.

While he overheard girls giggling over the trite expressions of the young men present, Phillip grimaced as he remembered how he'd once been so full of his own consequence and determined to have the ladies slavering at his feet. He'd almost succeeded too well. He discovered quickly that flirting and courting were a bit too close in the minds of many of the young misses and he experienced a few narrow escapes from traps set for him.

Much of that was before his brother's wife had given the family two heirs. Even now, older, although eight and twenty was not so great an age, he still found that his appearance and rumored wealth made him a worthy catch for those not in the market for a title. In many ways, he was grateful his courtesy title was all he could offer and that he only had the responsibilities of his own little piece of the kingdom, and not the heavier duties that fell to those with landed titles.

Many second sons were forced to choose a career, either in law, the military, or in the clergy. He avoided all three by simply having an adequate fortune with which to sustain himself. He almost failed when a few years of gambling and other frivolous activities found him at the brink of financial ruin.

It was his friend Marcus who gently counseled him about better ways to spend what was left of his fortune and his time. An unexpected inheritance from an aunt provided a small property which gave him new purpose...and a steady income.

He now discovered he wasn't as disappointed to be back in London as he thought he'd be. The busyness of all the balls, al fresco luncheons, dinners, and card games at White's, kept him from looking any deeper into himself, or any loneliness he pretended didn't exist.

He glanced over at his mother. He loved his parents dearly but found it difficult to escape the reputation he'd established years ago. He shrugged. Did it really matter what they thought anyway? He didn't need their approval for his successes to be any more real. Still, it galled him to be told over and over again his only real chance for a happy and settled life of any value, was to take a wife.

Beth. Elizabeth. He had desired to see her, to ascertain her safety and happiness. He shook his head at his own foolishness. There were no two people he could trust more than Lord and Lady Remington. He would have to bide his time in town before he could ride out to Rose Hill and find out more about the mysterious "tortures" that this young woman had endured. Anger surged within him at the fact that she would be forced to take such drastic actions. He inwardly shook himself for his reflections. He needed to pay attention if he wanted to learn anything of value.

Phillip scanned the crowd gathered in the room until he discovered the person who could be the most help to him. Lady Orion. An older matron of the *ton*, she wielded great power. She was rail thin, wiry, and shrewd. It was not easy to converse with this opinionated woman. Still, if anyone understood the truth of things, it would be her. He pushed away from the wall he'd been leaning against and crossed over to her, pulling up an empty chair nearby to sit for a coze.

"Lord Westcombe, what have you to say about the matter?" she queried.

"I'm afraid, dear lady that I am unaware of what you are referring to. Has King George recovered from the disaster of Prince Frederick, Duke of York, being forced to resign as Commander in Chief of the Army? I thought Sir Arthur Wellesley was an excellent choice to replace him. Has Prince George become frugal and gone on a diet? Just what have I missed?"

Lady Orion tittered. "Silly boy. I'm referring to Miss Follett's disappearance. Lord Wolton is now offering a huge reward for the return of his *supposed* fiancée."

"Really? Do you question whether she really is engaged to that man?"

"What woman would not suspect something havey-cavey about the affair." She tapped Phillip with her fan. "Anyone can see that Lord Wolton is not the man for any young girl, and definitely not as pretty an

English rose as Miss Elizabeth."

"She is a fair picture to look upon, to be sure, but what seems to be the concern? Where has she gone? Why the reward? A woman has the right to withdraw from even the most official of engagements and yet nothing was posted in the papers regarding theirs."

"You are astute, Lord Phillip, and I've said much the same thing. I'm glad she managed to escape. If she had come to me I would have been more than willing to face Follett and Wolton to protect her. Her rescue would have been something to behold. Wolton and Follett have no clue the wrath they've escaped."

"Other than marriage to an older man, which many young women undertake for various reasons, why do you think she is opposed to this one?"

"I have no proof, so I really shouldn't say anything," Lady Orion whispered, suddenly being quite circumspect, heightening Phillip's senses.

"I'm sure you can trust me with your suspicions, my lady. I am no gadabout, I can assure you."

Lady Orion looked into Phillip's eyes and he gazed back without wavering. She nodded her head. "You'll do."

"I'll do? For what, pray tell?"

"Yes. For Miss Follett. You must find her Phillip, and protect her."

Phillip's eyes grew wide and a hand flew to his chest. "Excuse me? I cannot have possibly heard you correctly. I only met her last night."

"You would make a handsome couple." Lady Orion winked.

"I'm not of a mind to marry."

"Oh, men always say that, but Cupid sometimes has other plans."

"Cupid, huh? Chubby little baby with wings and a bow and arrow who somehow predicts true love? I wasn't born yesterday and I don't believe in such nonsense."

"I think you protest too much." The woman grinned.

"Regardless, you still haven't answered my question about why you are so concerned regarding the circumstances of her disappearance. Perhaps she had a lover and ran off to Gretna Green."

"T'would be to her benefit if she had, but I don't believe that to be the case. She's been kept locked up at Lord Follett's estate for years and my footman has tales to tell of the doings at that place, events that no proper Englishmen should be associated with. Lord Wolton is a part of it, as well."

"Truly, you surprise me, ma'am. What kinds of *doings* have you heard about?"

Her voice lowered. "Evil things. Blood. Sacrifices. A secret society."

Phillip could barely hear her.

Her wide eyes reflected the horror of the words she had related. She then waited for his reaction.

Phillip schooled his face to show no emotion although a chill ran up his spine. "Interesting. I have heard of these kinds of activities going on, but usually much more to the north where superstition runs deep. Yet you say this is part of Miss Follett's problem? That this may be why she ran away?"

Lady Orion nodded, leaned over and patted his arm. "You must do what you can to save her, young man."

"It is not my role to assume."

"Something tells me you are wrong, Lord

Westcombe, but I'll pray for you."

"I will not refuse any prayers on my behalf although I'm not quite sure how active I believe God will be in my, or Miss Follett's life at this point, much less the two of us together."

"I don't think you will let Him down."

The idea that God desired to use him was ludicrous, but he wouldn't gainsay the older woman. "Let's hope not."

Phillip rose and bent over Lady Orion's hand. "Good day, my lady." He turned to make his farewells to his mother and sister and departed out into the street. He headed to Regent Park to walk and think.

4

Lord Wolton paced the study of the Follett house. He was red and perspired, frequently wiping his brow with a stained handkerchief while Lord Follett watched nervously.

The fire was unlit due to Lord Follett's straightened circumstances. Worn carpet, outmoded furniture, and moth-eaten draperies depressed him. A chill hung in the air. Or was that fear making him shiver? "I explained several times already. I don't know where she could have gone," Lord Follett pleaded with his importune visitor. Why had he ever become friends with this man years ago? He'd had no clue it would come to this.

"You certainly must," claimed Wolton firmly. "I hope you're not hiding her from me." The man glared at him.

Follett gulped. "Why would I? I've always allowed you free access to my home and grounds at Follett Hall. I have nothing to hide. I want Lizzy here as much or more than you do. I've also prevented any staff from spreading tales. I'm certain shame alone will keep Lizzy from doing so as well."

"Her disappearance has jeopardized our society. You realize she will not remain alive long after I've wed her. We cannot risk it. If Whitehall were to discover what we were about, you and I would both be locked in the tower. Only our titles keep us from having our own necks stretched. No. It is your daughter who will pay the price for breaking the silence whether she has done so or not. There is no other choice."

Lord Follett drank an entire glass of brandy and ended up hitting himself in the chest as he coughed in reaction to the burn of the liquor in his throat. "She is still my daughter. I don't believe she would risk her reputation by revealing our secrets. You will not be displeased with her and perhaps she would give you an heir. Would it not be worth it to keep her alive until then?"

Wolton turned, his eyes glittering and dark. "No life is worth the risk of exposure for the greater good of what we are trying to accomplish, Folly."

"I dislike it when you call me that."

"When I've wedded and bedded your daughter, I'll consider altering my name for you."

Lord Follett's dislike for this pompous lord increased. He was trapped and inwardly cursed Lizzy for placing him in this position. The consequences of her disappearance were vast. He was on the brink of certain ruin, financially as well as socially, if she were not found quickly.

"She might have returned home to Follett Hall. She appeared pale last evening."

"Do not make excuses for her, Folly. She must have known about the Special License I planned to use today. How did she discover that? Certainly, you've not been foolish enough to tell her."

"Certainly not. Everything was planned with precision to get her to the church and drugged just enough to ensure her cooperation. I'd no clue as to how she'd uncovered our plot, or if it was even the reason she left."

"What about her maid?"

"I questioned her extensively to no avail. She became a sniveling worthless heap. She has been dismissed but unable to spread tales." Follett didn't bother to share just how he tried to exact that information. He was becoming as horrid a creature as Wolton. He barely felt shame for his actions.

"Good."

"What else can we do? Did you want me to call in a Bow Street Runner?"

"Are you a fool?" Wolton bellowed. "Why would we want to attract more attention and scrutiny into our affairs? No. I will set my own men on her trail. There has to be a way to uncover her whereabouts."

"Do you still desire to wed her?"

Lord Wolton stopped pacing and an evil grimace appeared on his molted face. "Oh, yes, Follett. Your little girl will be my bride, and taught a lesson she will never forget. Not that she'll live very long to repent of her waywardness."

A shiver overtook Lord Follett. It wasn't because the house was cold.

~*~

Lord Westcombe attended luncheons, danced at balls, and went to routes and recitals, all in an effort to glean information on Lord Follett and Lord Wolton. He was becoming increasingly frustrated at how little he was able to uncover. Finally, he decided enough was enough. His sister was well established but nowhere close to selecting one of the men who flocked around her like bees to honey. It was time to head to Rose Hill. It had been a week. For some odd reason, he needed to see for himself that Beth, Miss Follett, was truly doing well.

At least, that's the lie he told himself.

~*~

Somehow, Lizzy found herself with a makeshift wardrobe manufactured out of older clothes from Lord Remington's sister's wardrobe. She never looked quite so fashionable even if the fashions were a season out of date. Anxiety made it difficult to sleep, much less keep herself gainfully occupied during the day. She took the dogs for walks in the garden with Duke. She sewed and listened to Lady Remington dream about the babe growing inside her. She wondered where Lord Phillip was. In spite of what little she knew of him, she longed to see him again. Even her nightmares were replaced with dangerous fantasies regarding her rescuer. The country air definitely held restorative powers.

~*~

Lord Phillip arrived at Rose Hill to find the household asleep. Having spent many years visiting Marcus' home, he was able to gain entrance to the house and stirred the fireplace in the library to warm up by the hearth. He relaxed with a glass of brandy after his long journey. He was surprised when Elizabeth entered the room. She wore a nightgown covered with an opaque robe. Her beauty and fragility were accented by her hair unbound and flowing like a soft red flame around her shoulders to her waist. Her green eyes sought his and he grinned at her. He surely must be dreaming. "Miss Elizabeth, I hope I find you well."

She didn't answer, only stared at him.

Phillip scanned her from head to toe. She was relatively tall and the top of her head came to his nose. It was rare to find a woman he didn't tower over. He set his now empty glass on the mantel behind him and waited for what she would do next.

She never spoke.

The sway of her hips and her elegant toes peeking from underneath the gown taunted him. Elizabeth stopped directly in front of him, closer than the distance he would have held her during a waltz. Her sweet scent clouded his senses. Or perhaps it was the brandy. Or wishful thinking.

Something was amiss. Elizabeth reached up with her right arm and caressed his hair. Her fingers traced the line of his jaw before her hand moved to the back of his head and her other arm came up over his shoulder. Before he realized it, she pulled his face towards hers—and kissed him.

Soft lips urged his eyes to close and he wrapped his arms around her. Surely, this was a dream. He'd known women in the past, but here was a sweet innocence and passion he'd never experienced before. He was no innocent himself but something inside him claimed that when it came to this woman, he was. He grew lost in the sensation of her in his arms. His fingers savored the silken strands of her hair. Time stood still as they were lost in this impassioned embrace. A line from Shakespeare's play, *A Midsummer Night's Dream*, taunted him in this madness.

If we shadows have offended,
think but this and all is mended,
that you have but slumber'd here,

while these visions did appear.
And this weak and idle theme,
No more yielding but a dream.

A throat cleared, breaking the spell, for surely that must be what it was.

Phillip reluctantly broke away from the kiss and looked past Elizabeth to discover Marcus standing in the doorway with a scowl on his face. Phillip gulped as he realized the source of his friend's anger. He'd been caught taking advantage of a young woman under Lord Remington's protection. Protection Phillip sought for her. He was trapped.

"I assume tomorrow you will return to London to procure a Special License." His friend's voice brooked no argument.

Phillip nodded and weakly pushed Elizabeth away from his body, yet her arms held fast. "Miss Follett, you must let go," he whispered urgently to her. He reached up to grab both of her arms still wrapped around his neck and yet, she said nothing. She looked at him and smiled sweetly as he returned her arms to her sides and stepped away from her.

Elizabeth stared at him for a moment with a soft smile playing on her well-kissed lips. Silently she turned and walked past Marcus without any hint of awareness of his presence.

"I'm well and truly caught, aren't I?" Phillip groaned.

Marcus' grim expression continued as he nodded and turned to leave. He stopped. "Your usual room is ready for you."

Phillip bent his head. He'd just spent a day on the road and now, due to one moment of indiscriminate passion, he'd be heading back to London. His single days were over. The noose tightened around his neck. He reached up to undo his cravat. When that didn't help, he poured another brandy and took it with him to his room. In the old days it would have been the entire bottle.

~*~

The sun teased through a gap in the drapes, falling across Lizzy's bed. She stretched and smiled. She'd had the most wonderful dream. Reluctantly she rose to face reality. Her dreams could never come true. It was pure folly to think about Lord Phillip as she had in her sleep.

The maid brought in fresh water and a cup of hot chocolate.

Soon Lizzy was gowned, coiffed and ready to join her hosts in the breakfast parlour. As she opened the door to leave, she discovered Josie there, hand raised to knock.

"I need to speak with you, Elizabeth." Josie entered, shooed the maid out, and closed the door firmly behind her. She motioned Elizabeth to the sitting room.

"Is something the matter?"

Josie frowned. "Can you tell me what happened last night?"

"When? After dinner when I left you to come to my room?"

Her hostess nodded.

"I came here and Elsa helped me ready for bed. I was exhausted, went to bed and slept better than I have in weeks."

"And..."

"And what? I enjoyed wonderful dreams and

awoke to sunshine."

"You don't remember anything else?"

"Why should I? Did something happen last night?" She bit her lip. Would they blame her for something she hadn't done? Would she be cast out?

"Yes. Marcus came upon you kissing Lord Westcombe in the library."

"Lord Westcombe arrived last night? I didn't know. As if he would ever dally with me. And how could he? I spent the night asleep in my bed."

"Aware or not, my husband walked in on the two of you locked in a passionate embrace."

Elizabeth's eyes grew wide and her hand went to cover her mouth. "So...it wasn't a dream." Lizzy rose to pace. "When I was younger I used to sleepwalk. I wasn't aware I still did that. If I came upon Phillip and kissed him, it was not done intentionally." Heat rose to her cheeks. "I must apologize."

"It'll have to wait. Phillip has already left to procure a Special License. In three days, we will have the minister come and you will wed here in the chapel."

Lizzy dropped back into the chair. "You cannot be serious. He does not want me or love me. I'm in no way appropriate for a man such as him."

Josie rose. "You may have initiated the contact, but Phillip did nothing to avoid you or to stop it. He understands his duty to a woman of noble birth whom he has compromised."

"My reputation is of no account and no one of our acquaintance need ever know of this. I will *not* marry the man."

"I wonder if you really mean that, Elizabeth." Josie's head tipped to one side.

"Excuse me?"

"Why would you select Phillip out of a crowded ballroom when other men were available to approach for assistance? Why would you, even in your sleep, kiss him if he were not the object of your heart's desire?"

"Desire does not equal love," Lizzy protested. "He must despise me. This is not a good way to start a marriage." She looked up at Josie. "What did you tell him about my past?"

"Not much. You'll have the pleasure of filling him in on the details."

Lizzy began to weep. This couldn't be happening. Arms wrapped around her, holding her.

"*Shhhhh!* Many marriages start out far worse than this and survive. There is no reason why yours couldn't grow to be a grand love match. This also resolves the dilemma of what to do to protect you from Lord Wolton. Your father cannot force you to marry one man when wed to another. Phillip is more than capable of defending what is his."

"So, I'm to wed in three days?" Lizzy hiccupped.

"Yes."

"Then I suppose I need to figure out how to look my best when he returns. I don't want him to regret this marriage." She wiped away the tears with her hands.

"That's the spirit. You will be the most beautiful bride and Phillip will wonder why he had never stumbled upon this solution from the start."

"I hope you are correct."

"I pray God will make this right somehow. He specializes in the impossible."

"I've not seen proof of that yet."

"That's because you haven't been looking." Josie rose and accompanied Lizzy to breakfast.

~*~

Phillip spent his journey back to London on horseback, contemplating his fate. She'd tricked him and he'd fallen straight into her trap. Those beguiling eyes, that soft hair…were enough to turn any man's head. So why had he succumbed in that moment? He really couldn't blame his fatigue or the alcohol. It would take far more than that small glass of brandy to dull his senses. It had been years since he'd been in his cups. He didn't like losing control over his life and too much drink did that to a man. *Blithering idiot!* He spurred his horse on.

Marcus didn't need to force the issue. How was he to face his noble friend when he returned? Shame washed over him in waves. He knew better than to be caught near a woman like that alone. Unless he were married. Well, he would soon be that way. Heaven help him if he let Miss Follett's womanly wiles captivate him again. She'd obviously planned this from the start. He'd fallen hard and fast, teased along by a sad story and a desire to help. Perhaps to prove he wasn't the wastrel his family thought he was.

Oh, like this would improve his reputation? A hasty marriage in the country by Special License to a woman who disappeared at his sister's come-out ball? A woman wanted by Lord Wolton for a wife. She'd be safer with Phillip, at least he could provide her sanctuary. He sighed as he came to the livery stable in the next town. Time to change horses.

Refreshing himself with a meal, he was soon back

on the road with his own horse that'd he'd left there only yesterday. When he returned to Rose Hill it would be with his carriage. Once wed, he'd spirit his wife off to his estate until the scandal in London died down. He'd provide the conniving beauty with a home and safety. He could not promise her more. The love he witnessed between Marcus and Josie would never be his to enjoy.

His memory of the previous night flooded his senses. She'd been soft in his arms. Why had he been so weak? Had it been too long since he'd been with a woman? He couldn't justify the expense. Well, now he'd be paying the piper, for sure. Women cost money, and even more so when they were a wife. At least she had an inheritance. Perhaps she could purchase her own trinkets and folderols with that. Once wed the money became his. If he allowed her access to those funds she wouldn't drain his own. He grinned and nodded to himself, satisfied at one solution to a problem.

But he'd have a wife cutting up his peace for the rest of his life.

He'd be safe from the fortune-hunting debutantes. He suddenly felt older than his years. Some of those young girls were barely out of the schoolroom. At least Beth was of an age. Not too much younger than himself. Obviously, she'd honed her wiles though or he wouldn't have been caught.

Resign yourself. It's over. His days of living only to please himself were through. The future stretched ahead with a heavy weight of doom. Where was this God that Marcus so often talked about? Certainly not interested in the life or desires of Phillip Westcombe.

Desire. He gave a wolfish grin. Well, at least that

would be one positive thing. He could slake his desires whenever he wanted. She'd come to him willingly enough. She was beautiful. Her kisses stirred to life something foreign within him. Something beyond lust that he didn't understand. She was his for the taking. He'd only have to guard his heart lest she steal that too.

He arrived at his room to discover his valet gone. And why wouldn't he be? Phillip told him he would be gone a few days. He left a note for the man for when he returned. Likely out enjoying his own comforts for a change. Fenway would commence packing for an extended stay in the country and they would leave in the morning after Phillip finished business at Doctor's Commons.

Collapsing into bed it hit him that from now on, if he wanted, he'd be sharing his bed with his wife. *Wife*. Daunting word. He'd have to give up his rooms here and purchase a house when he came to town next. There was no way he'd stay with his parents.

He rolled to his side. The Earl of Manchester was bound to be cross over this when he read it in the paper. He'd need to write to his mother to smooth things over. That would wait until after the deed was done. He'd send a letter at the same time as a notice to the papers of the marriage having taken place. He'd be setting the fox amongst the henhouse with that one action.

Fleeing to his estate would definitely be the best course of action. Regardless of how she had tricked him, he would not subject his wife to the sharp tongues of the *beau monde*. Eventually, they would be forced to come to town and face society together. He drifted into an uneasy sleep as dreams of Miss Follett teased and tantalized him. A noose hovered overhead as she led him there, pulling the lever to release the floor beneath him. The cord drew tight as his feet dangled and he gasped for breath.

5

Phillip awoke gasping for air. It was early but there was much to be done. He rang for Fenway, who stumbled into the room worse for wear after a night of debauchery.

"Did you get my message?" Phillip asked.

The valet frowned. "Carriage to Rose Hill and pack all your bags. You're giving up your rooms here?"

"Yes. I'll tell you more when we arrive at Rose Hill. From there we will be traveling to Stanton Hall for an extended stay. I have a few errands to run this morning and I'll be leaving on horseback. I expect to see you at Rose Hill by evening. Lay out my brown jacket and tan breeches for today and my riding boots."

"Yes, m'lord." The valet stumbled to the closet to assemble the wardrobe. Phillip rose and decided it was best to shave himself this morning given his valet's reduced competencies. He didn't trust the man with a knife to his throat.

Soon he was on his way out the door. Few people of the upper class milled around the streets of town at this early hour so he managed to procure his Special License without being accosted by anyone. He stopped to purchase a ring he thought suited his new bride-to-be. Returning to his rooms he found Fenway had departed. He made one last stop at his solicitor to draw up a new will and make arrangement for his wife's funds to be preserved in her control. His solicitor was a discreet man but an eyebrow raised at his demands.

"Mr. Hollenback, find me a house I can purchase here in town. With my upcoming marriage, I will need a suitable place to live."

"Yes, m'lord. May I inquire as to when this marriage is to take place?"

Phillip growled. "No. You may not. You can read about it in the papers with everyone else. I will send you a letter with my bride's name and information after the deed is done."

"Something havey-cavey about this, m'lord?"

"Not at all," Phillip asserted. "A love match, if you will." He stared at the man till the solicitor bowed and scraped away.

"Yes, m'lord."

"And not a word to anyone until it is in the papers. No one. Not even your partner." Phillip's eyes narrowed.

"Of course, m'lord. It shall be as you say."

"Very well. Carry on." Phillip turned and left, a small smile playing on his lips as he sought his horse. He had no doubt that before the news hit the papers rumors would be swirling about his marriage. By then the deed would be done. While he could have avoided all that by having his solicitor attend him at Stanton Hall, he did not want to leave his new bride unprotected. Life in this world was uncertain. There were never any guarantees. If he was to be wed, unwanted or not, he would do what was right by his wife.

A shiver overtook him. He glanced around the streets and mews, but seeing no one he shook his head and entered. Once his horse was ready, he mounted and they were on the road, and within a few hours overtook Fenway with the carriage. With a tip of his hat to his valet and coachman, he passed them and urged his horse onto Rose Hill.

He stopped in Didcot, the town just shy of Rose Hill and took a late repast. He wanted to avoid conversation with Marcus or Josie, much less his bride. His carriage passed and he waited an hour, nursing an ale, before heading on.

Marcus greeted him when he arrived and drew him into his study. "Good to see you, Phillip. I admit to some worry when your carriage showed up without you."

"Stopped for dinner at a pub."

"Cold feet?"

Phillip shrugged. "I'll do my duty, never fear that."

"I have some news that might make tomorrow easier to bear."

"Really? Do tell." He accepted a glass of brandy from his friend and took a sip. All he needed now was a bath.

"Your bride-to-be was sleepwalking. She didn't try to entrap you. Josie reports Elizabeth was horrified when she realized what had happened. She tried to beg off."

"Likely story."

"Don't enter marriage resenting her. You still are responsible for your own actions."

"I already told you I'll do my duty, Marcus, and you have every right to hold me to a code of honor, but you cannot tell me how I must feel about Miss Follett."

"Don't make the mistake of starting out poorly with something that could bring you great joy if you allowed it to."

"Is this another one of your God talks?"

"A woman can be a help-mate, a comfort, and definitely a delight. No more lonely nights, Phillip."

"How would you know if my nights have been lonely?"

Marcus raised an eyebrow. "If I've misjudged your more recent attitudes toward debauchery, I stand corrected. I only thought…"

"I'm being peevish. Forgive me, old friend. I've had better things to do with my money than invest in a lady of the night to slake temporary desires."

Marcus grew pink in the cheeks. For a married man, he was still far too virtuous to talk about sex or ladies-of-the-night. In spite of the fact he himself entered a brothel to protect Josie before they were wed.

"I'm assuming Fenway has a bath ready for me by now. I shall see my room and will see you in the morning. You will stand by my side as I speak my vows?"

"I'd be honored to do so."

Together the men left the room and went up the stairs, Phillip going to the room that had been for years set aside for his frequent visits there.

~*~

Lizzy startled awake, heart pounding. She glanced at the clock. She'd be expected at the chapel in two hours. Why had the maid allowed her to sleep so long? She tossed and turned most of the night, worried about how Phillip felt regarding their marriage. Did he resent her? Would he abandon her?

No. He was a gentleman. He'd be there. He would not spurn her now. But had he been informed of the sleep-walking or did he still believe she intentionally seduced him to trap him into this unwanted *mésalliance*? She took some deep breaths and rose.

Josie assured her everything would be resolved.

Lizzy feared that by marrying her, Lord Westcombe was placing himself in harm's way. No man deserved to be punished for her sins, and possibly die on her behalf. She tried to raise the issue with Josie yesterday but wasn't taken seriously. Josie instead spoke about how someone had already died for her sins. Jesus.

Yesterday afternoon, Lizzy read the holy scriptures, in the gospel of John. It confused her. Someone from ancient times died, but Phillip could as well. There was no promise she could find that her fiancé would be safe from harm. She asked if they would permit her to talk to Phillip last night, but they never told her when he had returned. She would only see him before the altar of God, and that fact alone caused her to wonder if he or she wouldn't be struck down dead before the final affirmation of vows.

~*~

Elsa soon arrived. A light breakfast was enjoyed as Elizabeth's hair was put up with small pearl pins to keep it in place. A lovely gown of lavender and white was found in the closet of Marcus' sister, Henrietta. Josie assured her that his sister would not mind if she took the dress. Now a married woman, she had a new wardrobe and didn't visit Rose Hill often.

Lizzy glanced down at her gown. Finally, a color that became her. The white dresses the debutantes wore during their season washed her out. Today she was marrying one of the most eligible and handsomest men of the *beau monde*. Her heart ached for her mother, whom she'd lost when she was five-years-old. She pirouetted around the room. *Mother, can see your little girl now?* She came to a stop before the window where Duke watched with his head characteristically tipped to the side.

"Pretty bird," he said.

"Shouldn't it be pretty lady, Duke?" She curtseyed to him, giggling.

"Pretty lady." He parroted back to her with a wolf whistle.

She grinned and placed a kiss on the top of his head. "Well, Duke, today I marry and become Mrs. Phillip Westcombe. Could anything be sillier than that?"

Duke nodded his head in agreement and gave a short laugh that sounded much like her own.

Lizzy kissed him again.

A knock on the door sent him flying away.

"Enter," Lizzy called out.

Josie came in. "Oh, Elizabeth, you look lovely."

"Does Phillip understand I didn't trap him?"

The young matron sat down, drawing Elizabeth to the seat beside her. "Marcus spoke with him last night and explained. Whether Phillip believes him or not, I don't know. We are both praying for your marriage. Phillip is an honorable man. He will treat you well."

"But will he ever come to love me?"

A soft smile played on the viscountess's lips. "I suspect he's already half-way there. How else would he have come to your rescue at that ball? He put his own reputation at risk to save you and he did that without any sense that you had manipulated him."

"But now he may view it all differently."

"He might. Your love can change all that."

"My...love?" Beth's hand went to cover her heart. "I don't love him."

"I think you must at some level, or you wouldn't be so worried about protecting him, having him think ill of you, or leaving you."

"Perhaps I only want safety."

"I think you desire more than that, Elizabeth. You long to be loved and cherished. Maybe Phillip's not there yet, but you have a sweet spirit about you. I suspect if he's not in love with you yet, he soon will be."

Elizabeth let her hand drop. She swallowed and blinked back tears. "I certainly hope so. I'd much rather be married to Phillip than Lord Wolton. I believe Lord Westcombe would never seek to harm me."

"Far from it. He would do anything to protect you."

"I fear marriage alone will not keep me safe from my father and his friends."

"Why do you say that?"

"They are evil, and associated with someone called the Black Diamond. I've never met the man but his name is spoken of with fear."

"All the more reason for us to keep praying for you. Try to enjoy this day."

"Thank you for all you've done for me, Josie."

"It's been my pleasure. I've looked forward to watching Marcus's friends fall to Cupid's arrow. Phillip is a good man. I'm happy for you both."

"You've treated me with more kindness than I deserve."

"Nonsense. You are a child of God, Elizabeth."

Josie gave her a hug and rose to her feet. "Come now. Dry those tears. We have a wedding to attend."

Beth rose as well and grabbed her bouquet. With one quick look in the mirror, she saw a beautiful woman. How could that ever be her? Would Phillip find her attractive? Pink colored her cheeks as she wondered if Phillip would later hold her, and kiss her as he had in her dream. Could reality compare to that? Oh, she hoped so.

~*~

A numbness settled over Phillip as he stood at the front of the chapel with the minister, who fidgeted next to him, more nervous than Phillip was. It'd soon be over. His cravat suddenly felt too tight.

Josie swept in accompanied by a maid.

Lord Remington walked Elizabeth down the aisle.

Her beauty took his breath away. Sunlight streamed in giving her an ethereal appearance. A lovely angel. As her eyes sought his, he held them. It was as if she spoke the same message from the ball. "Help me." He gave her a small smile and a nod. He'd not want her afraid of him, regardless of how she'd tricked him into this. He could almost believe what Marcus had told him was true, that it hadn't been a trick. Within the next hour, she'd be his. Apprehension about the ceremony vanished, and in its wake flowed a surge of protectiveness and warmth. His gaze tried to convey to her a depth of regard that was so new to him it shocked him to his toes. Reason struggled to find purchase there.

Don't be a fool.

~*~

The light filtering in the stained-glass windows fell across Lord Westcombe standing regally at the front of the small chapel, highlighting his blond hair. She was marrying a god. Dressed in all black with the exception of a brilliantly white waistcoat with silver embroidery, even his cravat was a masterpiece. A flash of emerald green from a pin there caught her attention. His eyes were bluer than she remembered. Lightheadedness assailed her.

The young minister bumbled through the long marriage ceremony.

She barely heard what the man said as she was keenly aware of Lord Westcombe standing next to her, his posture stiff. The vows were spoken. His were strong and firm. Hers soft, but certain. She would do her best to honor this man. When he slipped the emerald ring on her finger and spoke the final words, "With my body I thee worship," a shiver traveled through her, giving her hope.

Departing the chapel on his arm they returned to the breakfast room for a sumptuous brunch that had been prepared by Rose Hill's chef. When the meal finished, Marcus and Josie walked the minister to the door leaving the couple alone for the first time since that inauspicious night in the library.

Phillip leaned over, clasping her hand gently. "I'd like to leave soon to head to my estate, Stanton Hall. We could travel slow so you would be comfortable, but it will mean one night at a posting inn."

Finally, they'd be able to talk. They would have hours in a carriage to become acquainted. "That will be fine, m'lord."

Phillip smiled. "You may call me Phillip now, we

are married and I do not expect my wife to be 'my lording' me all day long."

Lizzy returned a weak smile. "You may call me Elizabeth, or Lizzy, if you like."

Phillip leaned back, gazing at her as he sipped from his glass of wine. He sat his glass down slowly, never taking his eyes off her. "Would you mind terribly if I called you Beth instead? For some reason, it seems to fit you better than Lizzy."

Lizzy nodded mutely. *Beth?* Only her mother had ever called her that. It pleased her that her new husband wanted to use that name. She fought back the tears memories of her mother evoked.

"Fine. Beth, can you be ready to travel within the hour? Your maid has already been packing your bags."

"I have no maid."

"Elsa has consented to travel with us and become your personal maid. It is a rise in position for her. Would that suit you?"

"Yes. I brought nothing with me so my belongings are few. I could be ready in half the time if you wish it."

"An hour will be sufficient so we can adequately say our farewells to Marcus and Josie."

~*~

An hour later Elizabeth waved good-bye to the only friend she'd known in her life. Duke perched on top of the carriage. She was surprised at how readily Phillip accepted her pet. What dismayed her, was her recently acquired husband chose to ride astride.

They still hadn't kissed.

At times, she could see him if she leaned forward

to the window, but soon found that fatiguing. She had to admit he was a fine specimen to look at with strong, lean muscles that showed to advantage on his dashing gelding.

~*~

Phillip had left a notice to be sent to the London papers with Marcus. He still needed to write to his parents. They'd be shocked when they read the news but there was little to be done. There'd been no time to pen a missive to them explaining everything. Not that he would tell them much of anything at this point. He wondered how Lord Follett and Lord Wolton would take the news of him stealing a march on them.

It was sure to be the scandal of the week amongst the *ton* to find the elusive Lord Phillip Westcombe quickly marrying a woman who had disappeared at his parents' ball.

He didn't have time to worry about that. What was done was done. In a few weeks, they could return for the end of the season. By then a new scandal would have taken over and he'd establish Beth as his chosen wife. His mother would likely be crowing over the announcement and start making claims that she'd been aware of the love-match all along. That was how the game was played. His father might be less enthusiastic.

He glanced at the carriage where his bride rode alone. A second carriage followed with his groom, the maid, and the luggage. He admitted his cowardice to himself. He had no clue how to become acquainted with this woman who was now his wife. They'd had no courtship. She was a stranger to him. Whenever he thought back to that kiss, he wondered anew whether he'd have the patience to forestall their wedding night until they arrived at Stanton Hall. Any time spent in proximity to her left his blood simmering with just one touch. He still wasn't sure what to believe about the sleep-walking.

Regardless of his reticence to wed, he could have done far worse than this beauty for his wife. He itched to hold her and kiss her. He'd promised himself not to do so until they were at Stanton Hall. He would make her his wife in his own bed, not at some posting house. The wait chafed at him.

At their next stop, he'd be forced to leave his horse behind and he'd be spending the remainder of the day in the carriage. Her presence was no reason to forgo the comfort of his own well-sprung equipage. The groom on the second carriage would return to Rose Hill and collect his horse to be housed there until his return. Thankfully he had a good stable even at Stanton Hall.

He only rode now to cool his passion for the woman inside the carriage. Two days of keeping his hands off a woman who was rightfully his. He owed her that honor as his wife.

After a late lunch, he joined her in the coach.

"Tell me about your pet," he asked as he sat across from her in the rear-facing seat. The space was a buffer to intimacy.

"Duke?" she smiled. "I found him last year, having fallen out of his nest. He'd been injured. I bandaged him up and kept him hidden in the barn where my father and his guests couldn't find him. They don't know he exists. Duke recovered and I found him as greatly attached to me as I was to him. I've never had pets and very little affection. He became a good friend. I taught him tricks and how to talk and he's been with me ever since."

"Your father allowed a crow to come with you to London?"

She shook her head. "He knew nothing about Duke. The coachman and footmen kept him a secret and helped me bring him to London, riding on the carriage much as he is doing now. My father slept most of the way and would never notice a bird riding on top of the luggage. Duke would fly off whenever we stopped and returned when we were safely inside and on the road. Crows are quite intelligent."

"I never realized that. You are a woman of many surprises, Beth."

"I'm afraid some of those surprises you will find less than pleasant." She stared out the window.

"I'm sure if I gave you every detail of my own sordid youth, especially before I befriended Lord Remington, you'd find much unpleasantness there as well. I'm prepared to like you Beth, and perhaps to even grow to love you in time. I cannot promise you a title, but I can vow to do all that is in my power to see you happy and safe."

She turned her gaze to him and bit her lip. "You must be an angel, but I need to warn you. The battle we face may become ugly and vicious. Lord Wolton will not give up easily and my father may seek vengeance as well."

"You are mine. As the son of a powerful earl, your father and Lord Wolton would be foolish to attempt to seek any vengeance against us. Even slander amongst the *ton* can be fought and overcome in time. Regardless, we are married, for better or for worse, and I am a man of honor. Trust me, Beth. It will be fine."

"I hope you're right, Phillip."

A shiver of unease traveled up his spine and he shook it off. He would do what he must to keep her safe.

~*~

Beth fidgeted as she awaited dinner in the parlour Phillip had acquired for their privacy and comfort. During the meal, she peppered Phillip with questions about his family so she would know something of them when next they met. After the final course was removed she took a deep breath. "I shall meet you in our room after you have your port." She rose and he stood as well.

"I have a separate room for tonight. I did not want to consummate our wedding night in a common inn. We will wait until we arrive at my estate." He lifted her hand and placed a kiss there. "Sleep well, Mrs. Westcombe."

"And you too, Phillip." She pulled her hand back and went to her room to find Elsa there to assist her in preparing for bed. Once under the covers, she fought her disappointment. At least he treated her well. Tomorrow night could not come soon enough for her. She fell asleep longing for those lips on her own instead of on her hand.

One more day.

6

Phillip stepped outside to check they were ready to depart.

Beth joined him. With a whistle, she extended her arm and a large black crow landed there. She moved him closer and he made a kissing noise as he brushed his beak against her cheek.

Phillip's eyes grew wide.

"Lord Westcombe," Beth began, her face turning a pretty shade of pink, "Phillip. I'd like to introduce you to Duke."

"Hello, Duke," the bird squawked.

"Hello." Phillip had no desire to get close to that sharp beak.

"We're traveling on today to Phillip's home. You may fly along with us or rest on the carriage as you've done previously. We might make stops but I hope you'll keep up with us."

The bird bobbed his head.

Beth gave him a kiss and the bird flew off, circling overhead before settling on an overhang to watch them.

"Do you really think he understands you?" Phillip extended his hand to help her up into the carriage and followed along.

"But of course. Well, maybe not every word, but he will follow. I needed to make sure he knew I was well. He can tell that by the tone of my voice."

"He looks as though he could be a formidable

defender. You say your father and Lord Wolton knew nothing of your pet?"

"I've learned to be circumspect." She looked down at her hands in her lap.

Phillip knocked on the roof of the carriage to let the driver know it was time to continue their journey.

"You are not a first-born son, are you?"

"No. If you hoped to snare the heir, you misjudged matters. My oldest brother already has two hardy sons to ascend to earldom should the need arise."

"So, you were the spare in your family."

He nodded.

"But you didn't choose the church, the law, or a military career?"

"I was fortunate in that I had no need to, although I considered the law or the military briefly. Not much need for the church, but Marcus and Josie would strongly disagree."

"Josie talked to me about God."

"I'm not surprised."

"You respect them and hold them in great affection but you disdain their faith?"

He sighed. "I respect their faith. It works for them. I just see no need of it in my own life."

Beth opened her mouth as if she were to speak but shut it again and looked out the window.

"You had something to say? Don't be afraid to share your views with me," Phillip urged, suddenly quite interested in his wife's perspective.

She turned back to him. "I've seen too much evil in this world to deny there are demons. So why would I deny the existence of a God as well?"

"Demons? I was just talking about going to

church."

Beth shook her head. "No. Faith in Jesus is more than that. It is a relationship with the God of the universe. It transcends a church building. From what I understood so far, there is a spiritual war being waged that takes place beyond our sight."

"I don't understand."

"I'm not saying I do either, but I shall keep reading the Bible Josie gave me in an effort to grasp this."

"Let me know if you figure it out." A small smile played on her lips and all he could do was remember kissing them, how many nights ago was that?

"I shall indeed do so."

The rest of the journey was quiet. Phillip kicked himself for not being courageous enough to seek to know his bride better. He reasoned he had the rest of his life and since he hadn't wanted a wife he didn't need to go out of his way to accommodate one. He'd treat her with respect and would most likely enjoy their nights together, but he needed little else. Something teased at the back of his conscience telling him that he was being selfish.

She trapped me.

You don't know that for sure.

It was as if a demon and angel were arguing from both sides of his head. He closed his eyes and shook his head willing them both to be quiet.

They arrived as the sun began to set.

Phillip was pleased to see his bride lean forward to get her first glimpse of their home. Honey colored stone with ivy growing up the sides and three stories high, Stanton Hall was an average-sized country manor. It was more than sufficient for his needs as a second son.

"I have only owned the place for two years and have yet to do any redecorating. You may undertake that task. The staff is small but you may supplement as you see fit."

"Phillip, it's wonderful. The grounds, the way the sun seems to illuminate the buildings and glisten off the stone, is enchanting."

"I'm delighted it meets with your approval."

By the time the carriage rolled to a stop in front of the main entrance, the staff managed to line up outside to meet the new mistress of the household.

Phillip made all the introductions and noted how every servant beamed their delight at having a mistress in residence. He was glad she was being greeted so warmly but regretted they would only be here for a week or two at the most. The season would end before long and they needed to make an appearance in town to ensure she was accepted by the *ton* for her future well-being. A new wardrobe and introductions to the right people were integral to that plan and time was short.

Mrs. Wilson escorted his bride to her chambers which were connected to Phillip's, so Beth could freshen up before dinner.

Phillip went to do the same but quickly arrived back in his study to glance through letters that had yet to be forwarded to his London address. He placed them on the desk and sat. His rooms in London were not fit for a bride. Gentleman's quarters only. They'd need to stay in a hotel until he arranged for his own house. If Marcus remained at Rose Hill they could possibly stay at his London home. Phillip was unsure. At least he had his solicitor looking into residences for him.

He pulled out some paper and dipped his quill to write letters to his mother and friends to confirm his marriage and apologize they were unable to be a part of the event. He promised his mother he'd bring his bride to town soon to meet the family. He finished sanding the last letter as his wife entered the room.

She stepped in slowly, taking in the surroundings.

This was the one room he had furnished to his specifications as he spent most of his days here. He rose to go to her. "Are your rooms to your satisfaction?"

"Everything is fine. So much nicer than I dared dream." She motioned to the bookshelves around her, the fireplace, and the desk. "This room suits you well."

He was only a step away but couldn't keep himself from closing the distance between them, gently touching her arm. "I'll give you a tour tomorrow and you can select a room to call your own."

"Thank you." Her eyes dropped to her hands.

He reached forward with his right hand to lift her chin so he could view those bewitching green eyes. He longed to give her words of comfort, and assurances that the night ahead…

A knock on the door led him to drop his hands to his side. Masters, the Stanton butler, entered to announce dinner. Phillip held out his arm and Beth placed her hand on it. He led her into the dining room with a table set for two.

The meal was quiet. His new wife didn't eat much but he attributed it to nerves. When they had finished, he stood to help her from her chair. Placing a kiss on her hand he gave her a gentle smile. "I'll be up in an hour."

She nodded, avoiding his gaze and left the room.

Phillip sat to savor his port as the staff removed the covers. He finished his drink and rose to go pace in his study. Was he a monster to expect her to gladly enter into a wedding night when they barely knew each other? He had not kissed her since that night in Rose Hill. He kept a tight rein on his passion but this was his by right. It was time. He was home. With mixed emotions of regret and anticipation, he rose to go to his room to prepare for his first night with his beautiful bride.

~*~

Beth was dressed in her night rail, much as she had been a week hence when she apparently accosted Phillip in his library. An hour had come and the closing of the door from the next room apprised her of her husband's imminent appearance. Her pulse raced and she took deep breaths. A quick glance in the mirror revealed long hair flowing down and her eyes bright in anticipation. She waited at his pleasure. But it was time. She couldn't help but smile in spite of her fears about the actual event. She strode to the fireplace and sat.

A soft door click preceded his arrival. He wore a dressing robe as he entered. Why would she expect anything else? He was as proper as ever. Did this man ever lose control?

"M'lord," she acknowledged him.

He came to stand by the fireplace mantel. "Beth."

"Would you care for something to drink?"

He shook his head. "Are you afraid of me?" he asked.

"No. But I want to know what I missed."

"I don't understand."

"I was told I kissed you."

"You did."

"I thought it was a dream. I'd like to do that while awake."

A soft smile played on his lips. "I'm willing to oblige you."

"Tell me what you saw that night?" She stood and strode to the door.

"You entered the room, dressed much like you are now."

She turned to face him

"You never said a word. Just slowly walked toward me."

She took a step forward. And another. "Yes?"

"You came to stand right in front of me."

He gulped as she drew near. His eyes watched her, traveled her entire body and back to her face.

"And then?"

"You reached up…"

"Like this?" She put an arm on his shoulder and snaked it around his head.

He nodded.

"Then what?"

"You kissed me."

She raised up on her toes and let her lips caress his. His arms went around her pulling her tight and she relaxed into his strength. She savored every moment of the kiss. He released her.

"Then what?"

"Marcus came in and found us."

"Let's pretend he didn't. What would have happened next?"

He didn't answer in words but drew her close

again and showed her, much to their mutual delight.

~*~

Elizabeth woke in bed alone the next morning but the depression on the pillow next to her made her smile. He'd spent the night enfolding her in his strength. After he'd dozed off she'd spent time staring at him. Even with his hair mussed up, he appeared perfect to her. Would he come to love her in spite of the inauspicious beginning to their marriage? Was that too much to hope for? She stretched languidly under the covers before tossing them off, grabbing her robe, and starting her ablutions. Eagerness to see her new home fueled her. And to spend that time in the presence of the man whom she'd spent the previous evening with, tantalized her. Would he kiss her again? Oh, she hoped so.

She found her husband at the breakfast table. Every hair was in its perfect place and she itched to run her fingers through it and leave it messy. Phillip took great pride in his appearance. Wearing her borrowed and remade clothing, she felt shabby sitting next to him.

"Is something concerning you, Beth?"

She nodded her acceptance of her coffee and a plate of food from the footman before answering. "Will you be ashamed of me when we arrive in London? I lack a wardrobe that could compare to your standard of dress."

"You could wear rags and be beautiful to me. However, I agree that you are in need of a new wardrobe and I am aware of an excellent modiste who we will contact when we arrive in town." He sipped his coffee. "Speaking of that, I realize my rooms in town will not be adequate for us. I've set my solicitor to the task of locating a suitable residence. We can inspect his choices once we are in London. I expect you to be honest about what you like or dislike."

"You are generous."

"Did you expect me to be an ogre? My parents have been happily married and my father was faithful to my mother. Very often they are caught acting like newlyweds and I have hoped that as we age we will not lose that sense of wonder with each other."

Her face grew warm. "You should not speak so in front of the servants," she whispered.

Phillip raised a brow at the footman who stood by the buffet ready to serve their needs. The man gave a curt nod and exited the room, silently closing the pocket door behind him. "There, is that better?"

Beth gave him a smile. "Thank you."

"My servants are circumspect. They will often be around. I do not let that hinder me as I go about my life. They are paid well to be of service. I hope you don't expect me to only kiss you in the privacy of our suite."

"I've little experience with managing a home and I would want them to respect me."

"Why wouldn't they? You are their mistress and I suspect they are rejoicing that a woman is now in charge. I'm afraid I've not been all that my housekeeper and butler would desire as far as taking care of the home. I've allowed them leeway. It is up to you to tell them how you wish for them to go on."

"Now? I hardly know where to begin."

"If you are finished with your food, I will give you a personal tour." One eyebrow raised as if challenging her. But to what? A tour was innocent enough and eagerness had her standing so quickly her chair almost tipped over.

Phillip rushed to grab it and push it back into the table. "See, that's what I pay the footman for." He winked at her.

Arm in arm they slowly made their way through the rooms. With every space, Phillip would close the door and kiss her, leaving her dizzy with need. So much so that when they finally came to their suite of rooms, she grabbed his cravat and dragged him inside.

Elsa was there.

"Elsa, you may leave us. I'll ring when I have need of you."

The young maid bobbed and ducked out the door, shutting it quietly behind her.

"I have work to do, my dear," Phillip protested.

"You most certainly do." She untied the cravat, tossed it to a chair, and proceeded to unbutton his waistcoat.

"You intend to ravage me in the middle of the day?"

"I'm making up for lost time." She pulled his head down and assaulted him with her kisses.

He capitulated much to Beth's delight.

7

Their week at Stanton Hall drew to an end and Phillip reluctantly handed his bride into the carriage to begin their journey south to London in easy stages. There would be no stop at Rose Hill. He wished he could stay away from the season longer but he understood the importance of establishing his bride amongst the *haute ton* and face down any gossip. Announcements would have been read and discussed and by now Lord Follett and Lord Wolton were aware that their plans for Beth had been foiled.

Phillip started out their journey on horseback but soon joined his wife in the carriage. He enjoyed stealing kisses from his bride and holding her as she rested against him. He'd never acted as a buffer against the bumps of a carriage—or life, but now it seemed he was that and more to this unexpected addition to his life.

When she wasn't dozing, they had stimulating conversations about politics and the issues facing the nation. She had even stayed abreast of the war effort.

"Lord Remington's brother, Jared Allendale, is an aide-de-camp to Sir Wellesley."

"A great commander. 'Tis a shame about Prince Frederick, Duke of York. Did you ever meet his mistress?"

Phillip's eyebrows rose. "It isn't proper conversation for a lady to discuss."

"There is only you and I here, and I'm curious."

"Next you'll want to know if I've had a mistress."

She frowned. "I'd never considered that. It is the norm for a gentleman of the *ton* to have one, if I'm not mistaken."

"It is done. And my past is simply that. My past. My future has no need of anyone other than my wife. I promised to be faithful and I fully intend to adhere to that principle."

Her gaze fell to her hands. "I'm sorry if I made you cross."

He lifted her chin with his finger and his lips met hers. Pulling away, he sighed. "You haven't made me cross. I desire none but you."

The next morning as they traveled, Phillip was once again on horseback. He would have invited his new wife to join him as well, but she lacked the appropriate clothing. The quiet soothed him and the exercise and space from his wife tempered the temptation she presented with her delectable lips. Marriage wasn't anything like he'd thought it would be.

Duke typically rode on the top of the carriage, occasionally flying off and returning, most often when they would stop to change horses. Phillip was startled when the bird swooped down at him forcing him to duck just as the report of a gun was heard. The carriage stopped and Phillip whirled around with his own pistol aimed to where he thought the shot had come from. His outriders were unsuccessful in locating the shooter.

Beth came running to him as he dismounted.

"What was that all about?" He shouted at the bird now sitting on top of the carriage watching the excitement.

"Are you all right, Phillip?"

"I'm well, just furious at that bird of yours for nearly knocking me off my horse."

Beth grabbed his arms and pain sliced through his shoulder. She moved around to his side. "You've been shot. Come, take off your coat." She helped him take off his greatcoat and then his suitcoat.

"Ma'am if you want me to undress further, I suggest we do this inside the carriage." He wiggled his eyebrows at her but she didn't laugh.

"You will come to the carriage so I can bind up that wound." She turned to the carriage. "Duke. Here darling." The bird flew awkwardly down to perch on her arm. She checked him over and found some flight feathers on one wing broken off. "He must have been hit by the bullet as well. I believe he was trying to save you, Phillip." She kissed the bird's beak. "You were my brave warrior, Duke. Thank you."

Phillip stood there stunned. Why was she kissing the bird and thanking it? He was the one shot and bleeding.

Beth turned to him. "Do you have anything to say to Duke?"

Sighing, Phillip said, "I'm sorry I was so hasty, Duke. It seems I owe you an apology. Thank you for saving me." Phillip gave a bow and handed off the reins to the tiger who assisted his coachman. "Perhaps we should seek the shelter of the carriage, dear wife, so you can tend to my wound."

"Certainly, dear husband. Allow me to bandage your injury and soothe your pride, hmm?"

He grabbed her as the world spun and righted itself. She assisted him to the carriage, this time helping him up the steps first and following behind. She drew the window covers shut. Soon Phillip forgot all about the scratch in his shoulder from the bullet as his wife cared for his every need.

~*~

Beth's heart raced as she settled next to her husband and tended his injury. His face grew pale as he relaxed against the squabs of the carriage. She bound his wound with a spare cravat. His shirt was ruined as was his coat. It struck her that if Duke had not intervened, she would be a widow after only a week of marriage. While she had not sought to wed this man, she could not imagine a future without him. Their compatibility surprised her.

A little bit of brandy and some love from her had gone a long way to relaxing him. Still the shadow of doom loomed over them as they ventured closer to London and the eventual confrontation with her father and Lord Wolton.

Phillip seemed to dismiss the threat. He believed the attack was only a random highwayman. He refused to listen to her pleas for protection for himself. Beth understood her husband was a marked man in mortal danger against evil forces he didn't understand. The one thing she'd yet to share with him was the ugly truth about her background.

It was that very negligence on her part that could cost him his life. She'd been a victim of evil since her mother's death. Did her mother accidentally die as her father claimed or had she been a victim of despicable acts by Lord Wolton and his men?

Phillip began to snore softly.

Warmth stole through her as she gazed at his

strong features. A man she'd summoned across a crowded ballroom. A man who'd given up his single life to spare her scandal. A man who brushed off danger as if it were commonplace. Sweet, naïve, Phillip. A man who was also her husband who now held her heart and their future in his hands.

She'd still been reading the Bible Josie had given her. Jesus said that if his followers needed anything, they only had to ask. Was it really that simple? What did one ask a holy God? *Lord, protect my husband and our marriage from the evil that threatens my first chance of happiness. I don't want Phillip to ever regret his choice to make me his wife. I'm not even convinced of Your existence yet. Help me understand. I'm so tired of the evils of this world. Thank You for glimpses of heaven through marriage to this man.*

Arriving in London they got rooms at Grillion's Hotel and immediately viewed a few potential residences.

Phillip grew pale from the exertion and Beth begged off further visits so he could rest.

~*~

Phillip was at a loss as to how to calm his wife's fears. He enjoyed having her fuss over him. He wondered if the attack really had been intended for him. A notice of their marriage had been sent to the papers and if his suspicions about Wolton and Follett were correct, they would stop at nothing to eliminate him to get at his wife. He sent out missives to his friends in town to discover if any were around to render assistance. More than anything he longed to be back at Stanton Hall, watching his estate flourish and filling the rooms with laughter and the joy of family. His own family. A dream he'd never really held dear, but now...now he could not imagine any other future for him than to have Beth by his side and a passel of children running through the halls of their home.

Thoughts of family brought about the concern about how his own parents and siblings would react to the news of his sudden marriage. Especially given the notoriety of the bride he'd acquired. He'd no regrets now. In spite of his earlier concerns he counted himself blessed to have a wife so in tune with him.

The next morning Phillip summoned a modiste to attend to Beth in their rented rooms.

"Please do not leave the hotel without me." He leaned over to kiss her cheek.

"But..."

"Beth. It is not safe and we don't know what your father or Lord Wolton might be planning. Honor me in this."

She straightened her shoulders and swallowed hard, but gave a nod of assent.

He wondered how compliant she would be. On his way out the door, he admonished his valet to keep watch over the new bride.

"Aye, m'lord. It shall be as you say."

Fenway handed him his hat and cane and with some trepidation, Phillip ventured out into society. His first stop was White's, where he had requested Sir Michael Tidley and Lord Theodore Harrow to join him. They had been friends since university where they'd become acquainted through their mutual friendship with Marcus.

"What, ho! Phillip, my good man, I didn't realize the wind blew in that direction. Congratulations you sly dog." Michael gave Phillip a hearty pat on the back, almost knocking him over as the force hit his injured shoulder.

Michael was wiry in build, shorter than the rest of them, but made up for it in his quickness on his feet. Whether with sword or fists, he was definitely the man to have by one's side in a fight. He was fearless and tenacious but there was a little of the devil-may-care attitude about him. He had dark hair and eyes and the unfortunate legacy of being baseborn. His mother was now deceased, as was his grandfather. Adrift in the world, he clung to his friends.

"Well met, Tidley. Yes. It is true I am well and truly caught and when you meet my lovely bride you will understand why the attraction was hard to resist." Phillip smiled as he sat down and raised two fingers to let the server know to bring them drinks.

"I believe I spied her at your sister's ball. Wasn't she the one who mysteriously disappeared? Interesting how she's now married to you." Michael gave a wink before he casually looked around as if life were boring. "Did you fall madly in love and spirit her away to be your bride, thus stealing a march on all of us?"

"Not quite the way it happened, but regardless, there is a very real danger I may have taken upon myself when I rescued her. I need help."

Theodore walked in, handed off his hat to the majordomo and gave the order for his own beverage. He sat as the drinks were brought. Once the footman left, Theo whispered. "I hate to say, 'I told you so,' Phillip, but when we last met, I did suspect you more attached to the young lady than you were willing to admit to."

Phillip smiled and lifted his glass. "I concede the

point. Regardless of how this came about, I am content with my new bride and hope you will accept her and help me protect her." He paused and tilted his head to Theo. "And no. I am not going to satisfy anyone's curiosity about just how I managed to find myself married. I don't need any more gossip than there likely already is."

"Why would you need us to help protect her? Isn't that your job?" Michael asked.

"I am also at risk. There was an attempt on my life on our return to town. I was shot, but wonder if I'd still be alive if it weren't for the actions of her pet crow, Duke."

Michael had been in the process of sipping his wine when this last was said and the liquid spewed from his mouth. He quickly wiped away the liquid from himself and the table. "A pet crow? And here I thought I was strange for having a ferret for a pet. Is she a witch?"

"She is not a witch. Yes, she has a crow. Why are you so superstitious? Ravens are kept at the Tower of London to ensure the safety of the monarchy. Think of it as more of a good-luck charm, although I don't believe in such."

"If I recall, your bride is not only beautiful but charming. You married Lord Folly's daughter and snatched her from the grasp of her affianced groom. Maybe that's all a blessing for her, but not necessarily for you, my good man," Theo stated.

"I've yet to meet Lord Follett. Have some respect, Theo. The crow has proven to be more useful than I would have guessed. I wouldn't be here now speaking with you and my bride would already be a widow, if it weren't for that bird."

"You're serious, aren't you? Where were you injured?" Michael asked.

"My shoulder. Thankfully I ducked before the bullet could pierce my heart."

Theo shook his head. "So, let me get this straight. You rescued the fair damsel in distress, stepped into the parson's mousetrap with nary a by-your-leave to us, inherited a pet crow, and now find yourself tangled in a web of evil. You want our help to protect your marital bliss."

Phillip nodded.

"What do you need from us?" Michael asked.

"Has there been any news around town with regard to Follett or Wolton? Has anyone uncovered why they were so eager for her to wed that creep?"

"I've heard nothing. Has Marcus uncovered anything?" asked Theo.

"I suspect he's still at Rose Hill but I will be sending him a letter."

"When is he due back in town?" Michael sipped his wine again but put the glass down as Phillip opened his mouth.

"Not sure. He may not be around much this season. Impending fatherhood has brought out his protective instinct."

Michael and Theodore grinned.

"Marcus will be unbearable now that he's about to be a father. I can only imagine how proud he must be." Michael tapped his finger on the table.

Theodore nudged Michael. "Should we be taking bets on how soon it will be before Phillip makes a similar announcement?"

Phillip scowled at his friends. "If we cannot stay alive it will be a moot point."

Both Michael and Theo sobered up and bent their minds to figuring out just how to protect Phillip's newfound bride. The discussion also centered on how to go about uncovering what was happening with Lords Follett and Wolton.

~*~

"Fenway tells me you tried to leave." Phillip sipped his tea while waiting for Beth to own up to what happened that morning.

"I told Fenway and Elsa I should be safe enough if they both came with me. I'm tired of being cooped up." She seethed inside at Phillip's tight watch over her. He was in more danger than she was yet he was free to come and go as he chose.

"We still don't know if your father or Lord Wolton might try to take you back."

"What would be the point? We're married. My inheritance is now yours. Even if I died the money wouldn't revert to my father," she protested.

Phillip sighed and set his cup on the table. "I understand you chafe at the way men have hedged you in. I'm only trying to protect you until we are certain we are both safe. Then you'll be able to shop with a maid and a footman with my blessing. But now I want you either here or by my side. Safe. I'd hate to return and find something had happened to you."

"That's fine for you, but I have to wait to see if you will return. I pace, anxious that some terrible fate has befallen you. You've not recovered from your wound yet. You cannot adequately defend yourself."

Phillip reached to take both her hands in his. "I've spoken with some of my friends who are working to help us resolve this. Everything will work out. You'll see."

"How can you have such faith?"

"Faith?"

"Josie spoke of trusting God for the future."

"Marcus has spoken of that as well. I only have faith in my own ability to survive. I am not without resources."

"But—"

His finger pressed against her lips. "No buts. We will be fine. I never sought to have a wife but now that you are in my life I will do everything I can to see you safe. Trust me." She nodded and he removed the finger. "I want to take you with me to visit my parents this afternoon. It is meant to be a private interview. They are not at home to guests."

"I'm too much of a scandal to traipse about society."

"I don't know about that. I'm sure we stirred up some gossip with our hasty marriage on the heels of your disappearance but it will settle down. My father is a powerful earl. Most of the *ton* will not want to be in his black books for alienating me even though I am not his heir."

"You have great faith in his powers."

"I do, even though my parents may not always understand me. I'm their ne'er-do-well son."

Her eyes grew wide. "What? You?"

"It's hard to live down my wilder days as a young man about town. Drinking, gambling, races... I was not in their good graces for some time. They still seem to view me that way. They've not visited Stanton Hall or understand that I am independently secure. Not wealthy by any means, but thanks to Marcus, I'm in better shape than I ever was. My father still insists on giving me an allowance. It's gone into an account. I don't spend it."

"I can't understand how they would fail to appreciate how good and honorable you are." She reached up to caress his cheek.

He gave a wry grin. "See, I even have you fooled." He winked at her. "Shall we go and scandalize them some more?"

Beth sighed. How could his parents not notice what a noble gentleman Phillip was? "Do you think they will shun us?"

"No. My mother will be crowing about my finally choosing a wife and start hinting at grandchildren. My father will likely lecture me on my new responsibilities as a husband and that I need to 'mend my ways.' He has never realized I had mended those years ago." He assisted her to her feet.

Elsa brought her shawl and parasol. Fenway handed Phillip his hat and cane and together they strode out to meet their carriage.

He helped her inside.

"Have you obtained more servants?"

"Consider them a protection for us both given what happened."

She nodded and settled back against the squabs for the short journey to the Manchester house. Phillip exited first and helped Elizabeth step down. She shook out the skirt of her day dress trimmed in lace. She was grateful the modiste had some ready-made dresses that could be quickly altered to fit her.

"You are beautiful. Don't be afraid, my dear," Phillip whispered.

She placed her hand on Phillip's extended arm and

together they took the steps to the front door that opened as they reached the top landing. A butler ushered them in, taking her parasol and Phillip's hat and cane. She glanced around at the vestibule of the home, even more imposing than the night of the ball when she'd been swallowed amongst the many people entering. The butler cleared his throat before escorting them to a drawing room.

I can do this for Phillip.

"Lord Phillip and Mrs. Elizabeth Westcombe to see you." The butler's intonation boomed with importance.

Beth fought back a giggle at being the center of attention as they entered the room.

The door closed behind them.

"Mother. Father. I'd like to introduce you to my bride, Mrs. Elizabeth Westcombe. Beth, these are my parents, the Earl and Countess of Manchester."

Beth managed a graceful curtsey the appropriate depth for their status. She remembered them vaguely from the night of the ball. Was that only a little over two weeks hence?

An elegant lady approached. Phillip's mother. "Oh, Phillip," she gushed, "she is lovely." Lady Manchester turned to Beth. "My dear, welcome to the family. You understand how shocking we found this news of your marriage to my son after your unseemly disappearance. I'm still not sure how this all came about. We didn't even realize he was courting anyone."

A loud harrumph came from across the room. "Sure, would like to know how it happened," the grumpy sounding earl said.

Phillip escorted Beth to his father. "My father, the

Earl of Manchester, may I present my bride, Mrs. Elizabeth Westcombe."

The older gentleman rose and stared up and down at Beth. She fought the urge to fidget. Suddenly he smiled, picked up her hand and placed a kiss above it.

"I'm not pleased with the circumstances surrounding your marriage. No banns. Whenever did a Westcombe do such a thing? But you might just be the making of my son. Come, sit, Elizabeth." He escorted her to a chair and Phillip and his mother followed.

Back straight, Beth struggled not to giggle again. The entire situation was preposterous. She was a baron's daughter and came from a horrid home life that made living in the stews of London seem like a vacation palace.

For the few balls she'd attended in town, she had no polish or training and only a short time at boarding school. Her mother died when she was young and she had little interaction with her peers. She was not worthy to be even a second son's wife. It was beyond silly. Phillip carried his regal bearing in every action. She was the imposter here.

Why had she agreed to this marriage? She glanced over at her husband who gave her a warm smile promising his love. And at night, she didn't need to pretend anything, for his attractiveness could not be denied. So how did she end up being fortunate enough to wed him? It still befuddled her.

"Phillip? May I meet her now?" The cry came from the door which was now open again.

Phillip rose to bring his sister over. "Lady Penelope, meet my wife, Elizabeth."

Penelope gave a curtsy and sat next to Beth. "Oh, I remember you from my come-out ball. No wonder

Phillip fell in love with you. You are beautiful."

"Well, I'm not—"

"—she's not accustomed to being gushed over, Penny."

"Oh, but we are sisters now and we can go to balls together and Mama won't have to shadow my every step." The last was said in a conspiratorial whisper.

Phillip shook his head. "Pen, we're not sure how long we'll be able to stay in town."

Lady Manchester interrupted. "Why? Why would you leave? It's the height of the season and you need to introduce your bride amongst the *ton*. Almacks. You need vouchers for there…"

"Mother…" Phillip warned. "Pen, as much as I'm delighted to see you—"

"Elizabeth is notorious right now, and it might not be to your advantage to be seen in your company, Penelope," Lord Manchester intoned.

The young woman blushed and Beth's face grew warm. She looked down at her hands folded demurely in her lap. Glancing at her husband, his expression betrayed no emotion.

"This will all blow over soon." Lady Manchester reached over to pat Beth's knee. "Once it does we will all be comfortable and enjoy the season." Glancing at her husband she continued. "Lord Manchester is correct, Penelope. We do need to make sure Phillip's precipitous plunge into the matrimonial waters do not hinder your own search for a suitable husband."

Phillip cleared his throat. "Where is the rest of the family?"

A look was exchanged between the earl and countess.

"So, the second son's marriage does not warrant a

full family gathering? Or is everyone piqued at my failure to wed at St. George's?"

"It was an insult to us all to read of your nuptials in the *Times*." His father's voice was now low and disapproving in tone.

Beth shivered as a fissure of fear flowed through her. She met Phillip's gaze and found comfort there.

"Father, I am certain when the whole is explained to you, you will agree I acted in a way that was honorable and in keeping with the values you instilled in me."

The blue eyes of the father met the identical set in the son from across the room and the tension sizzled.

Lord Manchester finally spoke. "I look forward to hearing it. We are an old and noble family and if there is justification for your actions, we can overcome this tittle-tattle currently spreading amongst our peers."

More might have been said, but the butler arrived to announce dinner was served.

Lord Manchester escorted his wife to the dining room and Lord Westcombe provided a double escort to his wife and sister.

~*~

Stilted conversation marked the meal, covering events among the *beau monde*.

Penelope delighted in detailing for them all the various men who had been vying for her attention.

Phillip dutifully gave his impressions on the worthiness of each seeking her hand.

When the ladies departed so the men could enjoy their port, Lord Manchester spoke. "Tell me all now, Phillip, so we may put this behind us."

Phillip bristled but hid his emotions as he sipped his wine. "Beth came to me at Penny's ball, seeking help. She was to be forced to marry Lord Wolton. She was terrified. Lord and Lady Remington provided a safe shelter for her and removed her to Rose Hill the next day.

"I came to visit out at Rose Hill a few days after and realized that I cared deeply for her. To keep her safe I obtained a Special License and wed her immediately before Follett or Wolton could force her. She is of age. Her inheritance is hers. I had no need of a dowry."

"No need? How could that be? You cannot expect to support a wife on your allowance."

"I've tried to tell you before, Father, that I am financially solvent. My estate prospers, as have my investments. I can support a wife with ease. Not luxury, but definitely with style."

"*Hrmppff.* As long as there were no dirty dealings on your part or inappropriate behavior. You didn't compromise the girl, did you? If you had I could have bought her off easily enough and spared you—"

"I did not bed her until our wedding night and I find I am well-pleased with my choice of bride."

"That remains to be seen."

"Will you support me in this?"

"For the sake of the family name, I will. I'm disappointed in you. I fully expected you to aim far higher in seeking a bride."

"I doubt I would have found one as well-suited to me as Beth is. I am content in my marriage."

"At least you are not foolish enough to be in love. What a disaster that could prove to be for you."

Phillip sighed inwardly. *Love?* Maybe he didn't go

into marriage in love, but he feared he might be well on his way there. He neglected to speak of the attack on the journey to London and the danger he and his wife might be in. "Have you heard anything about Lords Follett and Wolton?" Phillip asked.

"No. Strangely enough there's been no talk and it wasn't until the notice of your marriage appearing in the paper that speculation about the matter was resurrected. They've not been seen or heard from."

Whatever was going on with Elizabeth's father and erstwhile groom, they were keeping their secrets close. Phillip understood the danger of assuming their silence guaranteed any safety for him and his bride.

~*~

Beth sank into the squabs on the way home and he squeezed her hand. "Don't worry. They will come around to loving you as I do."

"I hope so, Phillip." The look she gave him indicated she doubted the veracity of his words. He had much to prove to her about just how much he really did care for her.

~*~

Lord Wolton,
You have failed to deliver on your promise. Where is Lizzy Follett? The wench was supposed to satisfy yours and Follet's debts. If she is not delivered to me soon my wrath will be terrible. No more delays or the next neck sacrificed to the Dark Lord will be yours.
Black Diamond
The Black Diamond sealed the letter with blood

red wax. He almost wished he could deliver the message in person to watch the man tremble in fear. But his identity must remain a secret and Lizzy needed to be found lest she share things she didn't even realize she knew. He settled back in his chair. Ah, the future would definitely be bright once he had her under his power.

8

"How dare she show her face back here in town!" shouted Lord Wolton as he once again paced the worn carpet of the Follett house.

Lord Follett was drunk. Insensibly inebriated since the notice appeared in the paper. The noose was tightening around his neck with every step Lord Wolton took. The letter from the Black Diamond only added to his despair. "It's all over," he moaned.

"No, it's not over. She will yet be mine. She has always been mine and I am at an end with the years of waiting you have put me through to get her. And now this?" Lord Wolton walked over and leaned down, nose to nose with Lord Follett who cowered at his approach. "If she is not back with me by the end of June and standing before a clergy pledging her troth to me, you, Folly, will be the one to pay dearly. And pay dearly you will. I have no problem serving you up to the Black Diamond on a silver platter with an apple in your mouth. I'll not take the fall should the truth be known. Your daughter knows too much and whether or not she has told Westcombe is irrelevant. He needs to be taken care of. Permanently."

He stood back up, red and panting. Taking out a handkerchief, Wolton wiped his balding head of the perspiration that arose from his ranting. The room was cool with no fire lit but his passions were high. Follett would be trembling if his extremities weren't already so numb from the cheap brandy he'd been drinking.

"Those goons botched the first job. Why didn't you tell me she had a crow keeping guard over her and her lover? We need to eliminate the bird as well."

"Crow? What crow? I've never allowed her to have a pet. Any animals that we've found have been used for sacrifices." Lord Follett again shivered before leaning over to retch onto the floor by his chair. The room possessed a dank stench from previous such episodes in recent days but neither man seemed inclined to clean up. Household staff remained out of sight.

Lord Wolton sneered. "She is mine and always has been." His eyes glittered pure evil. "From the very first time I touched her and she trembled with fear and begged me to leave her alone. Every time I tortured her to get her to submit I bound her to myself. It was her, and that glorious red hair and those terrified green eyes that were to be our ultimate sacrifice. But now the Black Diamond demands her of us due to your foolishness. She was to be mine!" The man bellowed and rushed at Follett, grabbing him by the coat and shaking the man before tossing him into a heap on the floor.

Lord Follett relaxed there hoping the rant would end so he could suffer in peace.

"I still believe you had some part in her leaving. You resented me from the day of your wife's 'accident.' What a weak man you are to not better protect your wife and daughter from such as I. Too late now. The web is wound too tight around you, Folly. She will be mine."

With that Lord Follett slipped into darkness.

~*~

Phillip escorted Beth around town to inspect various potential homes. Nothing pretentious, as Phillip did not anticipate spending too much time in London, and as a second son was not expected to be doing major entertaining. They finally settled on a place on St. Edmund's Terrace, just northwest of Regent's Park. The mews were conveniently a block away and sufficient for their stabling needs while in town. The fully furnished home allowed them to move in the following day as soon as Fenway could find a cook, housekeeper, and butler. As the modiste returned for another fitting on some of the gowns Beth ordered, he left her to deal with that and headed to White's.

Lord Remington appeared just as Phillip settled into his favorite spot with a cup of coffee.

"You've returned to town, Remy?" Phillip asked.

"I posted back as soon as I got notice from the Ministry of Defense at Whitehall. I realized a sheet of foolscap would fail to convey what I needed to share with you." Marcus sat across from him.

"Something to drink?" Phillip asked.

"Nothing. We have no time for such things."

Phillip's eyebrows rose. "What have you discovered?"

"There has been some illegal activity in the east near Ipswich." Marcus spoke in hushed tones.

"Near the Follett estate?"

Marcus nodded.

"What kind of dealings?"

"Treasonous. Lord Follett is up to his neck in debt and Lord Wolton is holding something over him." Marcus stared at Phillip. "I have a bad feeling about this, my friend. I'm beginning to believe your wife did not exaggerate the danger you are both in."

Phillip sat up a little straighter. "Perhaps that bullet was not just from a common highwayman," he mumbled.

"What bullet?"

"I was grazed as I rode behind the carriage on our return to town. Duke managed to save me from more serious injury."

"You need to remove her from town. Her life is in danger and we cannot investigate this and keep you and her both safe."

"Your proposal?"

"Take her to Rose Hill to stay with Josie. They seem to get along well and I will fare better knowing Josie is not alone while I'm assisting you."

Phillip nodded. "We were moving to our home tomorrow but I can take her to Rose Hill instead. I'll tell her the house needs work and I do not want her to be inconvenienced by the noise. I will not have her living in fear."

"Does she not already suspect the danger?"

"She does. I won't add to her anxieties on my behalf. You did not inform Josie of the danger she was in last year, did you?"

Marcus shook his head. "No. She would not have listened. At the time, she was furious with me for my alleged indiscretion."

Phillip gave a bark of laughter. "What a tangled web that was. In the end, you prevailed, have wed well, and are expecting a child. Perhaps I can look forward to such a future when we are past this."

"You surprise me, Phillip. I thought you were opposed to marriage yet here you are, concerned for the safety of your new wife. One might suspect you of being in love."

"One might."

~*~

Early the next morning a rented carriage left the nearby mews bearing Phillip and Elizabeth. Phillip had discovered men watching the hotel so they sneaked out the back and through several alleys before meeting up with the Remington equipage. Elizabeth yawned but relaxed against his good shoulder. Tomorrow, unbeknownst to her, he'd be returning to London. Alone. This would be their first separation as a married couple.

"Are you sure it's necessary to leave London? We haven't circulated amongst the *ton* as you desired."

"Your wardrobe has not been completed and I fear at this moment it might be counterproductive. Why? Were you eager to dance and flirt now as a married woman?"

She turned her face to his. "Only with you."

She kissed his cheek and he captured her lips with his. Their time together was limited and he was determined to enjoy every moment he could.

It was late afternoon when they arrived at Rose Hill.

"Phillip. Elizabeth. What a surprise. Here I was lamenting how alone I would be with Marcus gone and then you arrive to relieve my tedium." Josie helped them get settled and they had a quiet meal together.

"Did you meet with Marcus in town?" Josie asked.

"No," Beth answered.

"Yes," Phillip replied at the same time.

"You did?" Beth frowned.

"We met at White's. I didn't expect to share every conversation of my day with you."

Beth's eyes narrowed. "Did the conversation spur any actions on your part? For instance, taking a ride to the country with your wife?"

Phillip's face grew warm.

"He was well?" Josie asked after an uncomfortable silence.

"Marcus is in good health and hopes to return as soon as his business is finished."

Josie smiled. "At least I shall have Elizabeth to keep me company when you leave, Phillip."

Beth frowned. "You're leaving?"

"We'll discuss this later." Phillip's stern tone might have ruffled his wife's feathers but she didn't argue.

The reprieve only lasted until they were alone in their rooms. Phillip sat Beth down and joined her. His thumb caressed the back of the hand he held. "I return to London in the morning."

Her eyes glistened with unshed tears. "You're abandoning me here?"

"I'm sorry, my dear. I have work to do."

She gulped hard and pulled her hand away.

"I want you to be cautious. Even here. No riding without a groom or walking alone. I would prefer you did not leave the house."

"Rose Hill is my cage? Am I a prisoner here? For how long?"

He took a deep breath. "I do not know. I expect you to heed my request."

"I'm to obey you without understanding why?"

"Yes. I do this only because I care for you and long for you to be safe."

Beth turned to face him, eyes narrowed. "Am I chattel to you? A dog to do your bidding, put on a leash or secure in a pen? How dare you keep telling me to 'do this' and 'do not do that.' Commands. Not requests. No courtesy was given to me as a human being, much less as a wife." She stood and walked over to the unlit fireplace.

"I apologize if I came across as dictatorial. For too long I lived alone and have only had to consider my own needs and desires. I have had the obeisance of my staff. You are more to me than any mere servant could be. I am only concerned for your safety. I would be grieved if harm befell you."

"What harm? What do you know, Phillip?" She waited for him to speak.

"There is possible danger from Lord Wolton. I want to be cautious. In light of that will you give me your assurance you will obey?" He rose to his feet.

"I suppose." She turned to walk toward him. "In the future, please do not make demands of me. Ask. There have been too many instances in my past where I have been bullied into obedience and threatened." She tipped her head back and lifted up on her toes to kiss his cheek.

"Ah, dear wife, if that is what it takes to please you, then you find me your most obedient slave." Phillip wrapped his arms around her and grinned.

She pulled back, grabbed his cravat, and proceeded to drag him toward the bed. "In that case…"

~*~

Beth stretched under the sheet. The room was warm even with the breeze from the open window. Phillip indulged her by leaving the fire lit instead of banking it. Light streamed in. She was unable to spend an entire night locked in Phillip's embrace even though part of her longed for that kind of affection and security. She couldn't stand any sense of confinement. She rolled over lazily to reach for her husband.

He wasn't there.

She sat up and the room spun. She collapsed back into her pillows. He left? She slowly rose again and rang for Elsa to come and help her dress. Perhaps he was eating. She rushed down the stairs to the breakfast parlor to discover food on the sideboard and no one at the table. She served herself.

A footman pushed in her chair and left her in peace.

Beth stabbed at the eggs and attacked her toast with a vengeance as she buttered it and spread it with preserves. How dare he leave without saying a word.

"Good morning, Elizabeth!" greeted Josie cheerfully as she entered the room. "Has Phillip departed for town already?" Josie was serving herself and couldn't see Beth's scowl.

With a deep breath to calm herself, she replied, "Yes. He left."

"It's just the two of us. I'm grateful Marcus thought to have you join me here while they sort things out in London. I will enjoy more time with you." Josie frowned as she looked at Beth. "Are you well?"

"I am vexed that my husband departed without a fare-thee-well this morning."

"I think it is sweet that you miss him. It is an indication that your marriage, for all its inauspicious beginnings, is bearing fruit of potential happiness for you both."

Beth shook her head. "I believe you misunderstand me."

Josie set her cup down. "You share a strong affection for each other. That much is obvious or his departure would not be causing you grief. It is something I understand all too well."

"Perhaps. I lack friends, other than you and Marcus. Phillip is all I have to cling to." Beth let the lids fall over her eyes as they brimmed with tears. "I fear for him. He is in danger and I would be cast adrift should anything happen to him." She used her serviette to dab at her tears.

"My heart cracked wide open when Marcus almost died, having fought valiantly to rescue me. Phillip gave a good account of himself in that battle. Marcus, Lord Harrow, and Sir Tidley will all strive to protect Phillip from harm. Lord Westcombe is not without mettle either. While he may be a fastidious dresser with nary a hair out of place or wrinkle in his coat, he is strong and fierce in fighting for those he cares about."

"I have no doubt of Phillip's strengths. My fear is that he will underestimate the power of the enemy he faces. There are no rules to this fight. I wish I could shake this fear inside me."

"Let me help you with that since I cannot ease your fears regarding your husband's capabilities." Josie drank the last drop of her hot chocolate and rose.

The women walked to Josie's cozy retreat at the back of the house. The intimate room overlooked the gardens. She motioned Beth to a seat near the window.

Josie sat in a chair adjacent to Elizabeth's. "This battle you and Phillip face is spiritual as well as physical. Am I correct?"

Beth nodded. "How…?"

"The evil you described to me on the night we first met, didn't seem to be real. Something else had to be at work. Have you spoken to Phillip about your past?"

Beth shook her head. "I did not want to give him a disgust of me. As long as we were hidden away at his estate, I believed no harm could befall us. I hesitated to bring that darkness into our marriage and shatter our tentative happiness. Shame kept me quiet."

"How can Phillip go into battle for you when he does not fully understand the enemy? Did you believe you were protecting him by not sharing all you knew?" Josie leaned forward, hands clasped in her lap.

Beth settled back in her chair and inhaled the fragrance from the gardens coming through the open window. "I attempted to impress the gravity of the threat without the specifics from my past. He did not sense the same danger I feared. Perhaps he thought I was a silly female worried about nothing."

"I read something the other day from the Holy Bible that reminded me of you. 'For we wrestle not against flesh and blood, but against principalities, against powers, against the rules of the darkness of this world, against spiritual wickedness in high places.' That comes from Ephesians 6:12."

Hand to chest, Elizabeth gasped. "Yes. Those words are true."

"God has given us tools to fight the evil in this world. Evil is a spiritual force, but that battle can only be done when we place our faith and trust in Jesus."

"You mentioned something like this before. I've only ever heard curses toward God and His followers."

"Those who deny His lordship over their lives are cursed by their own choices. Either you deny Christ by ignoring him, or you admit you have sinned. If you accept the fact that Jesus, a man who was also God, came and died in your place and mine, then you can become a child of God and have a relationship with the Lord of the universe."

"Are you saying that if I don't accept Jesus, I'm siding with the evil that terrifies me and has marked my life?"

Josie nodded. "Yes."

Beth took a deep breath. "I want to choose God over the evil I've known. Will you help me?"

"It's as simple as that and reading the Bible I gave you."

Eyes closed, Beth sent up her silent prayer. *Lord, save me and my husband from those who would do us harm.* "I think I need time alone." Beth rose and returned to her room. Settling in a chair with the Bible, she read more. After that, she went to the desk in her room and pulled out stationary. Dipping her pen in the ink she began to write to her husband.

Dearest Phillip,

I was not pleased to find you gone this morning. There was so much more I failed to tell you about the evil you face. While you desire to keep me safe, I also long to protect you from any harm that might befall you. Lady Remington shared with me about spiritual warfare and the power of God to fight it. I am praying for your safe return.

Beth

~*~

Phillip's journey back to London was uneventful. He experienced some measure of guilt in leaving while Beth slept. Her soft strands of hair spilled across the pillow beckoning him. Everything inside him desired nothing more than to stay in bed with her this morning. Those lips slightly parted in sleep begged to be kissed. What a strange thing marriage was. He needed to stop thinking about her. Duty called and once he'd dispatched the threats to his marriage he'd be free to return to London with his bride or hide away at Stanton Hall whenever he pleased.

He didn't bother stopping at his new home, assuming it was probably being watched. He dropped his horse off at the Remington mews and walked to his friend's home. Handing his hat to the butler, he strode into Marcus's study unannounced.

"Marcus. I've returned."

Lord Remington set his pen aside and quickly sanded the parchment in front of him. He rose to greet his friend. "So, I see."

Phillip sighed and paced until Marcus handed him a glass of brandy. He stopped to sip it and savor the burn as a warm languor traversed his body. The fact that he even needed to leave his wife behind when all he longed for was to be with her at Stanton Hall, created a desire to dispatch this problem as soon as possible. Strange that he already missed the wife he never wanted in the first place. What spell had she over him? He bit back a grin. Who cared? He'd enjoy every moment he could when he once again had the opportunity to reunite with her. Emotions were not something he would spend time on.

"Beth is safely at Rose Hill with Josie?" Marcus

asked as he sat down.

"I'm concerned about leaving her there unprotected."

"Why do you think she'd be in danger?"

Phillip strode to the window and looked outside at the darkening sky. "Something deep inside I cannot shake. I'm uneasy." He sat the empty glass on the side table. "Not even that helps right now." He flopped into a seat. "I never desired a wife, Marcus. But now that I have her I would be loathe to lose her."

Marcus grinned. "Love has a funny way of taking over, doesn't it?"

"I didn't say anything about love," Phillip retorted.

"Really? Let me examine the evidence. You've gone out of your way to take care of her needs. You have endured multiple inconveniences to ensure her safety. You miss her, and are worried about her, and finally, the *coup de grace*, you've confessed your concern to a friend."

"I thought love was supposed to feel 'good' somehow. This is torture."

Marcus nodded, his face grim. "I don't think anyone other than the Lord understood the struggle I endured with everything that happened last year." He sighed. "It was worth it. I would go through it all again to have Josie safely by my side as my wife."

"Your confidence during that time is more than you're confessing to now. How is that possible?"

"I recognized that God had a plan. Didn't mean I liked it at the time. Her rejection, the slander, the distance, and of course that beating that almost killed me...in the end, I needed to trust Him."

"It is too simple. I respect your faith and

appreciate that you've not forced it on me, but I don't understand how some invisible God can give you peace when your world is falling apart around you and lives are at stake."

"Do you believe there is a God?" Marcus asked, his voice soft. The question was sincere.

Phillip shrugged. "Sure. I just don't believe He'll have anything to do with me."

"You perceive him as distant, off running the universe, and you can blissfully go on ignoring Him?"

"Something like that. I leave the holy living to you."

"A relationship with God is more than doing the right things. I've got my own areas of sin to struggle with. You don't see me acting like the Puritans condemning everyone who doesn't believe as I do."

"Having some experience with them, I can honestly say, no. Your talk of faith in Jesus seems more humane that some of the religious factions out there, with their sour faces and inability to enjoy life. Surely not all pleasure is sin is it?"

"I believe Jesus even laughed. He celebrated at a wedding feast and even provided the wine. He held children in his arms. He was more about grace and compassion than a list of do's and don't's. He became angry with those who put the law above care for others."

"A God who laughs and enjoys a good party? Now you have me interested." Phillip grinned at his friend.

"You just arrived in town and need to shake the dust off from your travels. Let me ring the cook to bring you some food and drink before we discuss matters further. You'll not think straight to strategize a plan for Beth's safety while your stomach is rumbling."

"Capital idea."

"I'll let the matter of faith drop for now, my friend. Consider what I've said. Read the book I gave you and test out my words. Test God. You might be surprised at what you discover."

Phillip rose and took a deep breath. "Fair enough. You've never pushed but what you've said along with how you have lived your life, merits consideration. The least I could do would be to investigate it further."

Marcus nodded as he walked with Phillip up the stairs. They parted in the hallway.

Phillip was a man of his word and he would think about God more…but not right now. He had too many other things vying for his attention.

Like how to keep his wife safe.

~*~

The Black Diamond paced, fury roiling within. His hands clenched. His servants were avoiding him in his foul mood. How could Wolton and Follett falter so completely? He'd guarantee Lizzy wouldn't be talking. She didn't know his identity. It was only Wolton's sect that was in danger. Minor loss to the cause. He'd leave his mark to remind her whose she really was.

Lord Remington was becoming a pest, however. First, his sister, Henrietta, escaped his clutches by marrying Lord Percy. Then Sir Bastian failed to bring Miss Storm to him. Both times Lord Remington had stepped in to interfere, along with his friends. Oh, he had plans for Sir Michael Tidley. He stopped to savor for a moment the delight that awaited that particular thorn in his flesh. He never suspected Lord Westcombe would get in his way. He'd make him suffer for that. His perfect wife wouldn't remain that way for long. He'd let Wolton take his due as well.

9

Phillip had eaten in silence and savored the glass of port, grateful to put his thoughts on hold for a time. All he could envision was his bride as she slept this morning. Sweet Beth. Had she been furious with him at his departure? Her hair spread like silk across the pillow, her long lashes resting against her cheek. Those lips. If he had awakened her he would have been tempted to stay longer and sample the delights she had for him. It was pure torture walking out that door. His own weakness forced him to skip that farewell kiss.

After all, it was a kiss like that which led him to marry her in the first place. A fortuitous event. How else could he protect her if not as her husband? And the benefits were beyond what he anticipated. He grinned. And he still couldn't stop thinking about her. Perhaps he was besotted.

His respite over, he rose to find Marcus, who had eaten earlier. The hour was late but he doubted he'd sleep well without his wife, or without having some clue about how to protect her better and eliminate the danger that still threatened.

Marcus rose from the chair he'd been sitting in, reading. "You're tired, Phillip. This can wait until morning."

Phillip shook his head. "No. I need a more positive direction for my thoughts. Perhaps some sort of plan could give me peace."

Marcus's eyebrows rose.

"Stop. Yes, I will consider what you said about God, but for now, can we focus on a plan?"

Marcus nodded. "Fair enough. Has Elizabeth shared with you anything about her family, her past, the experiences at Follett Hall?"

"She was evasive. Not that I blame her. If there was distasteful information to be shared it would have put a damper on our short time together. She made veiled references to evil, and dark forces haunting us, but I'm not sure what that means."

"It's hard to share the bad things when you're adjusting to marriage. Remember my brother Jared wrote to warn about evil afoot in England. Sir Bastian and Josie's uncle were definitely not saints and posed a significant threat to her last year. Just because they've been dealt with doesn't mean the danger has been eliminated. From what little Josie shared, it appears we are up against a selfish, misguided desire for them to claim her inheritance for themselves."

"Could it really only be about the money? It couldn't be that simple. I'd gladly pay for her to be free."

"The dowry is yours. You married her."

"I don't need the money. I've put it in trust for her to use as she wants. I'd gladly pay that amount for her to be free."

"Do you have that much?"

"Barely. I'd need to economize but it could be done."

"What if they only want her?"

"Why?" Phillip gaped. "I appreciate that she has value, but for what reason would Wolton need her when there are plenty of other debutantes with large dowries to be had?"

"Maybe it's Follett who needs the money and his daughter in trade for something else?" Marcus mused.

Phillip shook his head. "Without her telling me or me hearing it from them or from the runner you put in motion, I have nothing to work with."

"I'm sorry your life has been so unsettled by this. While you are the perfect agent to protect your wife from the dangers that threaten her or you, you are inadequately prepared."

Frowning, Phillip leaned forward, elbows on his knees. "I'm not sure if I should be insulted by that. If you weren't my friend, I would suspect you of denigrating my manhood and skill in the various masculine arts." An eyebrow went up as he glanced at his friend.

"Don't be offended. I meant no such slight and have great respect for your talents with your fist, sword, and ability to shoot. I could ask for no better friend to stand by my side in an attack, which you have done in the past. You've acquitted yourself admirably. However, the enemy you face is beyond the mere human shape of Lord Follett and Lord Wolton. There is evil afoot you are ill-equipped for."

"What? Ghosts, goblins, and demons?"

"Let me ask you this, Phillip. When you experience a sense of dread in your heart of the danger facing you and Beth, is that a physical or spiritual thing?"

"I never thought of it in those terms. I'd say spiritual."

"I believe your enemy is a spiritual being. They do not respond well to fists, swords, or pistols."

"How could I ever fight a battle like that?"

"There are two sides to the coin."

"Good and evil."

Marcus nodded. "More specifically, God versus Satan."

"You believe I'm up against the chief demon of the underworld?"

"It is possible."

"Follett and Wolton are human."

"Correct, as are the ruffians likely awaiting you outside your house. But we all serve a spiritual master, whether we acknowledge it or not."

"You said you wouldn't talk about this anymore."

"If you were drowning and I had a rope to toss you, would you want me to hide it away as you sink?"

"That's ridiculous. I'd hope you'd toss it and pull me to safety. Although I am a good swimmer."

"Beside the point. If I have information about spiritual things that could help you in your battle to protect and free your wife from her past, shouldn't I toss you that rope as well? I'd sure hate to watch you both end up dead because I feared your anger about broaching a subject you dislike."

Phillip sighed. "Fine. Throw me the rope." This should be interesting. In spite of his initial reticence, he found himself intrigued.

"Either you serve Jesus or Satan. If you refuse to make an intentional choice to repent of your sins and accept the free gift of God's forgiveness and eternal life, through Christ alone, who died on a cross for you and rose again on the third day—then you have, by default, sided with the enemy you fear, the devil."

Phillip shook his head. "You can't be serious."

"Dead serious. Understanding this means the difference between life and death for you and your lovely wife."

Rubbing his eyes, Phillip rose. "I'm sorry, Marcus. You mean well. I need to think on this and I'm more fatigued than I realized. Maybe tomorrow morning would be a better time to meet." He stretched. "I'll seek that bed you mentioned earlier."

Marcus rose too. "As long as you're not avoiding the question. Josie and I are praying for you both, for your salvation and your safety."

"I appreciate that. I really do. This is not avoidance. I must think on what you've said."

"Fair enough. Good night, Phillip."

"'Night, Marcus."

~*~

Phillip dismissed his valet and collapsed into bed. His arm reached across to the other pillow and he experienced a deep emptiness inside. Did Beth miss him? He smiled. Was he in love with his wife? Was it possible to be so quickly attached to a woman he didn't need or want to begin with and had only married out of a sense of honor? What a pompous fool he'd been to deny the very real void his wife filled in his life. One he'd failed to recognize before. He drifted to sleep, dreaming of holding her in his arms.

He awoke with a start. How long had he slept? He rose and listened. Nothing. The room was cloaked in darkness. The window draperies had been closed and the fire banked. Silence. Complete and utter silence. So why was his heart beating so wildly as if there was an imminent threat? Something was wrong. Terror gripped him and he couldn't shake it. He rose, threw his robe on, and stoked the fire. Striding to the window he opened it letting in the damp night air. The gas lights were lit, casting little puddles of light beneath them. Nothing moved outside.

He returned to sit by the fireplace and leaned back, deep in thought. On the table was the Bible. Of course. This was Marcus's home. He took this book seriously and strove to live by its words. Phillip picked it up and let his hand gently touch the cover. What was it about this book that gave Marcus so much confidence and trust in God? Phillip grabbed a branch of candles and lit them so he could see better. He opened the book. Where did one start? The pages fell open to Psalms, chapter five, which read:

To the chief Musician upon Nehiloth, A Psalm of David. *Give ear to my words, O LORD, consider my meditation. Hearken unto the voice of my cry, my King, and my God: for unto thee will I pray. My voice shalt thou hear in the morning, O LORD; in the morning will I direct my prayer unto thee, and will look up. For thou art not a God that hath pleasure in wickedness: neither shall evil dwell with thee. The foolish shall not stand in thy sight: thou hatest all workers of iniquity. Thou shalt destroy them that speak leasing: the LORD will abhor the bloody and deceitful man. But as for me, I will come into thy house in the multitude of thy mercy: and in thy fear will I worship toward thy holy temple. Lead me, O LORD, in thy righteousness because of mine enemies; make thy way straight before my face. For there is no faithfulness in their mouth; their inward part is very wickedness; their throat is an open sepulchre; they flatter with their tongue. Destroy thou them, O God; let them fall by their own counsels; cast them out in the multitude of their transgressions; for they* have *rebelled against thee. But let all those that put their trust in thee rejoice: let them ever shout for joy, because thou defendest them: let them also that love thy name be joyful in thee. For thou, LORD, wilt bless the righteous; with favour wilt thou compass him as with a shield.*

Phillip sat dumbfounded at the words he'd just read. As if God knew exactly what he and Beth were facing. He glanced at the clock on the mantel. It was after one in the morning. He read the chapter a second time. Something in the words of King David resonated within his heart.

He could avoid the truth no longer. Marcus's faith was real. At some level he'd recognized this but didn't want to accept that he himself needed to make a choice. He'd been avoiding it for years. He was not in control of his life. God was. The stakes were too high for him and Beth. He needed Jesus. It all made sense now. His own sin kept him from God and acknowledging his need of a Savior. The necessity of Christ's death on the cross. He wasn't ignorant of the facts. He'd gone to church on and off over the years. He might have had a period where he acted like a heathen and church seemed like a way to hedge his bets.

He'd heard enough sermons. He'd read the history. Suddenly it wasn't some far off event. A real man, flesh and blood, died for him, Phillip Jerome Allen Westcombe, a prideful sinner. Phillip dropped to his knees and prayed. A deep sense of peace invaded the room, driving out the darkness and terror that had originally awakened him. Phillip rose and read some more before returning to bed.

The battle had shifted, and Phillip had no doubt he was on the side of victory.

~*~

When Phillip arose in the morning, he was surprisingly refreshed considering his late night meeting with God. He grinned. His step was lighter as he headed downstairs to break his fast. He wanted to share the news with Marcus and anticipated his friend's happiness. This morning, instead of dread, joy overflowed his heart. He couldn't find a better word to describe it. Joy. He hugged it to himself and prayed he'd get a chance to share that with his bride soon.

Phillip entered the empty room, filled his plate and sat at the table to eat in silence. The footman arrived bearing a missive for him. Phillip tore it open as the man awaited a response.

Lord Westcombe,

There was a fire last night at your house. The servants managed to escape and attempts were made to put out the fire. We regret to inform you the upstairs suffered damage. Please come to advise what you'd like us to do next.

Sincerely,

Masters

Phillip addressed the footman as Marcus entered. "Convey to Masters that I shall arrive directly to survey the damage."

Marcus went to the sideboard to fill his plate. "What is amiss, Phillip?" He sat down and Phillip handed him the note.

"Fire at our new home."

"If you can wait a few minutes, I'll join you." Marcus called for the footman, whispered a message and dispatched him. He ate quickly. Dabbing his face with his serviette after his last sip of coffee he stood. "Let's depart. The carriage should be waiting out front for us."

Phillip followed Marcus into the carriage. "I had

some other news I wanted to share, but it will have to wait."

Marcus studied him. "Good news, for a change?"

Grinning, Phillip nodded. "Very good news."

"Must be since the fire hasn't dampened your spirits yet. It has been a long time since I've seen you this relaxed and at...peace."

As they pulled up there was evidence of smoke staining the upper stories and the windows were open, burnt drapes flapping into the breeze. The house was three stories high, tall and narrow but not as close to surrounding homes so as to have caused danger to them. They exited the carriage and entered the house.

The stench of burning wood assaulted them as smoke still hung in the air casting the hallway in eerie spookiness.

Masters led them to the bedroom.

"No one was injured?" Phillip asked his butler.

"No, my lord. We detected the smoke in enough time to evacuate the servants from the upper floor and developed a bucket brigade to douse the fire. We did the best we could but there is a lot of damage."

"Where was the fire?"

"It started from just inside the door to the master suite."

"The doors were locked?"

"Yes. We kept them locked and the drapes drawn every night as you requested to make it appear you and Mrs. Westcombe were in residence."

Phillip glanced at Marcus and motioned to the door as Masters opened it. "Shall we go see the damage?"

Marcus nodded. Phillip turned the knob and slowly opened the door, gasping as the odor of burnt wood and fabric grew overpowering.

The master suite of rooms had been well-preserved and it was less urgent to renovate those areas in the house. Phillip walked through to his wife's sitting room. The door to the hallway was similarly burned. Someone must have shoved something under the doors to start the blaze. Once the rugs caught fire the blaze had spread everywhere. Bedding was burnt and furniture was ruined. There would be no salvaging anything of value. Thankfully they hadn't yet moved into the home so personal treasures hadn't been destroyed.

Beth didn't own any personal treasures, other than her wedding ring. He'd be rectifying that soon he hoped.

"They anticipated you being here. If you had been asleep—" Marcus frowned as he inspected the damage.

"—we would likely not have survived this." Phillip strode to the hallway where his butler, Masters, stood waiting. "Were all the doors to the house locked? Were you able to discern how someone could enter and do this?"

Masters shook his head. "I checked all the doors and windows last night, my lord. Everything was secure. I was unable to determine how anyone could enter. 'Twern't one of us. We were all upstairs."

"I don't blame you. Thank you for your hard work in saving the house. Be careful in who you hire to assist in cleaning this up. Once we get the smell out we'll look at refurnishing the room."

"Yes, my lord."

Phillip headed down the stairs with Marcus at his side. He could barely wait to exit the house and breathe fresh air. A chill traveled down his spine at the methods their enemy would resort to. They didn't want Beth. They wanted her dead. *Lord, how do I keep her safe?*

~*~

Michael, Theo, and Phillip rose to their feet as a man entered the study at Marcus's home. Phillip's friend greeted the man like an old acquaintance. The face was familiar from when Josie was in trouble, but Phillip had no contact with the Bow Street Runner at that time. At least that was who he assumed this gentleman was.

"Lord Phillip Westcombe," Marcus intoned, "please meet Mr. Neville of Bow Street."

"A pleasure, m'lord." The hand extended was calloused and strong. The features on the man's face showed signs of hard work in the elements but his eyes conveyed genuine concern. The rest of the men were introduced.

"Thank you for coming, Mr. Neville," Phillip replied as they moved to sit down.

"Call me Nigel, please, Lord Westcombe." The Bow Street Runner sat down and pulled out some paper and a pencil.

Marcus gave an abbreviated version of the latest drama in Phillip's life.

Nigel leaned back, brows knit together in concentration. "You're obviously in danger. But it would be hard to hold Wolton or Follett responsible without proof. So far in my investigation, at Lord Remington's request, I've not found anything incriminating. Lord Follett is teetering on the brink of financial disaster, but how would paying out that dowry to Wolton have helped him? I cannot find a motive, unless Follett had sold her to him to get out of debt."

"Reprehensible," Phillip uttered.

"I agree, but it does happen. But why would Wolton desire a bride anyway? He's already had three, although they never seem to live very long and have never produced any heirs."

"Not another Henry the Eighth, I hope." Marcus shuddered.

"I've heard tales of satanic activity associated with Wolton," Theo offered.

"Satanic? As in demons and animal sacrifices? How would that have any bearing on this case?" Phillip asked.

Michael sighed. "I would also suspect he's somehow connected to the Black Diamond."

"How much has your wife explained of her life in Ipswitch?" Marcus inquired.

"Nothing. You asked me that before. Why is that relevant to the case?" Phillip crossed his arms as he reclined in his chair.

Marcus rose and paced. "I'm reluctant to say anything, because I've heard it from Josie, but I sense this could mean life or death for you, Phillip, so I must speak."

"Neither you nor Josie are prone to gossip. Speak." Phillip leaned forward, elbows on knees.

"When you brought Elizabeth to us, Josie spent time with her, remember? She spoke to my wife of dark things. Evil practices that occurred at Follett Hall. Did you know your wife is afraid of the dark?"

Phillip nodded.

"She used to be locked up for hours on end, bound, in a closet, and denied food, in order for them to make her more submissive to the tortures they would put her through. My wife has withheld details from me." Marcus sighed. "Your wife is a beautiful woman, Phillip. I would guess she was not a virgin on her wedding night, through no fault of her own."

Phillip leapt from his chair, fists clenched, growling.

Marcus held up a hand to keep him at bay. "Calm down, friend. I meant no dishonor to your bride."

"How could you know such a thing, much less bring it up?" Phillip's face grew warm and he paced, struggling to reign in his temper.

"You don't want to believe it's true. That perhaps others have taken what should have been rightly yours."

Michael and Theo were at Phillip's side holding him back from assaulting their mutual friend. *How dare he say these things in front of them all? Was nothing sacred?* His heart ached for his wife. He'd never stopped to question how or why...he wasn't an innocent himself when they'd wed. To think that someone forcibly took that from her filled him with rage and grief. *Beth.* He knew so little about his wife and he ached to know her better, to take away the horror of her past and give her a future with love and peace.

She needs Jesus.

The fight left him and his friends pushed him back into his chair. He bent over and buried his face in his hands. The room fell silent.

Nigel broke the silence. "Her knowledge of those events and the people involved, along with Lord Westcombe's, could put both their lives at risk. It still doesn't explain why Wolton wanted to marry her.

Granted, she is lovely and had a dowry, but Wolton has plenty. Why marry her when she was opposed to it?"

Marcus leaned against the fireplace. "I'm suspecting there is something else going on here. Wolton never seemed 'right' and his politics are slightly seditious. I'm not calling him a traitor—yet. He has sympathies for Napoleon and the 'little emperor's' efforts in France, although he is subtle in his expression of those views. It shows in the bills he supports or rails against on the rare occasions he ventures to town."

Neville sat up straighter. "You suspect there might be a link between this and the war?"

"I have no proof other than comments made by him that lead me to speculate he might not be supportive of England's monarchy."

"Not a lot of people are fond of Prince George right now—and his efforts to be named Regent," offered Sir Michael.

Phillip lifted his head, wearier than he could ever remember being. "Marcus, I'm sorry. I overreacted. I hadn't put the pieces together…I'm such an idiot."

"You know I'd never speak to cause you distress if I didn't believe it was pertinent to understanding this situation."

Phillip nodded at his friend. "Even if this is all true, how can I keep Beth safe?"

Nigel cleared his throat. "Where is she now?"

"Mrs. Westcombe is at Rose Hill with my wife and staff. She should be safe enough there and not as easy to track down as they would likely expect her to be at Stanton Hall," Marcus assured the Runner.

"Are you sure they are protected? These men seem determined."

Phillip broke in. "They aren't as smart as they believe themselves to be. Setting fire to empty rooms? That alone proves it wasn't one of my staff. If they intended to kill us from the smoke or the fire, they failed."

"I'm sorry for the damage done to your home," stated Mr. Neville. "I'm glad, however, that they didn't succeed in their objective. I'll be looking into this further. It may take time, but we will find out what's behind all this." Mr. Neville stood.

"Thank you," Phillip said as he rose to shake the Runner's hand. He turned to Marcus. "I hope you don't mind putting me up for a little longer."

"Not at all," Marcus said. "What are friends for anyway? I remember you going out of your way to help me with Josie. This is the least I can do. You are not alone."

Phillip took a deep breath and slowly released it and grinned. "I know. There's still something I need to share with you…later."

10

"Ha!" Phillip crowed as two balls landed in the pocket of the billiard table. They were passing time before attending a few balls later in the evening to listen to the gossip and perhaps spread a better tale amongst the *beau monde* regarding his marriage. Phillip's next ball missed its pocket and Marcus took his place at the billiard table.

"You had to miss some time." Marcus dropped a ball into the pocket. He lined up his next shot.

"I had something I was meaning to talk to you about, but in the flurry of this morning, I forgot." Phillip watched his friend assess the right angle. He muffed the shot and it was Phillip's turn.

"What was it you wanted to share?" Marcus asked as he stepped aside to let Phillip line up his next play.

"I prayed last night, confessing my need for a Savior. I'm a Christian." Phillip missed his shot and stepped back.

Marcus stared at him. "You...are? How? You were exhausted."

"It's hard to explain. I was tired and went to bed. I awoke in the middle of the night in a panic. I picked up the Bible in my room and soon I was praying and peace just washed over me. I've been to church countless times but never have had an experience like that before. The words on the page were real to me. God became real. I've always believed He existed... I had no trouble sleeping after that."

Marcus grinned. "I can't tell you how wonderful this is. I've prayed for years for you."

"I know. And you never pushed. You've lived your faith in front of me and shown me what a true man looks like."

"I have my father to thank for that."

"He was good man."

"Aye, that he was. Some days it's still hard to believe he and mother are gone. That they never saw Henrietta wed. That they will never hold their grandchild."

"They would be proud of you, Marcus."

"Enough about me. Your battle may have just increased because of your faith. If we are up against truly evil spiritual forces, they may become more determined now that you belong to Christ."

"I was already in a battle, but how do I arm myself for a spiritual war?" Phillip set his cue stick aside. The game was obviously over.

Marcus racked the balls and set his cue aside as the bell to dress for dinner rang. "Just in time, too. I suggest we stay in tonight and plan a strategy."

Phillip nodded. He knew from experience that if he were ever in battle, Marcus was the one he wanted fighting by his side and watching his back.

~*~

"Where is he?" Beth mumbled under her breath as she prepared to leave her room. She was a wife with no husband? Abandoned here for a fortnight in the country. While grateful for a safe place to stay, she was bored. Josie took frequent naps during the day. In spite of that, they had several conversations about the things Beth had been reading in the book of John.

She gazed at her room. Beautiful furnishings. The room she'd left at home boasted threadbare carpeting, an unused fireplace with missing bricks, and furniture that had been ill cared for over the years. She'd finally been given decent dresses upon arriving in town, and then only enough to be present at a handful of balls, and of course, for her marriage. There would have been no need for more. After the wedding Wolton would have whisked her away to his estate bordering Follett Hall and her own personal hell would have begun.

Lord, how could my father have ever done this to me? Did my mother suffer too? Protect me. Keep Phillip safe and return him to me. You have given me far more than I had ever dreamed of. Thank you for this haven and forgive me for my discontented heart.

She hated the fact that she even needed a man. Men had never been good to her, what few she'd known. But Phillip had been a revelation. A delightful fantasy she'd never dreamed or hoped for. When she'd sought him at that ball she'd never imagined being cared for as she'd experienced with her husband. She'd begun to even fancy herself in love with him. Was that possible upon such short acquaintance? Could he also find his way to loving her? Did a man go to such lengths to protect his wife as Phillip was doing, without love?

She desired for him to know of her faith but she feared writing to him lest her correspondence was intercepted and her location discovered by the wrong people.

She left her room and headed to breakfast. The

butler presented her with a salver upon which rested a letter. "Thank you." She picked it up and turned instead to the empty drawing room, closing the door behind her. She craved a message from her husband more than food. She snuggled into the chair to read the words written in his bold, distinctive script.

Dearest Beth,

We are still seeking to ensure your safety. I miss you.

Someone set fire to our new home. No one was injured. Our remodeling efforts will need to center on the master suite before anything else. I am more than grateful to God that you are safe at Rose Hill. I have come to know Christ and long to share with you all that God is teaching me. I wish you the same peace and joy I found. I pray for you often. I long for our days at Stanton Hall, where we could hide away from all our troubles. Perhaps our future holds more such days as that. Together, with God, we will overcome the evil that besets us. I hope to be able to visit soon. Stay safe, my love.

Phillip

Tears ran unchecked down Beth's cheeks and she dabbed at them with her handkerchief. Actually, it was one of Phillip's. Her fingers traced the fancy embroidered *P* and *W* on one corner. Deep joy filled her. Phillip was safe and had also come to know Christ. She'd not been in the new house more than once so the loss there was not difficult to bear. But if they had been there? A chill ran down her spine.

Someone was still after both of them.

She ran up to her suite, pulled out some paper, dipped the nib of the pen in ink and wrote her own letter to her husband. She sanded and sealed it and left it on her Bible to post later. She rang for her maid, Elsa.

Enough sitting around. She would go for a ride.

She'd only been out a few times since her marriage. She needed to be free of the walls that seemed to close in on her. She shivered. Forget the past.

He'd called her 'my love.' She hugged those words close to her heart as she donned her green riding habit Phillip had insisted she purchase saying it brought out the color of her eyes. She topped it with a jaunty little hat containing a feather dyed a pale gold. She glanced in the mirror. *Look how far you've come.* Her hand smoothed down the fabric of the skirt along her hips and came to settle over her stomach.

In the short span of their marriage, she was recently aware they had conceived a new life. Arising out of duty and desperation, this child would be raised with love. So much more than she'd ever experienced.

She'd shared the news in her letter to Phillip, longing to tell him in person. Phillip should be the first to know.

Soon Elsa and Josie would discover her secret.

Lightheaded and queasy in the morning and a fortnight past her monthly courses, she knew enough to diagnose herself. *God, please protect this little one and Phillip. You've made us a family neither of us ever dreamed of.*

She frowned as images of Lord Wolton and her father intruded. She would not let them ruin her happiness and peace. She took deep breaths, sipped her tea, and grabbed her riding crop before heading out to the stables to arrange for her favorite mare. Although she was an indifferent rider, she'd been trying to improve her skill to please Phillip.

"James, could you saddle up Sunshine for me today?" she asked the head groom.

"Ye be wanting a groom to ride with you? Lord

Westcombe insisted," the young groom asked.

"Don't worry. I know the basic riding paths and don't intend to go far. I just need to be alone."

The young man sighed and shook his head. "Yes, Mrs. Westcombe, but I be warning ye. Be careful."

She pointed to the railing where Duke sat. "I'll have Duke with me. He's a fierce protector."

James led the mare to her and gave her a leg up to the sidesaddle. "She's a bit frisky this morning. Ye sure you don't want Jem or Pete to come with you?"

"Thank you for the offer. I shan't be gone long." She nudged the horse and soon they were in the sunshine of a beautiful morning. Duke flew ahead and would perch in branches waiting for her before flying off again. The horse turned down a path Beth didn't remember, but as long as they were on Rose Hill property she should be safe enough. Marcus and Josie certainly owned a beautiful slice of England. She didn't worry about getting lost. Duke would help lead her home and Sunshine was always ready to return to the stable for food.

The pathway opened to a meadow where she urged the mare to a gallop. Such freedom! She laughed with pure joy. The powerful horse beneath her, the beauty around her, the wind in her face, unfettered by society's strictures. She pulled up before entering the woods they had reached. The heat of the sun on her habit caused sweat to run down her back and trickle from her hair. She let out a breath of contentment as she stroked the neck of her horse. *Thank you, God.*

She shivered. Was the air growing cooler? Clouds were moving in and the sky grew darker. She turned Sunshine around to head back to the path they'd previously taken. As she spurred the horse to a gallop again she came to the trees only to find the trail not as easy to find.

"Duke? Can you show me how to get home?"

The crow flew up high above the trees and disappeared before returning to her again. He landed on a branch on the edge and called to her. "Here! Here!"

"Thank you." She urged the horse toward that path and entered the woods. A chill crept up her spine as the sun no longer radiated through the leaves in droplets of light. She kept the horse at a slower pace. She didn't want Sunshine tripping over roots or being spooked by a rabbit. The path meandered. Time slowed. Nothing looked familiar.

Where was Duke?

Fear stalked her behind every tree. *Don't be silly. I'm safe on Lord Remington's land. God is watching over me and Duke is close. There is nothing to fear.*

Something struck her shoulders knocking her hat askew over her eyes and causing her to topple from her lofty perch. She crumpled to the ground gasping for breath as the air abandoned her. She tugged the hat off her head.

Strange burly men appeared as shadows. One slapped her horse on the rump and the mare bolted down the path.

It seemed forever before her lungs remembered to work. She struggled to rise but a boot placed against her chest forced her back. Faces wreathed in shadow, all she could tell was these men were large. *Lord, help me!*

"This is the little princess causing the master trouble?" one man asked.

"Red hair. It's her." Removing his foot, he reached

out his hand to grab hers and jerk her to her feet. "Ah, Mrs. Westcombe. At last, we have the pleasure." His breath reeked of stale ale and garlic. He leered at her. "I sez we all have a turn at her before we administer her punishment."

"We've no time for pleasure, my lad. Why did you send the horse off like that? They'll come looking for her the minute that beast shows up at the stables." The third man growled and swatted Beth's hand free from the man holding it. He grabbed her chin forcing her to look up at him. "Too bad. You are a delectable morsel to be sure." He turned back to his cohort. "You are an idiot."

He punched the other man in the arm and soon they were rolling on the ground pummeling each other.

Beth winced in pain as the third man gripped her upper arm tight. She refused to show them her fear. The man stooped down, grabbed a rock, and threw it at the two tussling on the path.

They halted, groaning. Rising to their feet they faced her.

Beth shivered and shook herself free. Three men. Thunder cracked through the silent woods. No birds chirped. No squirrels scampered. It grew deathly quiet as lightning danced across the sky, followed by another ominous boom.

"We've got time to do whatever we want. We can haul her off the path and truss her up. No one will discover her for some time," Stinky stated.

A shiver of fear rippled through her.

"Diamond doesn't want her dead."

"He's playing a deep game," said the tallest man she now dubbed Giant. "Still, if something were to happen because she didn't...obey, he can't get angry about that, can he?"

"We do the job first." This man was not as tall but had a large face. He looked like a gnome.

Stinky nodded. "The storm is moving in and I want to be a long way from here before they find her. Let's do the job we're to be paid for. We'll have money enough to get our pleasures elsewhere with plenty of comfort."

The other men grumbled and Gnome nodded. "I don't fancy hanging from a tree. Help me with the missus here." He pulled a long cloth from his back pocket and stepped toward her, raising it to her face.

Terror gripped Beth and she shook all over. She'd felt powerless long ago when she'd been bound and gagged. "I'll cooperate. Don't hurt me. Please don't tie me up."

"Cooperate, huh? Come on men, let's have some fun." Gnome grabbed her and dragged her into the woods, far from the path. The other two men followed. They stopped at a small clearing and she was tossed to the ground.

Knives appeared in the hands of all three men. Stinky pulled her to her knees. "No screamin', ya hear?"

She whimpered and nodded her head. Her arms were held tightly behind her back by Gnome as Giant stood over her with a rock, ready to knock her senseless if she screamed or struggled. Stinky took his knife and carved a swath of fabric away from the upper right corner of her back, exposing almost a fourth of her skin to the cooling air. Pushing her hair out of the way, the knife met her skin and pierced it. She jerked and Giant slapped her.

"Stay still or else."

She closed her eyes tight. All her muscles clenched tightly in response to the carving taking place. She was being marked. The outline of a shape ached but then the man worked to peel off the skin within the lines. She managed to disappear inside herself as trickles of blood flowed from the wound. Finished with their task, she was shoved face forward to the ground. They bound her hands behind her.

The men argued over who would get her first. She shivered as the temperature dropped further and sprinkles of rain made their way through the canopy of trees overhead. Soon the dirt beneath her was damp. From her tears or the rain, she couldn't be sure. A loud sound rent the darkness and the men cursed as they fought someone or something. She couldn't hold on anymore and slipped into the comfort of darkness.

~*~

Phillip grew uneasy. He paced the study while Marcus visited White's to pick up on any helpful news. By mid-morning, a note was delivered to the house by a street urchin. Phillip turned it over several times before ripping the seal open.

Lord Westcombe,

This is a warning. We found her and before you can reach her we will have dealt with her. The next time we touch your wife, she will certainly die. Cease the investigation.

There was no signature. Deep inside Phillip was certain something bad had happened. Beth was in danger. Right this minute. He called for the butler. "Dispatch someone to fetch your lord immediately. Tell him it's an emergency and to make haste."

Phillip took the stairs two at a time. He threw clothes in a bag and instructed Fenway to pack to return to Rose Hill by carriage on the morrow. *Lord, watch over Beth. Please keep her safe.* He ordered up two horses that stood outside by the time Marcus arrived.

"What's amiss, Phillip?"

Phillip dragged Marcus to the study and shut the door. "This was delivered less than an hour ago. We need to depart for Rose Hill immediately."

Marcus scanned the brief message. "Could this be a trap?"

"I don't care if it is. I must see Beth. If something happened to her because I failed to go... I need to make sure she's not been harmed by those..." He punched the air instead of filling in the profanity on the tip of his tongue.

Marcus smiled. "I applaud your restraint. God is at work in you. I will change and be with you in less than ten minutes. Make sure you grab your great coat. As warm as it is the scent of rain is in the air. It might be a wet journey."

Phillip paced as he waited for Marcus.

They were soon racing their horses out of town on the road to Rose Hill. Often Marcus would take Phillip on some cross-country paths he was aware of to cut the journey and also possibly avoid traps. The going was slower on those routes which chafed at Phillip's urge to hurry. He would not sacrifice his horse. Having the beast come up lame would not help either.

It was dark and the rain was coming down hard as they galloped up the drive to Rose Hill. Thunder rolled in the distance.

Phillip swore he'd be tearing someone's head off if he didn't see his wife soon. He was beyond worried over her safety.

Phillip was off his horse and tossing the reins to the stable boy before Marcus was able to dismount. Dashing up the steps to the house he threw open the door, not even waiting for the butler. "Beth! Beth!" he bellowed. He shook off his great coat and left it where it fell, casting his hat to the floor as well before rushing into the drawing room.

Josie was rising to her feet.

Marcus was behind him. "Josie. Where is Beth?"

"Phillip. Marcus. What a surprise. What's amiss?"

"Where is Beth?" Phillip asked again through gritted teeth.

"I've not encountered her today. She missed tea. She took a ride earlier on Sunshine but that was the last I've heard. She was despondent and missing you, Phillip so I figured she'd gone to rest after her ride. I was napping when she would have returned. I wouldn't worry."

Phillip's breathing was ragged.

Marcus strode to his wife and put an arm around her, kissing the top of her head. He glared at Phillip as if to warn him. Phillip caught the message. "Phillip received a letter this morning indicating Beth's life might be in danger."

Josie's eyes grew wide. "Oh, no. Talk with Stickney in the stables and see what he knows."

Phillip ran out the door, Marcus on his heels.

Entering the stables, they found Stickney rubbing down his horse, ridden to a lather getting them here. "Where is my wife?"

"Your wife?" the groom asked.

"Mrs. Westcombe. Where is she?"

Stickney called to one of the stable boys. "Have you seen Mrs. Westcombe?"

"Aye, sir. She rode out later this morning on Sunshine. I was coming to tell you that the horse was found in the western meadow with a strained fetlock. We thought you might want to come and check her out. It's raining and Jemmy is slowly leading her back."

"And Mrs. Westcombe?"

"No sign of her, sir."

Phillip was beside himself.

Marcus stepped in. "Who accompanied Mrs. Westcombe on her ride?"

James swallowed hard. "No one, m'lord. She insisted on being alone."

Phillip turned on the head groom. "And you allowed this?"

Marcus placed a hand on his friend's shoulder. "Intimidating my servants will not get you the result you want." He turned to the young boy. "What direction did she take?"

"She went north but the horse was west...so I'm not sure what path she took. Would you like me to saddle up some horses so we can search for her?"

"That'd be great." Marcus turned to Stickney and put an arm on the groom's shoulder. "You are not to blame."

The older man shook his head. "I was up all night helping Midnight give birth to her foal. I slept most of the morning. I'm sorry, m'lord. I didn't know. I'll round up all our hands to help in the search."

Phillip swung up into the saddle of the fresh

mount to find it skittish beneath him.

"You're making the horse nervous, Phillip," Marcus cautioned as his horse came up alongside him. "Stop a moment. Pray."

Phillip swallowed hard. "You're right. I've been running on my own power and haven't sought God with this. He loves her more than I do, right?"

Marcus grinned. "He does. It makes me happy to hear that you love her too."

Phillip took a deep breath and closed his eyes. *Lord, you know where Beth is. Please lead us to her. I love her and it would devastate me if something happened to her. Help me to entrust her to you until you bring her back to me.* Flickering his eyes open he urged his mount forward.

Soon Marcus was following as they headed into the trail Beth had first taken.

A black crow flew past Phillip and came to land on a tree branch, squawking. *Caw! Caw!* "Leezzeee! Help Leezzeee!" *Caw! Caw!*

Phillip pulled up close to the bird. "Duke. Where is Beth? Lead us to her."

Caw! Caw!

"You really think a crow can take you to your wife?" Marcus asked.

"That bird has saved my life before. He adores Beth and would never be away from her if she didn't need help. He knows where she is." Phillip addressed the crow. "Go. Find Beth."

The bird took off flying down the path turning off through rougher terrain.

"She must be off the path," Marcus stated.

"She'd never leave the path willingly," Phillip asserted as he skillfully maneuvered the horse around the underbrush. "At least it's drier under the covering of the trees."

They rode on in silence and time stretched thin.

Phillip continued to pray he'd find his wife alive and unharmed.

"Could this be a trap?" Marcus asked.

"Possibly. I don't care." Phillip knew he'd do anything to protect her. He took his marriage vows seriously. Even though he was a reluctant groom, God had done something wonderful when He'd given Beth to him as a wife. The wife he never knew he needed. The woman he didn't think he could live without.

Duke stopped on a branch and waited until they came alongside. He squawked and hopped to another branch further into the woods. Broken branches indicated others had been here before them.

"I think we need to walk. Why don't you wait here, Marcus. She must be close." Phillip dismounted and followed the crow into the underbrush, snagging his pants and coat. He almost tripped over her in the dim light as the sun was beginning to set.

"Leezzeeee! Help Leezzeeee!" Duke squawked.

"I found her!" He knelt down in the mud. "Good job, Duke." She was on her side, her right shoulder skyward. The bare skin and the bloodied wound in the shape of a rhombus sickened him. His finger touched her cold neck. She still had a steady pulse. "Beth? Sweetheart? It's Phillip."

She didn't respond. He touched her scalp and discovered a large bump there.

Marcus came up behind him. "Is she…?"

"She's alive, but not awake. The monsters tortured her. I can't take her back on the horse. Can you go get a cart and send for the doctor?"

"Sure. Here's my greatcoat, use this to help warm her up." Marcus took off his.

"I should be giving her mine."

"I can get another when I return back and I'll be traveling faster. It will get colder out here while you wait. Just take it. Guard your wife." Marcus turned to leave. "And pray."

Phillip pulled his wife up to wrap the long warm coat around her, taking great care with the exposed shoulder. He sat back against a tree and held her in his arms, resting on his lap while they waited so she wouldn't be on the cold damp ground. He shivered. Duke stood guard. "Thank you, again, Duke. You did a good job."

The crow nodded as if he understood the compliment.

Phillip couldn't help a smile. While he'd never objected to the strange pet, he'd been a bit surprised at how well Beth had trained the bird. Gratitude shook him as he hugged her close. Tears found their way down his cheeks.

"Beth, please come back to me. There is so much to tell you. I love you, Beth. I want to share with you about God. He brought me back to you. I'm sorry I was too late to stop this from happening. It won't change how I feel about you. You need to know that. You are beautiful to me. Precious. An unasked-for gift. Please wake up, Beth. I need you with me."

He pulled out a handkerchief, gently wiped mud off her face and placed a kiss on her forehead. *Lord, bring her back to me. Let her be all right. Thank you for leading me to her.*

Time dragged on while he waited, shivering in the cold and the eerie darkness of the woods. He wished he'd thought of bringing torches.

Light approached. Marcus arrived with servants and torches. Together they managed to carry Beth to the cart and Phillip sat in the back buffering his wife from the rugged bumpy ride to the manor house. When they returned he carried her up to her room and Josie took over, assisted by Elsa. Phillip was shooed away.

"Go get yourself cleaned up, Phillip. When your wife awakens, you don't want to scare her. A bath has been made ready in your room." Thankfully the suite was next door to his wife's. He'd not be staying there normally but would have preferred to share Beth's room. Given the circumstances, he acquiesced to the demand and went to clean himself up. Slipping into the hot water, he sighed and closed his eyes. With God's help, he'd found her. It'd be up to God now to save her.

11

Phillip paced in Marcus's study, nursing a glass of brandy.

The housekeeper promised a simple repast to be enjoyed as soon as they all knew how his wife fared.

Dr. Bruce Miller strode into the room, shutting the door behind him.

Surging forward, Phillip greeted the physician. "How is she, Bruce?"

"Nice to see you again too, Phillip." The man let his lip quirk on one end indicating he understood Phillip's anxiety.

"I'm sorry. I'm just—"

"—worried for your wife. Just as you should be. Sorry to give you a difficult time." He motioned to the chairs and both men sat. "Your wife took a hard knock to the head but has other bruises as well. I suspect she took a tumble from her horse. She'll be stiff and sore for some time, but nothing is broken that I can detect. I've done what I can to cleanse the wound on her shoulder. The cuts aren't terribly deep but she will have a scar with the skin they removed. The risk of infection is what concerns me the most." Bruce took a deep breath. "How long have you been married, Phillip?" the physician asked.

"We wed over a month ago. Why?"

"Congratulations."

"Is there anything I can do for her?"

"Pray. Make sure she gets fluids. Water, tea, weak broth. And lots of rest. I'll be back in the morning to check on her." Bruce rose and Phillip did as well.

"Thank you, Bruce."

Doctor Miller left the room. Phillip finished his brandy and took the stairs two at a time to his wife's room. He slipped in quietly and moved to the bed where she rested, so still. He didn't care what anyone said. He was staying with her tonight, by her side. It was where he should have been all along.

In spite of the bandage on her head, her red hair flowed over the pillows. She was still beautiful.

He turned to the maid. "Elsa, you may leave. I'll tend my wife tonight."

"Shall I bring you dinner?"

He shook his head. "I'm not hungry."

She bobbed a curtsy and left.

Phillip turned the key in the lock. Sitting on a chair by the fireplace he removed his boots and proceeded to undo his cravat. He tugged off his coat and waistcoat before bending to stir the flames. He understood why his wife needed it lit all night. It was the least he could do for her.

Striding to the bed, he sat in a chair to watch Beth sleep. The candles were lit by the bedside and next to them was a Bible. On top of that was a letter, addressed to him, in his wife's delicate script. Gingerly he picked it up, broke the seal, and read.

Dearest Phillip,

I was delighted to get your letter this morning. I have missed you terribly. I was overjoyed to learn you had found Jesus. I too have discovered great peace and joy in accepting Him as my Savior. I have been reading the Bible and long to share that with you when we are reunited.

I am sad about the house but grateful God led us to be away so the fire could not succeed in the plans set for either of us. I need to tell you more about my family and past so you can better understand the evil we are up against.

More than anything, I long to be in your arms and gaze into your eyes and remind you how much I love you and how grateful I am that God brought you into my life. I also long to share with you the joy of the new life we have created that I carry within me. You are a father.

All my love and devotion are yours,

Beth

Phillip read the letter several times before folding it and placing it back on the Bible. He stared at his wife. In a month's time, she had become vital to his happiness and now she carried his child. A child whose life was threatened by today's brutal attack. Love, joy, and anxiety stirred within him. He grabbed his wife's hand and began to pray.

When he finished, he blew out the candles and crawled into bed next to her, trying to enfold her into his embrace without hurting her further. His hand rested on her stomach as if by placing it there he could protect the little life growing within that now seemed so vital to their future happiness.

~*~

Everything ached but there was warmth around her. Safety and security she'd craved all her life enfolded her and she smiled to herself as she snuggled into the firm body next to her.

Body. Her eyes flashed open as her arm splayed across the chest of her husband. Phillip was here!

She allowed her gaze to travel up to his face. So

peaceful in repose. Stubble on his chin. His blond hair normally perfectly in place was messed up. She sighed. "Oh, Phillip. You came," she whispered.

His lids opened revealing the crystal blue of the sky on a cloudless day. "Of course I came. I will always come for you, sweetheart."

The throbbing in her shoulder caused the memory of her attack to flood in and she shivered as she clung to him. Tears filled her eyes.

"Beth? What's wrong? Are you in pain?"

"I just remembered the attack."

"I'm sorry I didn't get here in time. I never should have left you."

"This was not your fault. I didn't take a groom."

"That likely wouldn't have stopped them. They might have killed him rather than risk exposure."

She sniffed. "I believe you have the right of it. But Phillip?"

"Hmmm?"

"They branded me." She closed her eyes and tucked herself into him as if she could hide her shame.

He whispered, "I know." His finger lifted her chin so she was forced to open her eyes and meet his gaze. "I still find you beautiful and love you. If the Black Diamond thought to drive a wedge between us, he failed."

"I love you, Phillip. I have news…"

"Is it what you shared in the letter you didn't mail? I found and read it last night. You are with child."

"Are you happy?"

"Thrilled, my dear. I never planned for a wife and family but since God brought you into my life, I'm finding there are things I never hoped for that have become integral to my happiness. You. Finding God. And now a child we created."

"I was glad to hear you'd found God too. There is so much I long to share with you."

"And share we shall. In time. But for now, the doctor has ordered rest and I am determined to ensure you recover from this."

"Yes, m'lord." She kissed his lips, snuggled into him and drifted back to sleep.

~*~

Her heart rate slowed as her body relaxed. She had awakened in his arms. She would recover and knew his love and protection. Phillip had failed her, yet she seemed to forgive him. *Lord, help me to do better. To be the man she needs me to be. Protect us and our unborn child.*

He eventually rose and rang for food to be brought to the room. He did not want to leave Beth's side as she recovered.

Elsa entered with a tray.

Josie followed the maid in. "How does our patient fare?" Josie asked.

"She awoke this morning but rests now." Phillip poured a cup of coffee and took a sip before sitting.

"I can order a bath for her soon."

"That would be fine but I'll be taking care of my wife."

Josie nodded and gave a soft smile. "I'm happy for you, Phillip. True love has found you at last. Ring if you need anything. I'll leave you to your peace."

"Thank you, Josie."

"You are more than welcome. I remember all you did to help us. You're a good man." She exited the room.

Memories of watching Marcus fight off Josie's kidnappers returned. Was he as fierce in his love as his friend had been? Marcus was blessed that he'd survived that beating. His friend still had a slight limp, especially when he was tired. He never complained.

Thank you, Lord, for the example of Your sacrificial love shown to me in Marcus. You've blessed me in my friends as well as my wife. Help us fight this dark enemy.

Beth stirred and rolled to her back with a moan. Phillip set down his cup and saucer with a clatter as he rushed to her side. "Beth?"

She bit her lip. "Forgot about that hole in my shoulder."

"Let me help you." Phillip assisted her that morning and by the time she had bathed and put on a fresh nightgown, she was exhausted.

The doctor returned and shooed him out of the room.

Phillip wandered down to the study to seek out his friend. He walked in and shut the door.

Marcus looked up from his desk and rose to his feet. "How is Beth?"

"Bruce is with her now. She hurts, which is to be expected. Sleeping a lot. She gave me some news in all this."

Eyebrows rose on his friend's face.

"She is with child."

A wide smile emerged and Marcus rushed forward to pat him on the back. "Congratulations. What wonderful news in the midst of this trial. Josie told me Beth is also following Christ."

Phillip grinned. "Yes, I'm so relieved. I realize it doesn't guarantee things will be easy but it's a comfort."

A knock came to the door.

"Come in," Marcus called.

Bruce entered. "Gentlemen."

"You've news of my wife?" Phillip asked.

"Yes. The wound is clean and should heal well."

"I've already shared with Marcus the news that we are expecting a child."

The doctor grinned. "So far there is no indication her trauma has harmed the babe. That doesn't mean everything is fine, but for now, it looks good."

"Continue bed rest?"

"For at least another day. She will tire easily."

"Thank you," Phillip said.

"I'll return on the morrow, but send for me if anything changes." The physician left.

Phillip turned to Marcus. "I'm returning to Beth. I don't want her to be alone."

"I understand. For now, you are both as safe as we can make you here. At some point we'll have to figure out what, if any, our next steps are."

"I'll be praying about that."

"As will I. Go to your wife." Marcus motioned for his friend to leave the room.

Phillip took the steps to her room and found Josie there bursting with happiness having heard the news about the baby. She wrapped Phillip in a hug before she left them alone.

Beth yawned as she held out a hand to her husband. He strode to her and sat on the bed by her side. "I'll rest better with you beside me."

He removed his boots and coat. "You don't have to ask me twice."

~*~

Two days had passed and at last Beth was allowed out of bed.

Phillip hovered around, loathe to leave her.

As sweet as that was, she found it suffocating. There had been no indications that the baby had been injured in the attack. "Phillip, we must talk."

"We've been together for the past few days and have talked plenty."

"But not about what we really need to discuss."

"Which is?"

"The evil that haunts us."

"Interesting choice of words."

"The rhombus on my shoulder is a mark of death. It claims the Black Diamond owns my soul. At least in his mind. I have no clue who he even is so he can't fear exposure from me. The bigger concern is my father and Lord Wolton."

"That you'll expose them?"

"There are still things I've not told you about my past. I know disturbing things about Lord Wolton. If the truth of those things became public...he'd kill me without blinking twice."

"And yet you need to tell me these things?"

"You are my husband. I don't want secrets between us. Your life is in danger regardless. He'll assume you've already been informed of my past. You realize I wasn't pure on our wedding night, but what you don't know is why."

"I know how a woman loses her..."

She shook her head. "You were my first."

He stared at her.

She reached out to grasp his hand. "There are some things worse than being raped." Beth bit her lip.

Her husband enfolded her in his arms as her body shook from memories rising from the dead within her.

"Shhh. Beth. I still love you. I'm sorry you had to endure that."

"You don't even know what I endured."

"I don't need you to tell me specifics. As for the Black Diamond, we both belong to Christ now. His evil has no power over us. Nor does Wolton's."

"I know so little about how to fight this."

"We'll keep reading and learning. God can lead us through this."

She nodded and rested in the truth of her husband's love, as well as God's. Her past was washed clean and it no longer had the power to hurt her if she walked in her new truth. Oh, if she could only get her mind to understand and wipe it all away. But then, perhaps there was a benefit to remembering. She'd never be naïve about the very real physical danger they still faced.

~*~

Later in the day, Phillip led Beth downstairs for dinner with Marcus and Josie. Every muscle protested movement but she was grateful to be out of the room. After the meal, Josie escorted her to the drawing room in front of a cozy fire for the evening had grown cool outside.

"Is your health improving?" Josie asked.

"As much as it can when I ache as I do. It shall pass. Thankfully the baby is well from what we can tell."

Josie smiled. "I'm happy for you both. What a blessing." She rubbed her own bump.

Phillip and Marcus entered.

"You chose not to stay long over your port?" Beth inquired.

"No. I wanted to be with you." Phillip grinned and gave her a wink.

Her face grew warm.

"I wish we could get our hands on the men who tortured you, Beth," Marcus said as he sat next to his wife.

"It would do you no good. I suspect they are paid by the Black Diamond but have no clue who he is."

"I thought Wolton sent them." Marcus leaned forward.

"The diamond shape on her shoulder is a brand of the Black Diamond. Or so my wife informs me."

"I've heard of him. He was behind Sir Bastian's attack on Josie." Marcus clasped his wife's hand. "Thankfully you, Phillip, along with Theo and Michael, managed to stop that."

"He would have branded me?" Josie asked, growing pale.

"Possibly." Weariness flowed through Beth. "But I think in this case it was a warning. That doesn't mean Wolton still won't be after Phillip and me. I know too much about his activities for him to allow me to live."

"What kind of group is this?"

"Satanic. They believe this land is not the property of England or the monarchy, but belongs to members of a secret group. They long to undermine the government and encourage Napoleon to attack our shores. Sympathizers are scattered throughout the countryside to await the signal to stir up dissension and distract the government from the imminence of an attack."

"Wellesley won't be able to stop them? How do they think Napoleon will get that far north?" Josie asked.

"I doubt their plans will succeed as they've been missing a sacrificial offering to the overlord of their society."

"A handpicked virgin. I believe that was your destiny, Josie, as another escaped them the year before. These special offerings are carefully chosen. They wanted me this time, but as I am married...now I am only a threat. They are evil and twisted. They will still seek my destruction."

She swallowed. "I've witnessed some of their sacrifices in the past. I was not a willing participant but made to watch. Tied up and gagged and set in a corner to view their sadistic rituals. They've used live animals in the past. Now they need human sacrifices, but death is not all they would do to that individual."

"Wolton would have married you and killed you?" asked Marcus.

"He had three previous wives, and all mysteriously died. No one ever questioned how or why. None had family to defend them. My own mother may have been a victim."

"She wouldn't have been a virgin."

"No, but the very torture and murder...amongst other things...would have gained them favor if they were denied their ultimate sacrifice."

"This is too horrific to be believable." Josie shuddered. "Yet I believe you speak the truth."

"Thank you for sharing that information," Marcus stated.

She shook her head. "You know just enough to understand he's not a man to be trifled with. He serves an evil power and is under the authority of the Black Diamond. Wolton's master will not go out of his way to protect him, though. He'd sacrifice him if he ever believed his identity was about to be exposed."

"I'm concerned you'll be attacked again." Phillip stood and paced.

"I have no doubt they will make an attempt to take me from you, Phillip. They will never be satisfied with merely killing me."

"How could your father be party to any of this?" Josie asked.

"He's a mere puppet. Wolton is pulling his strings. I suspect Wolton is also responsible for my mother's death. My father was never the same after she died."

"I'm sorry you experienced that," Phillip said.

"Me, too."

"It will be difficult to get the Ministry of Defense at Whitehall to put more agents on this case to expose the secret society."

"Are you suggesting that leaves it up to us?" Phillip groaned. "I refuse to be party to setting a trap to expose them. I will not risk my wife and child."

Beth reached a hand out to him.

He strode over to her and held it before sitting next to her.

"Phillip, I've been marked for death. They will continue to pursue me until they have accomplished their goal. Once they've done that you will be next. Springing a trap might be a good idea. We can be prepared for them. It is not without risk, but we are in more danger by pretending that nothing bad could happen and going on our merry way."

Phillip let out a sigh. "We need Neville here along with Theodore and Michael to lend some wisdom."

"I've sent a message summoning them here. I will also get a letter to Jared to apprise him of what we know. He can pass it on to Wellesley."

"So now we wait?" Josie asked.

"We wait, but we will not be sitting ducks. We can lay low and release word you are still insensible, a story our staff has spread to the village. Word might reach Wolton and he will relax and bide his time until he's able to attack again. That gives us time to plan." Marcus squeezed Josie's hand.

She returned the squeeze with a smile. "And we will pray and 'take unto you the whole armour of God, that ye may be able to withstand the evil day, and having done all, to stand.'"

Josie bent her head and the group followed suit.

Marcus prayed, "Lord, You know the enemy that threatens our friends and we recognize that You are a greater power than the evil they represent. Guide and protect us all as we seek a way to make it through this trial. Thank You for bringing back Beth and helping her recover her health. Continue to be at work on our behalf to protect our friends and our nation. We are unable to do any of this without Your holy power at work in and through us."

A holy silence hung in the air as eyes opened and the fire crackled.

Peace settled over Beth's soul along with the freedom from the weight of the horror she'd carried within her for so long. God was in control. He'd blessed her with friends and a husband who would stand by her side for the battle ahead. She smoothed down her dress. "I'm fatigued. Would you excuse us?"

"Us?" Phillip asked.

"You are joining me, aren't you?"

"I thought I was being overly protective…"

She grinned. "You were, but tonight, I desire time with my husband. Alone." She gave him a wink their hosts couldn't catch.

Phillip's eyes brightened. He stood and assisted Beth to her feet. "We'll see you in the morning. We can strategize more at that time."

Beth grinned as she hooked her arm through Phillip's. "Thank you for a lovely evening. I'm sorry I had to spoil it with such terrible memories."

"Rest well," Marcus and Josie both chorused.

Once in the hallway, Phillip leaned toward Beth. "Are you really tired?"

"Of being in company. And being coddled. And revisiting the past. Tonight, I want to give my husband the welcome he deserved had I been prudent and stayed home."

"But of course, ma'am. Anything my lady desires." They reached the top of the stairs.

"Anything?" she teased.

He scooped her up in his arms and carried her down the hall. "Within reason. You are still recovering."

Once behind the closed and locked door to their bedroom, Beth slid to the floor and reached up to pull her husband's face to hers. "I've missed this." Their lips met and she was grateful once again, for a love that wiped away the shame of the past and gave her joy in ways she'd never imagined. There were no nightmares to bother her that night.

12

Lord Wolton sat alone in the dark study of his worn-down house. He turned over the green fabric in his hand, delivered to him as a gift from the Black Diamond. He held the material to his nose and sniffed. It smelled of her. He rubbed the cloth against his cheek. *She will pay.* He grinned. If the Black Diamond could track her down, he'd find her as well. He realized that sending the fabric was a way to show his superiority to Wolton, but Wolton assumed something was up when Lord Westcombe hastily departed town.

Too bad they hadn't been in residence when that fire started. Lord Westcombe was too crafty, but Wolton was a genius. He'd show who was superior. Westcombe might have Lizzy for now but she was ultimately Wolton's and he would possess her.

His tongue licked the fabric seeped in her blood. He could taste victory. It was within reach. He'd lull them into a false sense of security before he struck his final fatal blow. He couldn't take too much time as investigations were getting uncomfortably close. His lord was able to keep things hidden from the unsuspecting. The innocent and naïve would never uncover his secrets. Even if Lizzy did share, no one would believe her.

For now, he would pretend he was resigned to Lizzy's marriage and losing her to Westcombe. She would still be his in due time. He would make an offering. Another woman could suffice but Wolton could not and would not let Lizzy go. She was his. She would be his. Victory would be all the sweeter for the struggle to get there.

And he had no doubt she would struggle. The thought made him giddy. He would finish the task he set for himself—or die trying. He had no fear he might fail.

Holding the green cloth to the light of the window, he was assured of victory. She would be terrified and the thought of that excited him. He would delight in every scream of terror. His success would assure his climb to the top of the Society. Napoleon would reward him. He had wealth. What he longed for was power. He'd uncover the Black Diamond and become greater than him. He would establish himself as lord over England and fear and terror would reign to his great delight.

Oh, his fondest dream. He placed the green fabric on the table and smoothed it in front of him.

What should he do about Lord Follett? The man was tiresome in his doom and gloom whimpering. He'd outlived his usefulness. He'd keep him for now. Follett might be the one weakness that could bring Lizzy back into Wolton's waiting arms. A smile spread across his face. He would let her recover. Allow Lord and Mrs. Westcombe to believe he had given up. He'd strike when they least expected it. Perhaps he could make his move at the height of the little season when everyone returned from the sweltering heat of summer in the country.

What if Lizzy were with child?

He leaned back in his chair imagining her large and the perverse delight he'd take in torturing her and her pristine knight errant. Oh, yes. Victory would be sweet. He folded the green cloth and placed it in his inner breast pocket, right over his heart. He rose and closed the curtains and resigned himself to wait.

~*~

Sir Michael Tidley stared out the window of his coach as he headed to another ball. How many women would be victims of the despicable Black Diamond and his minions? Marcus had no clue that his sister Henrietta had been spared that fate due to the quick thinking of her husband, Lord Percy. And while Lord Remington was mildly aware of the Diamond's part in Bastion's attack, he had no clue the depths to which his depravity went.

Now Phillip's bride had been attacked and Michael had no doubt the Black Diamond was behind all of this again. Captain Jared Allendale, Marcus's brother and aide-de-camp to Sir Wellesley, was the only one who really understood the work Michael did and the threat to England these ne'er-do-wells presented.

Something about the Black Diamond haunted Michael. Attacks on people close to him made him question the identity of this elusive villain. Would they ever discover who he was and be able to stop him? If he really was a member of the aristocracy, the task was more difficult. One couldn't simply kill a member of the titled elite without repercussions. And punishment for titled lords was often tepid. It was becoming more difficult for Michael to keep his knowledge of the world within which he worked from his dearest friends. He'd do anything to ensure that Phillip and his bride got the happiness they so deserved. It'd never be a part of his own future but that didn't mean he couldn't help someone else.

He sighed as they pulled up to the Harrington ball. As a baseborn brat who only inherited a title through service to the king, he possessed a healthy income due to the reluctant generosity of his deceased grandfather. Michael understood his presence was tolerated as long as he was handsome, charming, and didn't cross a line with the debutantes. He wasn't sought after for more than that, which was fine with him. His place in the world was to make it safe for those he mingled amongst. It would likely be someone like Wolton or the Black Diamond who put a period to his own existence. He'd do the best he could to preserve the monarchy until that date came.

He handed his hat and cane to the butler and stood in the que to meet the host and hostess of this event as well as their newly presented daughter, the estimable Lady Eustace Harrington. He cringed as he viewed her. Probably wouldn't be a victim of the evil stalking London as they often sought more attractive targets. Once through the line he stepped into the ballroom and found Lord Harrow already present.

"Sir Michael, well met." Theodore puffed out his barrel-like chest.

"Will you be departing to Rose Hill?" Michael whispered.

The orchestra was beginning to play and one of the violins was out of tune, the screeching causing Michael to wince in pain.

"Aye, via carriage. Will you be joining me?"

"I'll likely go on horseback."

"Shady business with the attack on Beth."

"Shhhh."

"Oh, yes. Of course. Pardon me. Have you news of Follett or Wolton?"

Michael frowned and shook his head. "They've slunk back into whatever hole they came from. At least, for now. Don't be lulled into thinking they won't return."

"So why the summons to Rose Hill?"

"Guess we'll find the answers to that after our arrival."

"Don't mind visiting there. Remy's chef is one of the best."

Michael glanced at his friend's tight waistcoat. "You could do with a bit more exercises on horseback, my friend."

Theo grinned. "I can still hold my own if necessary."

"Good to know."

The substantial lord blanched. "You don't think we'll end up in a fight like we did to rescue Josie, do you?"

"You acquitted yourself well, there Theo. Just be alert to danger."

Theo sighed. "I don't know why I even come to these things. I've not found a woman who suits me yet."

"Do you ever wonder if you will someday encounter a woman who will cause you to willingly risk everything for her safety and happiness? It happened to Marcus and now Phillip. Do you anticipate falling into Cupid's lure?"

"I would hope we would both fall in love someday, Michael. I don't think either of us should settle for anything less than a woman for whom we would risk it all. Why enter the parson's mousetrap otherwise?"

"You're not cutting a swath through the town with the ladies. What have you to give up, Theo? Marcus longed for a 'home' and family and he got it with Josie. Phillip didn't want anything to upset his tidy life and Elizabeth came along—now look at him. What would love look like for you?"

"I would expect love might fill the loneliness that creeps in even at balls like this. Don't you ever wish you had someone to come home to? To sleep with every night in your home instead of sneaking out at dawn like a common criminal? Someone to buy pretty things for. To dance with. To look across a crowded room and share a private joke." Theo sounded wistful.

Michael's mouth hung agape.

"What? What did I say that has you looking like a cod starved for air?"

"First of all, I never sneak out like a common criminal. A mistress could give you almost everything you've mentioned. It seems that taking a wife like Marcus and Phillip have done can be a messy business. When your turn comes, focus on dancing with a girl, falling madly in love, and marrying her in three weeks after the banns are called. Have a nice reception and go to your estate for your happily-ever-after, filling the rooms with children and returning to the *beau monde* and the season whenever the mood strikes."

"I'm not ready for that. Not yet. You are correct. Marcus and Phillip had a fatiguing journey on their way to love and marriage."

"You don't hear them complaining, do you?" Michael joked and patted his friend on the shoulder. "Give it time, Theo. You're one of the good guys. Any woman here would be fortunate to have you as her husband."

"I'm not as attractive as some of the men..."

"You are a well-enough looking man with the kind of character that any father would be proud to entrust his daughter to. As for me, it shall never be my lot in life. A pointless endeavor. I don't begrudge Marcus and Phillip their marriages, though."

"Until it's my turn, I'll do everything in my power to ensure their happiness while awaiting mine in due time."

"Even though marriage isn't in my future, I stand with you in that pledge to protect theirs."

Theo yawned. "Long day hanging out at the clubs. Perhaps I'll leave after a few dances and head home to sleep."

"Might not be a bad idea, my friend. I doubt I'll stay around long either. I'll see you at Rose Hill."

"Safe travels, Michael."

"To you as well, Theo." Sir Tidley strode to the crowd to a woman often overlooked by the Corinthians on the strut. "Miss Sumpter, may I request your hand for the first dance?"

The young woman squinted at him, her pimply face turning red in appreciation of his singling her out. "Sir Tidley. Yes. Thank you." The band struck up the song in the already overcrowded and stuffy room as Michael led the young woman to the floor. At least for a few minutes, he would be someone's hero for the evening. He set himself out to be charming to the young woman as the steps of the dance would allow.

Tomorrow could not come soon enough.

When he escorted his partner back to her parents, he was accosted by Lady Orion.

"Sir Tidley. Walk with me, will you?"

"As you wish, my lady." He offered her his arm and they began a slow course around the ballroom.

"I wanted to inquire after your friend, Lord Westcombe."

"You want me to gossip about him and his lovely bride?"

She nodded with a prim smile of satisfaction. "You know me too well, Sir Tidley. Will you accommodate me?"

Michael smiled. What better way to help his friend than to boost the reputation of him and his bride amongst the *beau monde*? "They are in the country right now. I do not know when I have ever seen a more besotted and devoted husband than him."

"It truly was a love-match then?"

"You doubted it? Lord Westcombe was not of a mind to marry until he met Miss Follett. She was everything he didn't know he needed in his life."

She sighed and her free hand waved a fan in front of her face. "Oh, my romantic heart rejoices. That poor girl had an unfortunate father and what he was thinking to try to marry her off to that decrepit Wolton, well, I'd give him a piece of my mind were I to have the opportunity. A despicable business. I'm happy to hear it turned out well for them."

"I suspect they will return to town at some point in time."

"Oh, let them have their love for now. No need to parade it in front of society. Tell Lord Westcombe I am exceedingly proud of him."

Michael's eyebrows rose. "Why would that be, my lady?"

"I told him he would do. I suspected love was in the air from the start even though he was tight-lipped about it. To ensure her reputation, I'm certain."

"I will pass along the word to him."

"Don't be a stranger, young man."

"And why would you want me dancing attendance on you, Lady Orion?"

"An older woman can't enjoy the company of a scamp now and then? You are vastly entertaining when you set your mind to it, Sir Michael."

He grinned. "I'm glad to be of service m'lady."

"Return me to my seat now and find another young woman to dance with. You are delicious to watch on the floor. Thank you for our little tête-à-tête."

Heat rose in his cheeks as he helped her to her seat and placed a kiss about her hand before releasing it. "Your servant."

After a few more dances he finally left for home.

~*~

Lord Manchester had forgone his traditional visit to his countryside estate. He chose instead to stay in town, manage his investments and continue to seek a match for Penelope. She'd had a few suitors but none looked promising. Likely due to the precipitous and foolish marriage of Phillip's. He determined that a steady presence in town would settle the gossip. Perhaps come fall, Penelope would fare better during the little season. That was months away. They still needed to finish this one with their heads held high. His wife bore the brunt of the strain of that endeavor.

The butler appeared at the door to his study. "Lady Orion is begging an audience with you."

"Seat her in the drawing room, have tea brought

and tell Lady Manchester to come to me immediately."

"Aye, m'lord." The servant bowed and retreated.

Lady Orion was a dragon amongst the *ton*. This interview could make or break Penelope's chances to find a good match. The door opened and his wife entered.

"My lord?"

"Lady Orion is here. We will visit her together. Perhaps we can salvage what is left of this season with a modicum of grace."

His wife nodded, and taking his arm, accompanied him to the drawing room. They entered and Lady Orion rose to face them.

"It's about time you made an appearance. I'm not a mad dog with a thorn in my paw that you should feel the need for caution before entering your own drawing room." With a sniff, she returned to her seat.

Lord Manchester gave a minimal bow of his head before Lady Orion as his wife did likewise. He saw his bride seated and then found a chair for himself.

"Are we awaiting tea or may I simply state my business?" Lady Orion said.

The door opened and the tea tray appeared. Lady Manchester poured. Lord Manchester tugged at his cravat and clenched his teeth as he waited for their visitor to speak.

She took a bite of cake and gave his wife a nod. "You have a wonderful chef."

"Thank you, my lady. Why have you chosen to grace us with your presence?" Lady Manchester asked.

"I have been waiting for your son and his lovely bride to reappear in London. In spite of their hasty marriage, I wonder why you have not yet hosted a ball to welcome the lovely Elizabeth into the bosom of your family. Your son has done you great credit for many years now and it seems you have once again overlooked him. It appears he could use the assistance of his father, a great earl, and his mother, one of the premier hostesses of the *ton,* to establish your new daughter-in-law firmly under the Manchester umbrella of protection."

Lord Manchester sat stunned. This lady was taking him to task for not being a good father? How dare she!

His wife spoke. "I'm at a bit of a loss here, Lady Orion, but in what ways do you believe Phillip has done credit to his heritage? He has always gone his own way, much like many of the young bucks of society. Aimless and frivolous in his activities."

The matron sitting across from them shook her head as if in pity on them.

The earl was ready to burst.

"Do you see your son as a wastrel and a womanizer?" Lady Orion asked. "No. Do not answer me yet. I am well aware of his reputation in his younger days. But in recent years he has become the proud owner of Stanton Hall up in Milton Mowbray in Leicestershire. I hear it is a tidy and profitable estate. Were you aware that he'd been investing his allowance, and those investments have contributed to his wealth?"

Lord Manchester could stay quiet no longer. "Where do you come by your information? My sister left him a paltry estate up north. Nothing of repute. How could what you say be true?"

Lady Orion smiled. "There has been little to hear of your son's activities over the past five seasons, so I set out to discover what secrets he held. His pristine appearance and the lack of rumors surrounding him for the past few years piqued my interest. He has been living in such a circumspect way I suspected he was hiding something scandalous. Instead, I discovered a young man who has quietly turned his life and income around to become one of the premier gentlemen of the *ton*.

"He has been treated as such by most matrons and was lauded, before his marriage, as a highly eligible *parti* for a woman not seeking a title. From my understanding, Phillip could teach you and Lord Anthony a thing or two about managing estates and investments. His success in such a short time puts yours to shame, my lord."

Lady Manchester's hand flew to her chest. "We love Phillip. Why have we never heard any of this before?"

"Perhaps you've chosen to see him as he used to be, a scapegrace, as many young bucks fresh on the town from college are. He keeps honorable company which I'm sure has helped. I strongly encourage you to support your son and his new wife. Life is too short to be harbouring resentments. Lord and Mrs. Westcombe need your support if they are to weather the storm amongst the *ton*, which is by no means over. You owe it to your son and your future grandchildren."

Lady Manchester glanced at her husband and mouthed the word, 'grandchildren?'

Lord Manchester turned to their guest. "Why are you so concerned with our family affairs?"

"Unbeknownst to Lord Follett or his daughter, Lady Maria Follett was my dearest friend in finishing school. Before her death, she wrote a strange letter asking me to look after the future of her daughter should anything happen to Maria. Up until Elizabeth's advent here in town I've been denied access to her by her father. I am desirous of fulfilling my promise to her mother. I want to see Mrs. Westcombe gain the appropriate entrée to the *beau monde*. She will need all the help she can get with the dust Lord Wolton stirred up.

"I could do this on my own but it would look peculiar if I did so without your equal or primary participation. As you are an Earl, your approval has more weight than my own considerable influence."

"I thought the gossip had died down," Lady Manchester said.

"My dear Countess. The gossip will spring to life the minute they arrive back in town. If it is not dealt with, it will take on a life of its own and be more difficult for them to overcome. It will tarnish you and your daughter as well. Now that you understand the truth of the matter, will you, or will you not, hold a ball to celebrate your son's nuptials and welcome his new bride to your family?"

Lord Manchester glanced to his wife for approval of this proposal. They could well afford the expense but it would fall on her shoulders to plan and execute such an event.

She finally spoke up. "Of course, we will host a ball at the beginning of the little season. I will work to get the invitations ready and sent to summer estates so that our guests are prepared to arrive in town in time for the event. I will send for Phillip and his, um, er, bride."

"You mean your daughter-in-law, Mrs. Elizabeth Westcombe. She is a most delightful young lady if you were to take the time to become acquainted with her.

Your son has chosen wisely and I could not be more satisfied with the match if I were her own mother." Lady Orion rose to her feet. "You may remain seated. I'll see myself out. Our interview is done." With head held high and back stiff, she strode from the room.

The door to outside opened and closed.

They were now alone.

Lady Manchester rose from her seat. "Well, my dear, it seems I have a ball to plan."

"Yes, we do, and I believe we owe our son and his bride an apology for our treatment of them when they were here last."

The Countess nodded. "The ball will be easier to accomplish. Phillip can be stubborn."

"Do you think he'll forgive us?"

"I certainly hope so."

13

Phillip strode into the library to discover his wife curled up in a chair with her feet tucked underneath her as she read a novel. She looked up and smiled at him. He went to her and placed a kiss on her cheek before finding a chair for himself.

"Can we talk for a few minutes?"

"Yes." Beth put a piece of yarn in between the pages and set the book aside. "Did something happen?"

"A letter arrived this morning." He paused as he tapped the folded pages on his knee. "It's from my parents."

She sat up straighter. "Oh. What did they write?"

"I've been afraid to open it."

"Phillip. You have stood on your own for years without their approval. Why would their lack of enthusiasm over our hasty wedding surprise you?"

"I had somehow hoped that in time they would discover I'm not the useless son they used to think I was. That I had grown into a gentleman I hoped they could be proud of. I've tried to live my life in a way that would honor my heritage and name."

"Noble goals to be sure, but sometimes parents are blind to the realities around them. I doubt my father realizes the abuses I suffered at the hands of Wolton and others."

Phillip clenched his jaw tight. After hearing the heartbreaking details of all she'd endured in her father's home, he burned with anger and a desire for justice. They discussed their need to forgive, but the rage would overtake him at times like these. He gave a sigh and gazed into his wife's emerald eyes. "I'm not very good with this, Beth. I'm sorry. I fear if I were to see your father or Lord Wolton right now, I'd be tempted to kill them both. It is wrong…but they were wrong…"

"There is nothing you can do to bring back my childhood or innocence. All I need for justice is for you to love me as I am. God blessed me by bringing you to me. I never dreamed someone would love me as well as you do." She reached out a hand to grab the letter but he pulled it away. She grinned. "Do I need to fight you for it?" She moved to slip on her shoes.

Phillip held the letter further out of her reach. "I dare you to try."

"Those are fighting words, my lord." She stood as did he and they moved around each other. She jumped to try to grab the letter out of his fingers and he laughed at her failed attempt. She stopped and stood still in front of him, pondering.

He grew suspicious. "Ready to give up?"

"Not on your life." She gave him a sly smile that made his heart flip. She reached up to touch his nose, traced her finger down, along his chin, and then slowly down his neck under his cravat.

Phillip squirmed. "You're trying to trick me. It won't work."

"No?"

She continued to move her finger over the sensitive spot between his ear and shoulder, while the other one came up his side toward where his arm was raised high above her. Slowly her hand moved and

Phillip grimaced in his attempt to withstand the onslaught. She knew his ticklish spots. Soon he lowered his arm to stop her fingers from touching him underneath his coat. She grabbed the letter and moved around behind the settee.

Phillip chuckled. "Fine. You won that round, but you will pay later."

"Is that a promise or a threat?"

"Both."

"I look forward to it." She considered the paper she held, running her finger over the seal. "Shall I?"

"Please do. I don't have the courage to read the words alone. You may have the honor." He collapsed into a chair and waited as she walked around to sit across from him. "Let's get it over with."

Beth broke the seal with her fingernail. Opening the foolscap, she stared at the page. "Are you sure?"

He nodded.

"I think this might be your mother's handwriting."

Dearest Phillip,

Your father and I regret how we treated you and your new bride when you last visited us. To say that your wedding was a shock is mild. However, you are our son and we love you and recognize our error in not extending that same love and acceptance to your wife. We hope in time you will find it in your heart to forgive us for being foolish in this regard.

We would, with your permission, like to hold a ball in honor of your marriage, the second week in September. Please inform us if this would be agreeable to you and Elizabeth.

Fondest regards,

Lady Manchester

Elizabeth set the paper down.

"Stiff and formal. I suspected no less from Mother." Phillip reached for the pages and read the script himself. "I should be grateful, right? It's something. I've never heard my parents apologize or admit wrongdoing for anything in all my years. But here she has done so on paper. Unbelievable."

"She wants to give a ball. This may be the opportunity we've looked for to engage Wolton."

"I'd prefer we leave the continent than to seek out this man and risk your life."

"And what about yours, Phillip? Yours might be in more danger than mine. Do you think I would willingly give you up?" She rose and eased her way onto his lap.

His arm went around her, holding her tight as if she could disappear in any moment. He bent his head into her chest and her steady heartbeat forced him to calm down. "Do we dare use my parents' ball, in our honor, for such a thing?"

"It would be the highlight of the season to be sure, topping my disappearance at your sister's come-out." Elizabeth kissed his hair and hugged him in return.

He looked up at her and their lips met. Breaking away Elizabeth whispered, "I remember seeing a tall, handsome blond rogue, with sparkling blue eyes. He cast every man there in the shade. When he glanced my way, it sent shivers all the way to my toes."

"Really? Does he still do that?" Phillip grinned.

"Most definitely." She leaned forward for another kiss.

The letter was forgotten for the nonce.

~*~

Phillip escorted Beth for a walk in the gardens. She enjoyed his presence and this slower pace of life where they could enjoy being together. He carried a gun in his coat, just in case. She teased him about his overprotectiveness, but inwardly the fact it was there gave her a sense of safety she'd lived for too long without. Hoofbeats racing to the house put him on high alert.

"I wonder who is coming?" she asked.

"We should go inside."

"Wolton won't ride up and snatch me. It's probably one of your friends." She started down the path, dragging him behind her, toward the front of the manor.

"Michael?" Phillip stared.

"Is this your lovely bride, Phillip?" Michael dismounted from his horse as a groom ran out to take it to the stables.

"Beth, this is Sir Michael Tidley, a rascal and a friend. Michael, may I introduce Mrs. Elizabeth Westcombe."

"Ah, dear Mrs. Westcombe. I didn't think you could be lovelier than I remembered, but obviously, my mind is faulty for here you are, glowing, and casting the roses in the shade."

Phillip growled.

"You are too kind, but I should warn you, since my attack Phillip has become a fierce protector and I don't think he likes your flattery. Maybe I should be offended that he doesn't agree?" Her eyebrows rose.

Michael's head fell back as he laughed. "Oh, Phillip. She has you wound up tight." He strode to Beth and placed a kiss on her cheek. "Well met, Beth." He reached out a hand and Phillip shook it.

Turning back to Beth, the knight grinned and whispered, "And don't worry, in spite of my diminutive height, I'm quite the scrapper in a fight, as Phillip knows all too well." With a wink, he stepped back. "I'm off to find my quarters and see about cleaning up before dinner. I suspect Theo will arrive on the morrow." He went up the steps and disappeared from sight.

"I like your friends, Phillip. You've chosen well."

"As long as you love me best."

"Could you have any doubts? Do you need to be reminded?"

"Always." He wiggled his eyebrows.

"Naughty boy. Come with me then." She led him into the house to their room.

~*~

The dinner bell rang. "Hurry up, Phillip. We'll be late." She tugged at his cravat and gave him a pat on his chest. "There. You look wonderful."

"You look well-loved."

"Do not put me to the blush. I look like a proper wife. Now come." They went down the stairs and came to the drawing room to find Marcus and Josie before them.

"Where's Michael?"

"He arrived?" Josie asked as she glanced at her husband.

"Sorry. I thought you knew."

"I need to make sure the table is set for an extra guest." She swept from the room.

"Brandy?" Marcus offered Phillip.

"Yes." The drink was handed off.

Beth wandered around the room, surprised they managed to arrive in time. Phillip would glance at her and she couldn't help but smile. She hugged herself but released it as the skin on her shoulder pulled tight. Her injury was healing which was the best she could hope for.

Michael arrived at the door as Josie returned and he gave her his arm.

"Ah, Rose Hill hospitality. Nowhere on earth quite like it," Michael said. "I remember when Marcus longed for a wife to greet him when he returned home and a family to fill these halls with laughter. You are well on your way, my good man."

Josie blushed and came to stand with Beth. "He's a scamp."

"Delightful, nonetheless. Does he ever take anything seriously?"

"I believe so, but I rarely see that side of him. He is handy with his fists though and a good friend to have in a crisis. There is no laughter then. He helped Marcus rescue me when I'd been trapped in a carriage."

"How horrid."

"For them, perhaps. I was unconscious for some time. It was during my recovery that I fell in love with Lord Remington, before I'd ever seen his face."

"Excuse me?"

"The accident had rendered me blind. Thankfully it was temporary. That man prayed over me for nights on end."

"He's a good man."

"I'm a blessed woman," Josie said.

"As am I."

The bell rang and they headed into dinner.

Michael entertained them with tales from balls and

other events in London.

When the meal ended, Josie and Beth rose and left the men to their port.

Josie linked her arm through Beth's as they strode to the drawing room. "You seem far more content since Phillip arrived."

"I am. I long for us to go to Stanton Hall, but I understand that here there are people who can help us."

"Marcus doesn't want to travel far with the baby coming, even though I have some time yet before it arrives."

"It is equally sweet and annoying when they become so protective."

"Exactly." Josie sat and Beth found a loveseat in the hopes that Phillip would join her when he arrived.

"Are you worried about Wolton?" Josie asked.

"For the moment, no. But he is a threat. In time, he will attack. The terror is in not knowing when. I have peace that it won't be soon. Phillip and I disagree about how to bring resolution to this."

"I'm sure when Theodore arrives, the men will discuss a variety of options to help. In the meantime, I'm grateful for the company. Soon this house will be ringing with the laughter of children, but until then, it's nice to have it filled with the love and conversation of friends."

"I'm grateful for your hospitality. Phillip told me he has spent many summers here during his college breaks."

"He is a close friend to Marcus, Michael, and Theodore. I pray that as we start a family, and now you as well with Phillip, that the men don't lose the precious friendship that has sustained them for so long."

"I suspect it will be up to their devoted wives to ensure that never happens."

Josie grinned. "I wholeheartedly agree."

"Agree with what?" Marcus asked as he strode into the room with the men.

Phillip came to sit by Beth. A shiver of delight ran through her as his thigh brushed against hers. She hoped she never became immune to his touch.

"Agree that your friendships are worth preserving long into the future," Beth stated.

Phillip frowned. "Why wouldn't they?"

"Life is changing for us and for Marcus and Josie. That impacts everyone. It doesn't have to preclude time spent together, though. Thankfully, Josie and I have become great friends. Now we only have to hope that Michael finds someone we like and then Theodore as well."

Marcus grinned. "Plotting to marry off all my friends? Don't forget Jared. When he returns from war, it would be wonderful if he could find someone to love as well."

"We'll pray for God to open those doors."

"Forget about planning my marriage. I'm not interested. I'm happy for you and will delight in being an uncle to all the children you'll be having." Michael protested.

"The uncle who leads them into trouble?" Marcus asked.

"But of course," Michael smirked. "Listen, it's been a long day and I'm bushed. I'll see you in the morning. Hopefully, Theo will be arriving soon so we can plot what needs to happen to keep Beth and Phillip safe."

"Good night, Michael," Beth said as the others echoed her comment.

The knight strode from the room. Beth hooked her arm to Phillip's. "I'm fatigued as well. Shall we call it a night?"

Marcus grinned to Josie. "Rose Hill has that impact on people." He rose and held out a hand helping his wife to her feet.

The two couples took the stairs and when Beth and Phillip reached their room she pulled him in and locked the door behind her. She strode to him and began to untie his cravat as he unbuttoned his waistcoat.

"Not as tired as you indicated?"

"Oh, I'm tired, m'lord. Tired of talking." She gave him a sly grin and he bent to kiss her.

Beth slept well that night, never realizing the fireplace hadn't been lit.

~*~

Lord Follett sat at his desk and sorted through the pile of letters from his creditors. They had been hounding him. He'd needed to leave London in hopes they wouldn't follow him north. There had been no word from Lord Wolton for several weeks and that alone made him nervous. The man terrified him and always had. Folly took a sip of whiskey. His hair was unkempt, cravat untied and his waistcoat stained with gravy. A disreputable mess. He hadn't left home in over a week lest a creditor stalked him outside the gates.

He was aware there were people watching. Who sent them he didn't know and that terrified him more.

He'd gotten word of the fire at Lord Westcombe's home and was glad Lizzy hadn't been in residence at the time.

He wondered where his daughter had gone. As angry as he was at her double-crossing him, part of him was hopeful she'd find happiness with her new husband. His little girl had grown up timid and reserved. He hardly knew the woman she was within the beautiful shell she carried over her soul. She looked so much like her mother it hurt.

Ever since watching his wife die in a horrific way, he'd regretted his association with Wolton. He'd wondered if the man had ever touched Lizzy. Why else would she have been so repulsed and bolt like that? The thought of his precious daughter being harmed as a young girl, through the activities of the society, made him ill. He drank more whiskey.

It seemed there was never enough of the alcohol to keep him as numb as he longed to be. After years of imbibing, and times where he couldn't remember, it took more and more drink to get him through each miserable day. He'd only wanted Lizzy to marry Wolton so his debts would be taken care of and he could drink himself to oblivion. For years he'd been impotent to save himself much less his daughter. Would anyone even miss him if he died now?

The estate was mortgaged to the hilt with no heirs. The baronetcy would die with him. It was a minor title anyway. No great loss to the crown and he'd done nothing of value in his life. The only bright light had been having a daughter, but she was now haunted by an evil predator. He emptied the bottle and reached for another.

Was there anything he could do at this late date to

redeem himself? Could he perhaps change the course of evil that was set in motion? Even if he lost his life trying, it wouldn't matter. He was a dead man anyway. If, for once in his life, he could do something right with regards to his daughter, would he be redeemed in her eyes at least?

He set to tidying up his desk and wrote a letter. When he was finished, he sanded the letter, affixed the seal and locked it in the top drawer of his desk. On unsteady feet, he rose to seek his bed. Events would move along quickly enough. He needed to sleep and sober up if he was to do at least one positive thing in his life.

14

September

Beth hugged Josie tight. "Thank you for all you've done for us."

"I will continue to hold you both in prayer. We'll join you in time for the ball. I wouldn't want to miss the celebration of your marriage."

"You'll be coming close to your confinement."

"After the ball, I'm sure Marcus will spirit me away to Rose Hill and hover until our child is born."

The women grinned at each other and with one more hug, Beth moved toward the coach.

The men shook hands and Phillip assisted her into the carriage. Settling next to her she held his hand as the carriage lurched forward. Outriders surrounded them. Marcus had insisted on those. Duke rode proudly on top, a celebrated creature by all the stable hands. He'd truly found a home for himself at Rose Hill.

The journey was slow. Phillip demanded the trip take two days due to Beth's "condition." While she believed it unnecessary she gave in with grace. Her husband loved her and she relished every minute of it.

They stopped that night at the Red Boar Inn and enjoyed a cozy dinner in a private parlour before sharing their room. Such a different experience from her wedding night when she'd slept alone, hurt, and frustrated. How far they had come in such a few short months.

They arrived in London the next day and made their way to their house. The master suite had been repaired and decorated.

Beth looked forward to seeing it and taking up residence in their own space outside of Stanton Hall.

Phillip's friends hired ex-soldiers to stand guard as they took on duties in and around the house. They were armed, determined to protect her, and keep an eye out for danger.

Beth sensed that things with her father and Wolton were drawing near which led to increased anxiety. Every night as she snuggled in her husband's arms, she was able to set aside those fears and leave them in the hands of their capable God.

~*~

"Good morning, love." Phillip had already dressed but came to rouse her from sleep.

"Why are you waking me up?"

"I have a surprise for you."

"Really?"

"Madame Celeste will be arriving shortly to make you a gown for the ball."

She sighed.

"What's wrong?" He sat next to her.

"The scar is high enough to make designing a gown difficult if I want to hide it and I do."

"I'm sure she'll work wonders."

"And if you haven't noticed, your son or daughter is taking up more space."

His hand caressed her stomach, hidden by her night rail. "I happen to love every part of you. By the way, I requested she design your gown in an emerald green to match your lovely eyes."

"Ah, the joys of being married. No more sallow pastels for me."

"Exactly. I'm headed out but I trust you'll find Madame Celeste more than competent to have a gown ready for you in time for the ball. Order anything else you would like as well."

Her eyebrows rose. "Really?"

"Yes, my dear. As my wife, you need to look well cared for and please your husband by dressing in the most recent fashions."

"I could dress in nothing and make you happy."

His gaze grew warm. "Very true, but that's not an outfit I want to share with anyone else." He kissed her and pulled away leaving her longing for more. "Later."

"Promise?"

"Have I failed you yet?"

She shook her head. She delighted in watching him move. God had blessed her with a fine figure of a man and he knew how to dress well. Now it was her turn to return the favor. Oh, this could be fun!

~*~

Madame Celeste clucked as she moved around Beth. "Your husband did not lie about your beauty. We will design a gown as unique as the woman wearing it. Red hair is considered unfashionable but I suspect after the ball women will be trying to find a way to look as stunning as you."

They chose to design a bold emerald gown with a high back and modest front, trimmed with gold accents and a filmy golden overskirt. Beth would feel like a princess wearing it, but would her story have a fairy tale ending? After more gowns were ordered the seamstress left and Beth fell into bed to rest. Even shopping from home could be exhausting.

~*~

The next day Phillip enjoyed breakfast with his wife. He'd gotten into the habit of discussing news from the paper with her and found she had some insightful thoughts on the struggles facing the country. Too bad women weren't allowed in Parliament.

A footman stepped into the room clearing his throat.

"Yes, Jem?"

"You have a visitor."

"Who is it?" Beth asked.

"Lord Follett."

Phillip's fork fell, clattering against the plate. He looked to his wife. "You don't have to see him if you don't want to."

"If I don't, I'll always wonder…"

"I insist on staying with you."

Beth reached to give his hand a squeeze. "I wouldn't have it any other way."

Phillip rose and helped his wife to her feet. Together they went in to see Lord Follett, the man his wife hadn't seen since she'd run away into Phillip's arms.

~*~

Beth clung tightly to Phillip. Why should she fear her father? She was married to Phillip. In every way, she was now his.

Phillip stopped just inside the doorway giving her a chance to take a breath. Phillip whispered to the footman to keep the door open.

Lord Follett ceased pacing and stared at his daughter as if seeing her for the first time. Beth had to admit that she'd filled out since her marriage. Being well-loved, well-fed, and with child had given her curves. Her gaunt features were a faint memory.

"Lord Follett. Welcome to our home," Phillip stated coolly as he assessed the man.

"Thank you for receiving me. I would not have blamed you if you had denied me entrance."

"I'm surprised you came at all if you were so unsure of your reception." The ice remained in Phillip's tone. He led Beth to the settee and motioned for Lord Follett to take a seat across from them.

"How are you, Father?" Beth asked, still clinging to her husband's arm.

"Not well, but that is not why I've come."

"State your business," Phillip said.

Lord Follett considered his son-in-law for a moment, and sighed. "I have come to apologize to my daughter. I was initially furious when she flouted my plans and married you, Lord Westcombe. I didn't even realize she was acquainted with you. However," he now turned to Beth. "I've come to realize how blind I have been to who you really are, Lizzy, and what you needed. I overlooked many important things as you grew. I suspect I was blind to much happening under my very nose."

Beth silently assessed him. She nodded for him to continue.

"Yes. Well, I'm sorry, Lizzy, that I was not a better father to you. I cannot change the past. There is no way to redeem my mistakes. I hope that someday you'll find it in your heart to forgive an ignorant old man."

"I have forgiven you, Father."

His eyes grew wide. "You have?"

"I found forgiveness at the foot of the cross of Jesus Christ. If He has forgiven my sins, how can I withhold forgiveness for yours?"

"Jesus?" The man shivered and glanced over his shoulder.

"Yes."

He rose to pace across the room. On his third trip, he stopped. "You have surprised me, Lizzy, in so many ways. I am seeing you through new eyes. You are a beautiful woman, much like your mother was. I wish you a long, happy, and fruitful marriage to Lord Westcombe."

"Thank you."

"What about Lord Wolton? Why did you want an alliance between your house and his? How could you sacrifice your only daughter to him?" Phillip asked.

Lord Follett resumed pacing. "Sacrifice is a strong word." His hand now tapped his leg as he moved. "I thought he would be good for Lizzy, and financially, he agreed to assist me in stabilizing my fortunes."

"You intended to sell your daughter, without consulting her, to rectify your own financial mismanagement of your estate? Abominable."

Beth squeezed Phillip's hand in an attempt to get him to relax. He was tightly wound and ready to spring. His distaste for her father was clear.

"You are correct. There is much for me to atone for. I grew desperate and was not thinking clearly. I was in error and I have come to apologize. You, Lord Westcombe, have won the prize of my daughter along with her inheritance. I understand you didn't need the money so I hope that means you married her for love."

Phillip remained silent.

Lord Follett continued. "She deserves to be cherished and I hope you will do it well, to compensate for my many mistakes. It is a burden neither of you should have had to bear, but I cannot undo the past."

"Where does that leave us now, Father?" Beth asked.

"I do not deserve to be a part of your life and I will not ask it of you. Lord Westcombe, you are proper and within your rights to deny me any future contact with Lizzy. Your anger is reasonable. I failed. Lizzy, you have your new life. I wish you joy. I mean that with all my heart. I have no expectations of either of you beyond the hope of forgiveness, which you have so graciously given."

"She has forgiven you more than you deserve," Phillip said as he rose to his feet. "I, however, have a harder time finding it in my heart to forgive a man who would so callously allow others to abuse and torture his daughter and then seek to sell her as a piece of property for your own gain. We are not in the dark ages, my lord. My wife is a precious jewel, a human being. Worthy of love, being cared for, and protected. You have failed her on all counts. You are a miserable excuse of a parent." Phillip's hands were clenched.

Lord Follett stopped by the fireplace and considered his host. The baron's eyes filled with tears. "You are correct. Your sentiments do you justice and in what is left of my shriveled-up heart, I am grateful my girl has a man such as you to stand by her side and defend her honor, even from myself. Do you need more? Would a duel assuage our need for revenge? I blindly allowed harm to come to her under my own roof. I would meet you if it made a difference, but I will say this—I will not defend myself. There is no defense to be had for my sins.

"If you must kill me for the sake of justice, so be it. If you choose to let me live the rest of my days with the newly discovered horror of what I have done to Lizzy, you will also be avenged. Death would be preferable."

Elizabeth rose to her feet and stood in front of her husband. "Phillip will not be battling you on a field of honor. My dignity is not found in your death for past sins. It is only found in Christ. Father, do not spend the rest of your earthly days in recriminations over the past. Jesus longs to take that from you, cleanse you of all of your sins, and instead give you eternal life with Him as well as joy in your remaining here on earth."

Lord Follett dropped his head. "I'm sorry, Lizzy. I made my choice long ago, which master I would serve. Severing that alliance to follow Christ would mean my certain death."

Lizzy took a step forward. "Yet refusing Christ will mean an eternity with that master you serve. Why would you choose to give up now when you could be free?"

"Freedom means death, Lizzy."

"We all die at some time."

The baron scanned the room, avoiding looking at her. "I have overstayed my welcome. Thank you for listening. I will not seek you out again." He stepped forward, lifted Beth's hand to his lips and placed a kiss on the back of it. He glanced at Phillip. "I could think of no better man to entrust her to." With a short bow, he stalked out of the room and left the house.

Beth turned and walked into her husband's arms,

resting her head on his chest. The beat of his strong heart assured her of his protection and strength. She wept.

Phillip sat, pulling her onto his lap, cradling her as pent up emotions leaked out. He gave her his handkerchief.

When she calmed down enough she spoke through the sobs that still racked her body. "He is choosing an eternity in hell. Phillip, he is making that choice and it breaks my heart."

"It should. We can pray for him. Pray that the Holy Ghost will bring him to the foot of the cross and help him give up his need to hold on to his sin and self-condemnation."

Beth placed her hand over her husband's heart and smiled through her tears. "You have finally forgiven him."

Phillip nodded.

"I will be content. You are correct. We can pray. It is God's place to bring someone to Himself. My father was right about one thing, though."

"He was?"

"You are the best man for me. I am blessed." She gave him a tender kiss which he returned. Sorrow turned to comfort. They walked to their rooms and were not at home to visitors for the rest of the morning.

~*~

"It's been quiet," Phillip said.

"What do you mean?"

"Since your father left. Men have searched and Lord Wolton is nowhere to be found. How can we be prepared if we don't know where he is?"

"Maybe God's already taken care of him?"

"That'd be nice, but until we've located him, we can't guarantee your safety."

Beth sipped her tea. "All I need is right now. With you. That's enough for me to know I'm safe."

"I must leave you for a short time today."

"That's fine. Madame Celeste is due to deliver my ball gown. With the other gowns you've encouraged me to purchase, she may be here for a time for the final fittings."

"You'll be well occupied and won't even miss me." He pretended to pout.

"Silly man. I like having you around. Where are you off to?"

"My father has requested an audience with him."

"Has he ever done that before?"

"Never."

"Why does he want to meet?"

"He didn't say." Phillip let out a sigh. "I've always been a disappointment to them. Perhaps this is my dressing down for our hasty marriage. I cannot think of anything else he could find fault with."

"Perhaps you are worried for nothing."

"Perhaps. I shall go and discover what this is about." He leaned over and kissed her before rising. "You won't leave the house unless someone armed is with you, right?"

"I have nowhere to go," Beth said. "Now leave so I can spend more of your money with Madame Celeste."

He chuckled and made his way out to the carriage to take him to the Manchester townhome.

Once he arrived he was escorted into his father's study. The place brought back many memories—none of them pleasant. The scoldings and dire warnings he'd received in this room still echoed in his memory. He hoped he wouldn't be as severe with his own son someday.

His father was seated behind the desk that seemed much smaller than it had as a child. The scent of leather and cigar smoke permeated the place, a habit Phillip had never acquired. His father appeared frailer. Aged. Weathered. He'd only seen the man a few months past when he and Beth visited after their wedding. Was he looking at his father through new eyes? Or had he really changed?

The Earl looked up. "Ah, Phillip. You've arrived early I see. Very well." He placed his fountain pen in its holder and sanded the letter he'd been writing, setting it aside. He rose to stand before his son. "Thank you for coming. Have a seat." Lord Manchester motioned to the leather chairs arranged near the empty fireplace.

"What is it you wanted to talk to me about?"

"I've heard rumors that you've been making headway on some investments. I was wondering if you could enlighten me as to your strategy."

"My...strategy?"

"Yes, for investing money as well as turning a profit on your land. I'm curious. I believe I may need to make some changes and wanted your thoughts on the matter."

Phillip swallowed. "I can tell you what I've learned but there's still much I don't know. Lord Remington was the one who turned me on to how to be a better steward of the resources God had entrusted me with."

"Interesting perspective. Tell me more..."

And Phillip did.

~*~

The next day Elsa bustled into the dressing room as Beth finished her hair. While Elsa wanted to help, Beth found it easier to do it herself when she was staying at home.

"Ma'am?"

"Yes?" Beth turned.

"You have a visitor."

"Does this visitor have a name?"

"Lady Penelope Westcombe."

"Have you informed Phillip? He's gone to break his fast already."

"She requests an audience with you."

"Oh, well. I'll come down to greet our guest." Beth rose and made her way to the drawing room where Lady Penelope paced. "Penelope?"

The young woman turned with a big smile. "Oh, thank you for agreeing to see me. When you and Phillip visited after your marriage, mother and father forbade me contact with you. Now Mother says it is fine for me to know you. I hope I haven't come too early."

"I've yet to break my fast but you are welcome to join us. Your brother is already at the table."

"I'd hate to impose."

"You are family. What kind of imposition could it be?"

Penelope nodded and together they went in to eat.

"Phillip, look who has come to visit us."

Phillip rose to his feet. "Penny." He stepped forward to enfold her in a hug. "Do our parents know you are here?"

"Not right this minute but they said it was acceptable for me to visit with you."

"Grab a plate and get some food. Sit and join us." Phillip sat down and motioned to the footman who assisted Penelope and Beth with their plates and helped them sit at the table. "Send for some chocolate, Jem. It's Penny's favorite."

"Yes, m'lord." The footman left.

"This is a pleasant surprise." Phillip sipped his coffee.

"Father couldn't stop talking last night about all the ideas he had after meeting with you. It has been a long time since I've seen him that excited over anything. What did you tell him?"

"He asked questions and I answered them. I'm glad it was helpful."

"The ball is just around the corner. Do you have your gown, Beth?"

"It was delivered yesterday. I'm quite pleased with it. I've never owned anything quite so fine. Your brother is spoiling me."

Penelope grinned. "Phillip has always been the best of brothers. I was sad I missed your wedding. I know if things had been different I would have been allowed to be there."

"You're here now. A wedding is a short amount of time. A marriage is much longer," Beth said. "I've never had a sister before."

Penny's eyes grew bright. "Oh, how wonderful."

The chocolate was brought and soon the meal ended.

"If you ladies will excuse me, I've got some correspondence to attend to in my study."

"I'm sure we'll be fine, Phillip. Would you like a

tour of the house, Penny?"

"Oh, yes!" The young woman joined arms with Beth.

Beth gave her the tour and talked about the changes yet to be made.

Later, after their guest had left, Beth waylaid her husband. "God must be at work in your family."

"Something happened. I wish I knew what," Phillip stated.

"I might be able to shed some light on that." The older woman's voice rang from the doorway.

Phillip shot to his feet.

Beth followed at a slower pace.

"Lady Orion. To what do we owe the pleasure?" Phillip asked. "Have you been introduced to my wife, Mrs. Elizabeth Westcombe?"

"Not until now. How are you, Elizabeth? My, you are the image of your mother. She and I were dear friends. I came because I wanted to show you something." She waved a hand at Phillip. "You may leave if you wish. No harm will come to your wife. I only want to share with her my memories of her mother."

"Beth?" Phillip asked.

"I'm sure I'll be fine. Can you have tea sent in?"

Phillip nodded and left.

Beth settled in to hear about the mother she barely remembered.

~*~

Phillip locked the door to the bedroom and drew Beth into his arms. "It's been an interesting few days."

Hands on his chest she began to untie his cravat.

"A mild statement."

"My father, your father, my sister, and now, Lady Orion...I hate to imagine what tomorrow might bring."

"I must not be doing this right."

"Hmmm?" The cravat fell to the floor and she pushed his coat off. Her fingers began to undo his buttons.

"You are thinking about tomorrow. I'll have to work harder to get your attention." She reached up, pulled his head down to hers, and their lips met. She released him and stepped back.

"You were saying?" He grinned as he pulled her into his embrace.

"You were thinking about tomorrow."

He nuzzled her neck and nibbled at her ear sending shivers through her body. "Tomorrow will take care of itself. I have other things to occupy my mind."

She turned around so he could undo the back of her dress. "You do?"

He kissed the back of her neck. "Most definitely. Enough talking, my dear. I'll show you."

She grinned. She had no doubt he would.

15

Sun streamed in through cracks in the draperies. Beth stretched and rolled over to find her husband watching her. "Mornin'."

"I never tire of gazing at you, Beth."

"You're not too hard on the eyes either."

"Guess God gave us both what we didn't deserve or expect."

"I, for one, am grateful." Beth snuggled into her husband. "Tonight is the ball."

"Think Wolton will show?"

She shrugged. "I doubt it. I just hope this does what your parents hope it does."

"And what is that? Celebrate my brilliance in making the match of the year?"

"Silly man."

"From my perspective, that is the truth." He kissed her and all conversation ceased for some time.

~*~

Elizabeth sat in the garden having her breakfast with Duke. She had wanted to allow him in the house but Phillip refused saying a bird flying around would terrify the servants, and finding little 'surprises' from the bird would likely cause them all to quit.

"Tonight is the ball at the Manchester home. Remember the first time? That's when Phillip rescued me. I want you there again. Just in case. I'd feel safer knowing you were around. I know God watches out for me, but in some ways it's as if you are here at His bequest." She worked loose a pin feather on the crow's neck.

Taking a deep breath, she prayed. She'd been meditating on Scripture about the Lord being a sword and a shield around her. In spite of that anxiety haunted her. *Please don't let harm come to Phillip or me this evening.* Various armed servants would keep guard. Phillip's friends were on the lookout for Wolton, but no one expected he would do his own dirty work. It had been well over a month since the last attack. It was only a matter of time before something happened. It would be wise to never relax her guard.

A few more pin feathers were free. Duke flew up to the tree and shook his feathers out. He nodded his head and squawked.

She rose to return indoors. Too much sun was bad for her complexion.

When lunch came, Phillip had not returned from a visit to White's where he planned to meet with Lord Harrow, Sir Tidley, Mr. Neville, and of course Lord Remington. Elizabeth sat to eat by herself, toying with her food. Even her favorite rolls didn't tempt her and she went back outside to give one to Duke who tore it apart eagerly. Soon it was gone. With one last caress of his head, she went inside to rest so she would be prepared for the evening's event.

~*~

Phillip returned to the house mid-afternoon and went immediately to the master suite to peek in on his sleeping wife. How he wished he could stretch out next to her. Tonight would be a turning point in their acceptance amongst the *ton*. Phillip went to his study to look over some paperwork from Stanton Hall. When all of this was over he looked forward to returning there with Beth. The tension and wait for Lord Wolton to attack was wearing him down.

An hour later a knock on the door interrupted his work. "Come in."

His valet, Fenway, entered.

"What's amiss? Do I need to purchase more cravats?" Phillip teased.

"No, my lord."

"Well, then. What it is?"

"I was in the garden a few moments ago and came across a disturbing sight I thought you would want to see."

Phillip rose. "Disturbing?"

Fenway nodded and motioned for Phillip to follow him. Together they traveled through the kitchens to the small garden that was part of the property. Beth enjoyed sitting amongst the flowers here. Tall walls provided security and the previous owners had taken great care with the plants. Fenway led Philip around a tree to a bench where Beth often sat. The valet pointed to the ground.

A large black bird sprawled lifeless on the path.

Phillip bent down. The bird was warm, but most definitely dead. He checked for injuries or broken bones. There were none. "Has anyone seen Duke lately?"

All of the household staff were acquainted with the bird. "I've been calling for him. The footman over at the mews has as well. He doesn't stray far and always responds when summoned." The valet dipped his head and made the sign of the cross.

Phillip stretched out the wings again for a closer look. He found a spot where feathers were missing and hadn't grown back yet. It was the spot where Duke had been shot while keeping Phillip from getting killed. It was most certainly Duke. "He's probably been poisoned, but how?" Phillip rose. "Mrs. Westcombe will be devastated."

"May I suggest, my lord, that she not be told until after the ball?"

Phillip stared at the bird as if it would give him an answer. "I don't want to lie to her. She will likely be looking for the bird later and grow worried if he doesn't come when summoned. I'd hate for her to be sad on tonight of all nights."

"How could he have been poisoned?"

"Excellent question. He either finds his own food or takes what Beth or the stable hands offer him. I doubt he'd take anything from a stranger."

"Certainly not."

Phillip looked around and saw crumbs on the bench. "Was he here earlier with Beth?"

"The cook reported she'd come out twice. She spent time with him this morning and then brought him a treat after lunch."

Phillip scooped up the crumbs and returned to the kitchen to find Cook. He showed her the crumbs. "Would this be something from Mrs. Westcombe's lunch?"

The Cook nodded. "She didn't eat much today. Those rolls are her favorite."

"Did you make them?"

"Sarah bought them from a peddler down the

street."

"Had she ever purchased from that person before?"

"No. The man was new to the area. Why?"

"I believe someone intended to poison your mistress."

Cook's eyes grew wide and her hand flew over her mouth.

"Did anyone else eat these?" Phillip asked.

"No. They are over there in the galley."

Phillip strode to the bowl, pulled out a bun, and marched down the alley to the mews where stray cats abounded. He hated having to test his theory on a hapless animal, but if his wife was meant to be poisoned, he needed to know. He didn't know if animals had souls, but he sent a prayer heavenward for what he was about to do. "Come here, kitty." The scrawny, matted animal inched forward. Phillip tossed the bun to the cat. The feline pounced on it and eagerly ate. Phillip instructed the stable hands to watch the cat and let him know if anything happened to it. Brushing off his hands he returned to the house. In the kitchen, he pointed to the buns. "To be safe, do not let anyone eat those."

"Should I burn them?" Cook asked.

"Might be a good idea. Mrs. Westcombe did not eat any of these?"

"No. There were six buns. She gave one to Duke and took one. The four left are the rest."

He heaved a sigh of relief. If the buns were the method of poisoning, she'd escaped. He washed his hands, dried them and took the back stairs to their room. He had to see for sure she was well. He slipped into the room and walked to her bedside. A soft smile was on her face. He lifted her wrist. Her pulse was steady. God had obviously spared her life today. Phillip fell to his knees, continued to hold her hand, and bent his head to pray. *Thank You, Lord, for sparing Beth and our child. Continue to protect her and give me wisdom with telling her about Duke. I don't know if crows go to heaven, but Lord that one was a faithful friend to her during dark days. He saved my life. He led me to Beth when she was injured and now paid the ultimate price in giving his life for her. Thank You for the gift that he was to both of us. Continue to be with us as we attend the ball and face friends and possible enemies. Protect her heart as well as her body, Lord. Thank You for the gift you've given me in having her as a wife. I don't deserve such grace.*

~*~

Beth twirled around in front of the mirror. Phillip hadn't seen her in her new gown and she was pleased with how well it looked on her. She could proudly stand by his side and not shame him or his family. She'd called for Duke but he hadn't shown up. He was probably busy hunting a mouse. Silly bird. He'd come with the carriage, though. He loved his friends at the stable.

Phillip entered the room and gave a low whistle. "I'm tempted to lock you in for the night, lest any other man at the ball realize the treasure they lost out on and try to steal you away."

She turned to see that he'd managed to order a waistcoat in a matching emerald green with gold embroidery. Combined with his crisp white shirt, cravat, and black coat, she wanted to swoon herself. She lifted her fan and slowly waved it in front of her.

"It is you I might need to lock away, my lord. A dashing Corinthian in the first stare of fashion. All the ladies will be lamenting their failure to bring you up to scratch."

"And you did it without even trying."

"At least I don't wander in my sleep anymore."

"Because I keep you locked in my arms all night long. Any kisses you are determined to give in your sleep belong to me alone."

She grinned. "Thank you for loving me so well."

"I have a gift for you." He handed her a velvet covered box.

"You didn't need to give me anything."

"A jewel of a woman should have more than a ring to show the depth of her husband's affection for her."

She opened the lid and gasped. In a delicate gold setting was an emerald necklace. "Will you do the honors?"

Phillip lifted the chain from the box, came behind her, and fastened it behind her neck. The stone was not huge, but a beautiful addition to her ensemble. She fingered the gem and turned.

"Thank you." She reached up to kiss him but he stepped back, shaking his head.

"You'll have to show your appreciation later, my dear, lest we be late for our own ball. You are far too much of a temptation for me to stay alone with you for much longer." He held out his arm, guided her to the hall, and down the stairs where he helped her with a wrap that matched her dress. They left the house and he assisted her into the carriage, joining her inside, but sitting across from her.

"Why won't you sit next to me?"

"I don't want to mess your dress, or succumb to the temptation to kiss you and tell the groom to turn around and take us back home."

She smiled. "You flatter me. Where is Duke? It's not like him to miss an outing."

Phillip gazed out the door, saying nothing.

"Phillip?"

"Hmmm?"

"Do you know what has happened to Duke?"

"Why would I know? He's your pet."

"You have information. Tell me."

"I don't want to share with you anything that might tarnish the beauty of this evening."

"Something bad occurred." She looked away from her husband. "I could slap you. How dare you keep something important from me?" Her gloved hands were fisted in her lap.

"He ate some poison. We found him dead in the garden."

"Poison?"

"The buns you were given with your meal. The poison was meant for us."

Her heart surely stopped beating. She blinked her eyes to stop tears from forming.

"Beth?"

"I never expected poison. I fed Duke that roll as I prayed God would protect you and be a sword and a shield around us. He answered that prayer by taking Duke instead."

He reached for her hand and slid to the seat next to her. "I am sorry. If I could have kept this sorrow from you tonight of all nights I would have."

"Why? He was my pet. I had a right to know. Duke was a bird and I will miss him. God wants me to trust Him more and not rely on the actions of a crow who thrice came to our rescue."

Phillip was about to pull a handkerchief out of his pocket when Beth pulled out an identical one. She showed it to him with a sad smile. "I've had this since the night you rescued me."

"I'm honored that you kept it and that it continues to prove useful."

"It was your second gift to me."

"What was the first?"

"You listened." She dabbed her eyes gently, folded the fabric and tucked it back into her reticule.

"You can overcome your grief so soon?"

She reached over to clasp his hand. "I've had years of experience at hiding my emotions so others would not take advantage of perceived weaknesses. I do not do that with you, Phillip. Tonight, we enter a field of battle. I cannot let Duke's death sway us from our purpose. I can grieve him later in privacy."

"You are an incredible woman. And what is our purpose?"

"To show the world how besotted we are with one another. The match of the year. And for that, I do not need to pretend."

"I love you, Beth. Have I told you that today?"

"It has been a few hours, but you may tell me as often as you like without complaint from me for I love you more than words can express. If I had to choose between you and a crow, you would win every time."

The carriage rolled to a stop. They had arrived.

Beth took a deep breath and allowed the footman to help her down the steps. Linking an arm through her husband's they proceeded into his parents' home. *Chin up. Back straight. I can do this. For Phillip.* The battle had begun. She hoped they were ready.

~*~

Phillip hid his surprise at his parents' effusive greeting. The dinner before the ball was a mere sixty people. He was blessed to be able to sit next to Beth at the table. He'd begged his mother for that favor telling her that celebrating a couple's marriage wouldn't benefit by splitting them before the celebration started. People needed to see them together. He couldn't hide his affection for his wife. It might be unfashionable to be in love but he wouldn't pretend to be cool and indifferent when what he really wanted to do was whisk her away to a room where they could be private. Every rake in the kingdom would be ogling his wife and plotting to steal her from him. He had no fears over her faithfulness. Her devotion to him was true. Her pregnancy was obvious now as well, but she glowed with a beauty that captivated him.

Dinner was exceptionally grand. The chef had outdone himself on the various removes, but he noticed Beth ate little. Anxiety over the evening ahead or grief over the loss of Duke? He recalled his cook reporting that she'd not eaten well at mid-day either. He glanced at her. She seemed healthy, if a bit pale.

She glanced his way and gave him a soft smile. "Phillip," she whispered. "If you keep looking at me like that people will talk."

Phillip gave her a wolfish grin and leaned to whisper in her ear. "Let them talk. You are my wife and I don't care who knows it."

Her cheeks became infused with a lovely peach color as she turned away to tend to a conversation with the person sitting on her other side.

After the meal, his mother and father flanked them in the receiving line to give solid evidence of their support for the marriage.

Phillip kept a hand at his wife's back. She glowed, and her gracious interactions with all the strangers impressed him. She was born to be a Countess, not the wife of a second-born son. The thought humbled him.

Marcus and Josie entered soon followed by Lord Harrow, Sir Tidley, and Mr. Neville. When it was acceptable to do so, Phillip led Beth from the receiving line to speak with their friends.

Josie was with Beth as Phillip took Marcus aside.

"Is something amiss?" Lord Remington asked.

"There was an attempt on our life today."

The viscount's jaw fell slack. "What happened?"

"Poison. I missed lunch and Beth wasn't hungry and fed one of the buns from the meal to Duke. He was found dead in the garden with no visible wounds. I tested another roll on a stray cat and it too died. The buns have been destroyed and no one else ate them."

"We never suspected something so underhanded. How is Beth taking the news?"

"She only found out on the way here. I didn't want to tell her but she pursued her inquiry. She's not pleased but grateful neither of us—obviously—the intended victims, ate those rolls."

"I'm assuming they were not made by your cook."

"No. They were purchased from a street merchant. We've been searching but haven't found the person. I don't expect him to reappear."

"All the more reason to stay diligent tonight."

"Yes. Can you inform Michael, Theo, and Nigel?"

Marcus nodded and the men returned to their

wives as the orchestra warmed up.

Phillip bowed over his wife's hand, placing a kiss firmly on her glove. "Will you honor me with the first dance, Mrs. Westcombe?"

Beth did a graceful dip and a soft smile curved her luscious lips. Oh, he wanted to do more than dance. "I'd be delighted, my lord."

He led her out to the floor as the couples formed around them. "And don't forget, I claim three dances tonight."

"You will cause a scandal, Lord Westcombe. People might think you are enamored of me and will talk."

"I suppose I'll need to marry you then." The music started and they began the figures of the dance, conversation forgotten in the joy of being together.

~*~

Beth begged off a dance to rest. Phillip left her to sit with Lady Orion.

"You acquit yourself well, Mrs. Westcombe."

"Thank you, my lady. I appreciated your visit the other day, and learning about my mother."

"She would have loved to have seen you this day. Tonight is not the time, but remind me to share some of her letters with you. You have nothing to be ashamed of in her. You were a delight to her heart."

Beth swallowed hard. "There are moments when I wonder what it would have been like to have her love and guidance. I missed so much growing up without her."

"Watching you, no one would ever guess you lacked any of the finer refinements of a lady. Your husband certainly is not complaining. Even as he dances with other guests, his gaze is often on you. I, for one, am pleased with your match. Lord Phillip is one of the catches of the *beau monde* if a title means nothing to you. Handsome as can be." She winked at Beth. "Are you content?"

Beth's heart beat faster. She nodded to Lady Orion. "I do not take for granted the blessing Lord Westcombe has been to me."

Lady Orion leaned closer and whispered, "A healthy specimen of manhood, isn't he? You keep leading him a merry dance and you'll never have a fear over his faithfulness to you. Someday you will tell me how you brought him up to scratch." Lady Orion's eyebrows wiggled.

Fighting the urge to giggle, Beth hid her lips behind her fan, pretending to cool herself off. "That, my lady, will remain a mystery."

"Which will make you all the more intriguing to the *beau monde*. Beauty, poise, and a doting husband? You'll set the town on their ears."

"Does everything need to revolve around the opinions of others? It is a wearisome task to be so concerned about that. The trouble and expense of this ball alone could have helped so many hurting people instead."

"Do not minimize the power of public opinion, Elizabeth. It has the power to raise someone from obscurity or put them beyond the pale destroying future hopes of marital alliances and income."

"I just long for a peaceful life, raising a family at Stanton Hall with my husband."

"And someday your daughters will be brought to London to events such as this to find a prospective husband. Your sons, if they have a good reputation will also seek wives amongst society's elect. Everything you do today, has an impact on them. A disreputable name can last for generations."

"I need to overcome mine?" Sorrow lanced her at the image of her broken father asking for forgiveness and walking away in the hopelessness of his past sins.

"You have come a long way in accomplishing that."

"Thank you, my lady. Lord Harrow approaches. This next dance is his."

"Enjoy every moment, my dear." The older woman patted Beth's hand and released it so Lord Harrow could take it for the dance.

Beth glanced back at the woman who gave her a smile and a wink. Maybe her mother wasn't around but God had sent someone to provide the support and encouragement she needed in this moment.

~*~

Phillip had claimed the hand of his bride and they were approaching the dance floor when a clanking glass at the front of the ballroom drew the attention of the throng of visitors crowding the overheated space.

Lord Manchester stood there with his wife. "I wanted to proclaim that Lady Manchester and myself are pleased with our son, Phillip's, choice of a bride. I propose a toast to Lord Phillip and Mrs. Elizabeth Westcombe."

"Huzzah!" Glasses clinked throughout the room.

The crowd parted around Phillip and Beth. He looked at her. The people closest cheered again. Phillip beamed at her blush. "I am determined to dance a third time with you tonight."

She placed her hand in his. He led her to the floor.

"You'll scandalize the *ton*, my lord." She protested as she tried to put more space between them.

"I care not for the opinions of men in this moment. This ball is to celebrate our marriage and I will claim my right to dance with you as I see fit."

She relaxed as the music, and his body, twirled them around the floor in the figures of the dance as other couples joined them. Gold flecks sparkled in her eyes as she gazed up at him and her rosy lips parted as if begging to be kissed. He longed to talk about her night or any perceived threats but he couldn't break the magic of their time here with that kind of discussion. "You are the most beautiful jewel in this room, Beth. I am proud to claim you as my bride."

"As I am dancing with the most handsome man in town, I consider myself blessed to call you husband."

His voice lowered. "I called the carriage. We can make our escape for home. I long to have you to myself. I find myself jealous of all the men dumping the butter boat over you."

"Are you saying their flattery is excessive or untrue?"

"Never that my dear, only that I want to be the only one to woo you with words of love."

"Woo away..."

Phillip did just as he proposed. They soon escaped the stifling heat of the ballroom and were shut in their carriage. Phillip pulled the shades and dragged his wife into his lap. She didn't fight him but initiated the first kiss.

"Did you enjoy the evening, Beth?"

"Yes. Only because you were by my side for much

of it."

"Missing Duke?"

"Of course. I am grateful, however, that nothing happened this evening to spoil all your family has done to establish our reputation."

"It makes me wonder what might be next."

"I don't know, Phillip, but I have a suggestion."

"You do?"

She leaned closer to kiss him. Soon they were home and scampering up the stairs to the house. Once inside, Phillip whisked her into his arms and carried her to their room, and from that point on it was debatable who initiated what.

16

Beth longed for the country. The next few days of hosting a sea of faces in their drawing room drained her. She had become the toast of the *ton*. For now, anyway. She wanted Phillip to be present for the at-home visits but he was often at his club. She wondered if he only went there to escape. Thankfully, Josie or Lady Manchester and Penelope, would join her for these events and help her navigate the treacherous waters hidden underneath the swirl of questions.

Lord Wolton was forgotten and she'd heard naught of her father. She worried for him and had sent him a letter once again begging he reconsider his stance on matters of faith. She'd received no reply.

Duke's absence was felt daily. She'd sit outside in the garden and automatically searched for him. Phillip offered to get her a new pet, even a bird she could keep in the house. Apparently, Lord Remington's sister, Lady Percy, possessed a parrot. They had withdrawn to their country estate as she'd just given birth to their first child.

Trying to keep track of Phillip's friends and acquaintances exhausted her. After a few days of this, she finally took a stand. "I am not at home to visitors today," she told Masters.

"Ma'am?"

"No one. Please. It's been too much."

Masters nodded and left her to break her fast in

peace. She selected a book from the library and returned to her room. Phillip would be at Gentleman Jackson's today for a bout of fisticuffs. Phillip? Fighting? Josie had told her about how he had fought to help Lord Remington save Josie's life. She knew he was strong underneath the custom tailored suits. His strength was a comfort to her.

Elsa strode into the room. "Lady Orion has called."

"I can't. Send her away, please."

The maid bowed and after she left Beth rose and locked the door to the room. She wouldn't put it past the grande dame of the *beau monde* to force her way in. Sure enough, the woman was pounding on the door as the butler tried to calm her and get her to leave. Beth fought the urge to give in. No. She needed rest. She napped and later sat and read her book.

A knock came at the door.

"Beth?"

Phillip! She rose and unlocked it to let him in. He closed the door and put his hands on her arms.

"Are you well? Masters told me you were not at home to visitors today and even refused Lady Orion."

"I'm just tired, Phillip." She reached up to touch his jaw where a bruise was forming. "Someone got a punch past you."

Phillip grinned. "Theodore will be sporting a black eye tomorrow. Trust me, I won that fight."

"Why do you do it?" She eased his coat off and helped him untie his cravat.

"Exercise. A way to blow off some steam."

"I could think of other ways." She winked at him as she began to unbutton his shirt.

"I'm sure you could but we are due to attend a

recital this evening. I need to bathe and change..."

She walked away and sat back down in her chair. "I'm not going."

He stopped what he was doing and came to sit in the chair adjacent to her. "Why?"

"I'm tired. Phillip, I spent years in isolation except for the brief times my dad sent me to boarding school so I would gain some of the finer aspects of being a 'lady.' You leave me alone to meet with people who would chew me up and spit me out for the smallest violation of their rules. They are sniffing for something to use to bring me down—to discredit you."

"Surely you exaggerate."

She gave him a look that said otherwise. "You've lived amongst these people. You were raised in society. I was not. They might accept me as your wife, but as your equal? They test me constantly. I long for Stanton Hall."

"So do I. Shall I send regrets and spend the evening home with you?"

"I would hate for you to miss out on something you enjoy."

His eyebrows rose. "Enjoy? Perhaps if Josie were there to play her violin or the pianoforte, but most of the performers are either overpaid opera stars or the daughters of the *ton* who possess little skill or wit to recommend them. As if hearing a woman screech will bring the suitors out of their hiding places? No. It is more a place to see and be seen than to attend for pure enjoyment."

"It sounds torturous."

"When professional musicians and singers are performing, it can be enjoyable, but tonight is not of that same caliber. It will not pain me to miss it, especially if I cannot have you on my arm and by my side."

"Thank you, Phillip."

"I still long for a bath. Shall I have dinner served here in our room?"

Beth grinned. "I would like that."

"I shall arrange it all. Rest." He rose, called for his valet, and made arrangements.

Beth listened to him speak with his servant as water was brought up. She yawned. A sharp pain in her stomach startled her. She rose and climbed into bed, kicking off her slippers and rested on her side. The pain left. Perhaps she really had been too busy lately.

~*~

Phillip finished bathing and came to the bedroom to discover his wife asleep. Food had been brought in and candles lit. He built up the fire and poured himself a glass of wine. He walked over to the bed and sat, tracing his wife's jaw with his finger. She didn't respond.

"Beth?"

Her chest rose and fell. He pulled the blanket up over her and resigned himself to dining alone. He grabbed the Bible Marcus had given him and spent some time reading. Joshua had walked around the walls of Jericho day after day. Somehow Phillip felt like that was exactly what he was doing staying in town, waiting for something to fall. For Wolton to strike or show his hand. But maybe the real courage was in heading home for Stanton Hall. Perhaps the battle was the Lord's and had been taken care of for them. *Lord, please guide me and help me know what is best for Beth and our child. I, too, long for Stanton Hall and the life we could live there. Is it time to go home?*

After he'd eaten he blew out the candles and climbed into bed to hold his wife as she slept. Somehow God would show them the next steps they should take.

~*~

Beth awoke the next morning to find Phillip had already left. It was later than she was used to rising. She rang for Elsa to bring her some chocolate.

"Would you like me to bring you food?"

"I'm not hungry." Beth frowned as she rose. Something wasn't right. She began to prepare for the day but the brush got caught in her tangles.

"Here, let me help you," Elsa offered, coming back with her drink.

Beth almost threw the brush at the maid. Instead, she slammed it down on the table. "Please do. I'm ready to cut it all off."

"Oh, your hair is so pretty. You would not want to do that."

"I'll do what I want," Beth groused.

Elsa silently began to work the tangles loose. That's what came of falling asleep without taking her pins out and braiding her hair. Phillip preferred it loose, but then he would be the one to sometimes brush through the tangles. There was something sweet about him doing that for her. She suspected he preferred it when she shaved him too instead of his valet or himself. She'd been missing him in the mornings.

"Is my husband home?"

"He left a short time ago with Sir Tidley."

Beth's shoulders slumped.

"How would you like your hair today?" Else asked.

"A simple braid down the back. I don't plan to leave my room."

"Ma'am? Are you unwell?"

"I don't think so. Just tired."

"I'll let Masters know you are not home to visitors again."

"Thank you, Elsa."

The maid left and Beth rose to sit by the fire and sip her chocolate. Sharp pain cut deep and she stumbled back to the bed, the drink forgotten. She crawled under the cover and rested on her side as the pain subsided. She sucked in a breath and placed her hand on her stomach. It moved. The baby had to be well. She couldn't let anything happen to their child. Pain rippled through her as she struggled to breathe. Tears fell to her pillow and as the pain subsided she closed her eyes to rest.

Mid-afternoon sharp pain ripped through her again. She rose to relieve herself and discovered blood everywhere. She began to sweat and grew dizzy. She tugged the chord for Elsa and collapsed into bed.

The maid arrived in the room within minutes. "You rang."

"Elsa, I think I'm losing the baby. Please send for the doctor and send someone to find Phillip."

"Aye, Mrs. Westcombe." The maid scampered out the door and soon the housekeeper, a kindly older woman, Mrs. Wilson, was there beside her.

"Let's get you more comfortable my dear." The

older woman helped her change and placed a cool wet compress on her forehead. The pain stabbed through her periodically.

"Send for Mrs. Remington, please."

Josie was the closest person she had as a friend.

"Yes, ma'am." The housekeeper left to send a message and returned.

Beth tried to rest even as fear spiraled out of control within. She groaned.

"Just rest, ma'am."

Josie burst into the room a short time later. "Mrs. Wilson, I'll sit with her while you see to why the doctor has not yet arrived, nor her husband." Josie cleared out the room and came to sit by Beth's side on the bed. "You are in pain?"

"I'm afraid I'm losing the baby."

Josie blanched as her hand caressed the evidence of her own imminent arrival. She'd only just entered her confinement and would soon be departing for Rose Hill to wait out the rest of her pregnancy there.

"Pray for me please, Josie. I'm scared."

"Of course." Josie bent her head as she held Beth's hands in her own. "Heavenly Father, You are the creator of life and the beginning and the end are in Your hands. You have sustained Phillip and Beth through some difficult times and You know how their love has grown for each other and for You. I ask that You would spare their child and give healing to Beth. Ease her pain and fear. And if we don't get what we want Lord, help us to trust You for the future and not lose hope in Your love and goodness to us even when we cannot understand the pain we suffer. We love You, Jesus."

Beth sighed and closed her eyes. "Thank you,

Josie."

The hours passed.

The doctor finally arrived, evicted everyone else from the room and examined her. "Mrs. Westcombe. I'm sorry, but it seems you are losing the baby." He gave instructions for the staff and left.

Josie frowned. "He can't be bothered to stay with you?"

"What more can he do? You need to go home yourself and rest and care for your own baby. Please continue to pray."

"I don't want to leave you alone."

"I have Elsa and Mrs. Wilson. Hopefully, Phillip will arrive soon." Beth had lost energy and refused the broth Elsa had brought for her. "I just want to sleep."

Josie stood. "I'm sorry this is happening, Beth."

"I am too."

"I'll return tomorrow morning."

"Thank you, Josie."

The room sank into darkness with the exception of the fireplace. The drapes were drawn and Beth fell into an uneasy sleep.

~*~

Phillip groaned. "I've been gone all day, Michael. We've chased one lead after another and we lack any credible information about Wolton. I really should get home."

Michael led Phillip into a pub. "First, let's eat. I'm famished. I'm sorry none of my leads have netted any potential information."

They acquired a table and sat with a glass of the beer brewed locally.

Phillip sipped it and grimaced. "I prefer wine."

"Or brandy, I suspect."

Phillip shrugged. "Hard to get the best stuff with the war on."

"I'm sorry I took you on a wild-goose chase. Neville gave me leads I thought sounded worthwhile, but some of these areas are not as safe to travel in. Safety in numbers, and all that."

"I'm sure you could have handled it fine, but I am grateful for the occupation. Sitting and waiting has grown old."

"Maybe the threat is gone?"

"Perhaps, but I fear that letting our guard down is exactly what he is waiting for."

"So, what now?"

"Beth wants to leave London and travel to Stanton Hall. I long to go home, too. She's tired of all the at-homes and balls. There is much work to be done at the hall to prepare for our child. She will likely want to do some redecorating. There will be plenty to keep her busy along with meeting the neighbors and getting to know our tenants."

"Sounds like the perfect place for you." Michael paid the waitress right away as she bought the food.

"My own slice of heaven on earth."

"Do your parents understand you're not the wastrel and rake they thought you were?"

"I never descended to the depths of depravity as some do. Hard to do with a friend like Marcus. I wasn't as afraid of my parents finding out as I was of him."

"I think he always knew exactly what we were up to."

"Perhaps, but he never mentioned it or shamed us."

"He told me once that it didn't matter what he thought. He couldn't expect us to live up to a standard set by a God we didn't believe in. He still cared about us as his friends."

"Sometimes I think he was always a better friend to any of us than we were to him. I often wondered why he hung around us."

Michael shrugged. "I don't know either. You are a second son, I'm baseborn, Theodore is alone in the world. Perhaps we all just needed each other."

"But Marcus? We might have needed him but why did he need us?"

"Perhaps some things are better to not question. We were there for him when his parents died and Jared went off to war."

"You were around for Henrietta's wedding too, right?"

"Yes. Only because it happened quickly, otherwise you would have been invited."

"Lord Percy is a good chap. Marcus was relieved to have her off his hands." Phillip grinned.

"If you have a daughter, that might be you some day."

Phillip sighed. "I still can't believe I'm going to be a father. I never thought I wanted a family and now I can't hardly wait until Stanton Hall is filled with the laughter of children."

"I believe they do a lot of crying before they ever laugh."

"Someday, Michael—you might find love has some surprises in store for you as well."

"Good thing I like you and your lovely bride too much to make her a widow so soon," Michael growled.

They finished the meal and Phillip left to call a

carriage. "Sure you don't want a ride?"

"No. It's a nice evening for a walk. Never know what news I might uncover."

"Be careful, Michael."

"I always am. You, as well. Give my regards to Beth."

Phillip nodded and then closed the door, tapping the roof for the hackney to take him home. It had grown later than he expected and he hoped Elizabeth wasn't worried about him or missing him too terribly. Guilt assailed him. He should have been taking her to see parts of town she'd never experienced before instead of traipsing around with Michael or fighting Theo at Gentleman Jackson's or practicing his fencing with Marcus. Although he'd also been investigating Wolton to no avail. It was time to quit and prepare to go home.

The carriage pulled up to the house.

He paid the fare and strode up the steps. The door flung open.

"My lord. We've been looking for you everywhere." The door shut behind him.

Phillip's heart raced at the alarm his normally placid butler showed. "What's amiss, Masters?"

"Your wife—"

"Beth? Is she well?"

Masters shook his head.

Phillip was already running up the stairs two steps at a time until he came to the master suite. He opened the door to a darkened room.

Mrs. Wilson stepped forward, biting her lip.

"At last you've arrived, m'lord." Censure colored her words.

"What happened?" He moved to step further in

the room but she blocked him.

Her voice was soft. "She lost the baby. She's been in terrible pain and crying out for you, m'lord. Mrs. Remington was here for some time."

"The doctor?"

"Came and left. Said nothing could be done to stop nature."

"The baby?"

"Dead."

"What was it?" he asked in a whisper.

"A son." The housekeeper touched his arm and bent her head. "I'm sorry, m'lord. Go to her now. She needs you. Ring if you need anything."

"Thank you, Mrs. Wilson." The door shut behind him and he wandered over to the bed. His wife was pale as she rested on the pillows. Sallow cheeks were stained with tears. He'd been out fighting a useless battle when she'd been here all alone, needing him. He sat and removed his clothes quickly, stoked the fire and climbed into bed to hold her tight.

"I'm so sorry I wasn't here, Beth. Please forgive me."

"Phillip?" She stirred and placed a hand on his chest. "You came." Tears fell fresh as she leaned into him. His own joined hers.

~*~

The doctor had finished and spoke with Phillip in the hallway. "It's over, but she'll need time to recover the loss, physically and emotionally."

"Will she—"

"As far as I can tell she should be able to conceive again at some point. I wouldn't rush it. Healing takes time."

Phillip gulped. "Why did the baby die?"

The doctor shrugged. "We rarely know in cases like this."

Phillip could only nod. "Thank you, Doctor."

"You're welcome. Give her time. She'll be fine." He patted Phillip's arm and departed.

Phillip returned to the bedroom where his wife sat up in bed. He hurried over to her and held her hand. What could he say to ease her pain or make sense of his own loss?

"I'm sorry, Phillip."

"It wasn't your fault."

She sighed.

"I was thinking that perhaps in a week or so, whenever you are feeling well enough, we could travel home to Stanton Hall."

She gave him a wan smile. "I'd like that."

Phillip leaned forward and kissed her. She returned the kiss but not with the enthusiasm of the past. *Fool, she just lost a child. She's won't want to kiss or be touched.* He backed away. "Rest, dear. I'll be here." He helped her settle into the covers and sat on a chair near the bed to pray as she slept.

He picked up the Bible. Where was his courage now? Abraham was told to sacrifice his son, but at least he was given a choice. God took their baby without a reason or an alternative. It wasn't fair.

But life wasn't fair so why did God need to be? Ridiculous notion. God was God and could do as he pleased. Phillip remembered hearing about Job and how he'd lost all his children, his land, his businesses...and how the man continued to bless and praise God. Phillip was so new in understanding all this. But God pointed out in that book that Job didn't have the right to question God. Well, he could ask the questions but God wasn't obligated to answer. And in the end, God blessed him many times more. But that was an historical event. Not a promise for Beth and himself.

God gave them a child. God took the child away. If Job's story was an example, Phillip should be able to say, "Blessed be the name of the Lord." He could make his lips move to say the words, but did he believe them in his heart? He wasn't so sure. *God, forgive me. I've failed You.*

17

Darkness descended over Beth's soul. Even though the fireplace always held a blaze and the windows were open to let in the sun, a dark shadow covered everything. She had failed. She'd never dreamed of being married or having children but now that she'd lost the baby, all she could think about was her failure. Surely Phillip would despise her now. What good was she for? She'd only brought trouble to his life. He'd been so gentle with her. Almost tiptoeing around her, avoiding the subject.

She moaned and rolled over but he was gone this morning. He mentioned traveling to Stanton Hall when she had recovered enough to make the trip.

Elsa bustled into the room. "I have your chocolate, ma'am. Are you ready for me to help you dress? How about the blue gown today?"

Blue. Suited her mood. Too bad she didn't own black or grey. "That'll be fine, Elsa. Am I to receive visitors today? Or expected somewhere that I need to rise and dress?"

"Lady Remington is planning to visit you later this morning. Remember? She sent a note to you yesterday with the beautiful flowers."

Ah, yes. The white roses. The sweet note of condolence for their loss.

Beth sighed, rose from the bed, and began her morning ablutions, allowing Elsa to assist her with everything. Dressed and sitting in front of the mirror to have her hair arranged she looked at herself critically. Green eyes were dull and dark circles hung below them. Her complexion was pale. She told herself to smile but her mouth refused to respond. There was no reason for joy or happiness. She closed her eyes rather than look at herself while her maid arranged her hair.

"There, ma'am. Pretty as a picture," Elsa said as she stepped back.

"You did a fine job." Beth couldn't find more to praise and she didn't open her eyes again until she'd faced away from the reflection of grief that taunted her. She rose and left the room, taking the steps slowly to the drawing room.

The butler stopped her before she entered. "Will you not break your fast? Lord Westcombe awaits you in the breakfast parlour."

"I'm not hungry. Thank you, Masters." She pushed past him and entered the drawing room. A low flame was in the fireplace but she added kindling to bring it to a full roaring fire. She sat in a chair further away, wreathed in shadows. The drapes had not been pulled back and the room was dark. It suited her mood.

The door opened and light seeped in from the hallway.

"Beth?" Phillip called out to her. He stepped further in and went to the windows to pull back the covering allowing sunlight to brighten the space. He turned. "Ah, there you are. Hiding, are you?"

She shrugged.

He strode across the room to sit near her. "Beth?"

"Hmmm?"

"We will get through this."

"Will we?" She finally turned to him. He had dark circles under his eyes as well. His hair was still in place and everything about him spoke of tidy splendor. She was dirty rags next to him.

He reached for her hand. "I love you, Beth."

Her gaze fell to the floor.

"When will you be ready to travel to Stanton Hall?"

"As soon as Elsa can pack my things."

"Do you want to leave tomorrow or the day after?"

"Tomorrow is fine."

"Are you really well enough to travel?"

"If I can lay in bed all day I can recline in a carriage for two or more."

"We can take it slow."

"I'd rather just get there."

"It'll be as you wish. Is there anything you'd like me to arrange for you to have before we leave? I can send a footman or Elsa to pick up books for you or material. Whatever you desire."

"I lack nothing. You've done more for me than I deserve."

"You are my wife. I'd do more if you'd allow me."

"Thank you, Phillip."

He sighed. "I realize you're grieving. We lost a child. But you haven't lost me. I'm still here. Waiting. I'll return in a few hours."

She nodded and he let her hand drop. She pulled it back to her lap. When she finally raised her face he was gone.

The butler stepped in a short time later. "Lady Remington to see you, ma'am."

"Send her in."

Josie strode into the room, radiant. She stopped and scanned the area until she spied Beth in the shadows. "Beth." She rushed forward and sat in the seat Phillip had vacated. "I longed to visit but Phillip told us you needed rest. Did you get my note and the flowers?"

"Yes. Thank you. They were lovely."

"I'm so sorry for what you're going through."

Beth sighed. "I never even considered that something like this could happen. Especially after we survived the trauma when the Black Diamond's men attacked me at Rose Hill."

"That was a terrible time. I had hoped that once past that you'd not have to fear any problems with this child. Maybe our blessing most of the time is believing everything will be well."

"And yet..." Beth swallowed, trying to hold back the tears.

"Did you know what the child was?" Josie whispered.

"A son. We lost a son."

Josie sat in silence with Beth, her own tears falling as the fire crackled in the dim room.

Beth savored the quiet. Sometimes there were no words.

~*~

After Josie left, Beth went to her room to assist with packing for the trip to the country. She was soon resting.

Phillip returned home and oversaw some of the packing of his own belongings. He stopped to sit on the bed next to her. He held her hand and spoke not a word. After a few minutes, he bent to kiss her cheek and with a squeeze of the hand left her alone.

Always alone. Trapped inside a mind that swirled in danger and darkness. She did make it to the dinner table that evening and the meal with her husband was eaten in silence. When she finished she placed her serviette on the table. "I'll leave you to your port."

"You don't need to. You could join me." He motioned for another glass and poured some of the wine for her. He gave her a nod to try it.

Beth sipped the wine and closed her eyes to savor the flavor. This was not the watered-down stuff she'd only ever been offered. Warmth spread through her and her body relaxed. "I can see why you enjoy this."

His grin held sadness. How was that possible? His eyes didn't dance as they normally did. Fine lines were etched around them and on his forehead. He'd not had those a few months past when he'd first rescued her and took her as his bride. They were her fault. She reached over and ran a finger over his forehead. "What worries you, Phillip?"

His eyes flashed a momentary surprise. "You of course. Everything we've done has been to protect you. But I couldn't keep you from—"

"—losing our child?"

He nodded and took another sip.

"Even had you been here, there was naught you could've done."

"I should have been here regardless."

"You were searching for Wolton?"

"Following leads to no avail."

"I don't blame you, Phillip. None of this was your fault."

"It wasn't yours either, Beth. Why can't you

forgive yourself?"

Her shoulders slumped and she sipped more wine. "I'm trapped in darkness. I cannot escape."

"I long to have my wife back."

"Maybe you lost her too." She finished the wine and rose to leave.

"Beth?"

She stopped and waited.

"I never wanted a wife, but don't mistake that for not wanting you. I do. Please don't forget that. You are central to my life and happiness."

She departed the room and took the stairs to their suite. She shooed Elsa away for the evening. She dressed for bed and brushed out her hair, leaving it long and loose, the way Phillip liked it. She blew out the candles, left the fireplace burning, and sat near the fire to wait.

She thought about her husband. Her heart hurt at failing him in losing the baby. But she'd also failed him in being so focused on herself she'd never considered all he was going through. He'd suspended his life to protect hers. He would have been at Stanton Hall for the longest time, content and working on his estate if he'd not been hunting Wolton and protecting her reputation.

She owed him more than her grief. She owed him her life. Her gratitude. She vowed she wouldn't ignore him tonight.

~*~

Phillip finished his port and rose to go to his study. He had a few letters yet to write before they traveled the next two days to Stanton Hall. He poured some brandy and sipped it as he worked, the warmth an inadequate substitute for his wife's affections, which had disappeared along with their baby. He sealed the last letter and sat by the fire, this time with the bottle. He poured another glass.

They'd lost a child. A son he never knew he longed for. It could have been a daughter, he'd still be heartbroken. He imagined a little girl with red hair like her mother's dancing around Stanton Hall calling, "Daddy!" Or a son with his blond hair learning to pitch, or fish and someday, shoot.

The tears came. He'd lost more than a child. He'd lost his future. Dreams he didn't realize he'd held. And it seemed he'd lost his wife's love as well. The future loomed ahead as dark, even without the threat of Wolton hovering in the periphery. He sighed and sipped the drink and let it soothe the ache deep within. *Lord, how did we get here to this place? Why? I don't understand at all.*

~*~

A scream of terror ripped through his dreamless slumber. He shook himself awake. He was still in his study, the empty brandy bottle on the table next to him. He swayed to his feet and followed the ruckus up the stairs.

Beth! He sprinted to her room and tried the door. It was locked. He ran to his suite, through to the adjoining door, and stumbled into pitch black. He paused. Her whimpers were coming from somewhere. He moved to the bed. Empty. Slowly his eyes adjusted to the dark. He pulled a drapery open to let in the moonlight.

The fire had gone out. Where was his wife?

"Beth?" he moved with caution. If she was in the throes of a nightmare would she be violent? She'd been horribly abused in the dark. He found the other window and threw open the drapes to let in more moonlight. He lit a brace of candles and slowly made his way to the fireplace. He started a fire but it would take time before it would have a calming effect.

Silence greeted him. He scanned the furniture. She wasn't there. Finally, he spotted her in the corner of the room where the shadows were greatest even with the fireplace and windows open. Curled up like a child, she wept. Her hair had been left down and hung as a curtain over her face. Had she waited up for him?

"Oh, Beth. I'm sorry. I didn't realize you waited for me." He approached her slowly.

Elsa entered the room having found a master key. "Is my lady all right?" the maid asked.

"I believe she'll be fine. You may leave. Tell everyone to return to their beds."

The maid left, shutting the door firmly behind her.

"Beth? Sweetheart, I'm here."

"Phillip?" The voice sounded lost and childlike.

"Yes. Come to me." He held out a hand, giving her space. She reached for him and he helped her to her feet.

"It was dark."

"It is not dark any more. I'm here. Come. You need to rest." He led her to the bed and wrapped her in the blanket. She sighed and he placed a kiss on her forehead.

He strode back to the fire and stoked it until it was a healthy blaze. He placed more wood on it to keep it going until morning. He glanced at the bed. Had he failed her by not coming? It seemed he couldn't do anything to help his wife. He strode to the adjoining bedroom and the bed he'd never used before. He collapsed on top of the covers, fully clothed, and fell asleep.

~*~

In the morning, his mouth was dry and his head ached. He dragged himself out of bed and called for Fenway. He peeked in on his wife who still slept. Finishing his own grooming and ensuring all was packed for the journey he finally went to rouse his wife.

"Beth? We must leave soon. You can sleep in the carriage if you like."

She stretched and looked at him, her brow wrinkled. "Phillip?"

"Yes. 'Tis I. We need to start our journey to Stanton Hall. Pray, get up and let Elsa prepare you for the trip. All is ready."

She heaved a sigh and rose, glancing at the bed and the rest of the room. A chair was tipped over and the drapes remained open. "Did something happen last night?"

"You had a nightmare."

"Oh. I'll be down before you can finish breaking your fast."

Phillip left her in Elsa's capable hands and went down to eat. "Fenway. That special drink you make for hangovers, please. And have my horse saddled. I believe the fresh air will be more beneficial than being cooped up in a carriage all day."

His valet bowed and left to get the drink.

Phillip ate some toast and drank coffee while reading through the morning paper. The drink was brought and he gulped it down. He closed his eyes and willed his stomach not to rebel. It was foolishness to have drunk as much as he had the previous night.

Beth appeared in the doorway as her trunk was carried out by the footmen. "I'm ready to depart."

Phillip rose and shrugged on his greatcoat. "We can stop as many times as you deem necessary for your comfort."

Beth nodded and preceded him out the door, waiting for him to hand her into the carriage. "You'll not ride with me?"

"Perhaps later. I need the fresh air at the moment."

"Are you unwell? You appear pale."

"I appreciate your concern, ma'am. I shall be fine." He shut the door while inwardly kicking himself for not being forthcoming with his bride. Mounting his horse, he led the procession out of town.

Miles passed and hours dragged on. Phillip's headache only grew in power. At the first stop, he gave up riding his horse and joined Beth in the carriage, sitting facing forward and trying not to invade her space. She'd pushed him away and yet he longed to hold her. The memory of her kisses and soft curves tempted him. Her cool attitude reminded him of all he'd lost.

Reaching their destination for the night he procured two rooms and arranged for her meal to be brought to her. He ate in the pub by himself. When he finished, he made his way to his own room and the lonely bed there. Why did that bother him now? He'd been single for years. But he'd grown used to having Beth by his side at night. Her rejection stung.

The next morning, he was better and decided to spend the rest of the journey riding his horse.

Finally arriving at Stanton Hall, he dismounted and rushed to assist Beth from the carriage. Together they walked into the house and he escorted her to their suite.

The footmen brought in her boxes and Elsa was busy unpacking.

"It's been a long day. I can have a meal brought to you tonight."

"That would be lovely."

"Remember, these are your rooms to redecorate as you wish."

"I remember."

He bowed and left her alone, going to his own room and ordering a bath and a meal.

When he finished, he crawled into bed and stared at the ceiling. He was back to where he began. Yes, his wife was in the house but he was as alone now as he'd been before he met her. Perhaps even more so because her very presence would remind him of all he'd won and lost since spring.

Sleep did not come easy.

"You shall die for taking what is mine," the sinister voice growled.

His heart raced. He reached for his gun but couldn't find it. The room was dark. He gasped for air, went to the window, and opened it to let in the cooler evening breeze. A nightmare. Was God warning him the battle wasn't over? His bride might not care for him anymore but he still loved her and would do all in his power to keep her safe. Or die trying. Without her he had nothing else to live for. His future was secure in Christ. He didn't need to fear death any longer. His enemies failed to understand that made him the more dangerous foe.

18

First Duke, then the baby. Didn't trouble come in threes? She shouldn't believe in the superstitious darkness that was her friend of old. They were at Stanton Hall. She was safe here.

The journey north had been lonely. Phillip stayed in a separate room each night on the road and had taken to sleeping in his own bed in their suite instead of joining her. She missed his touch. What happened to them? She'd longed to be close to him again but the words would never come. They'd sit for a meal and she'd suddenly be struck with shyness.

They developed a routine. He worked and spent time on the estate while she took walks in the garden, became better acquainted with running the household and began taking an inventory to ascertain just what she really needed to improve the interior of the Hall. She pulled things out of the attics and debated color schemes. She didn't want to spend money if she didn't need to. Phillip had given her free rein but she refused to take advantage of his generosity. The fact that he'd married her at all was more than she deserved.

She was not able to regain her figure. She imagined the baby was still moving within her. Elsa had been silent about needing to let the clothes out more. She had little appetite. Every twinge inside her, every flutter she experienced, magnified her loss. While she missed her husband at night, she was grateful he wasn't able to witness her descent into madness. She debated cleaning out a space in the attic for her to stay when she'd truly gone insane.

~*~

"My parents have invited us to Manchester Manor for Christmas." Phillip broke the silence at breakfast.

"I don't want to leave Stanton Hall."

"Are you unwell?" Phillip asked.

Beth shrugged. "I do not need a doctor but I do not want to travel either. If you desire to go, you should. I can remain here."

"I would not leave you." Phillip sipped his coffee and watched his wife move food around her plate. As if he didn't notice she did not each much. She wasn't withering away, however. Staff reported she spent her days redecorating the Hall, room by room. She'd yet to do her own or select a space for herself on the main floor. She was either busy cleaning or resting. There was little in between from what he could tell.

She continually rejected any suggestion of bringing in the local physician.

"Beth, what happened between us? I love you. I won't force myself upon you."

She patted his hand. "You are a kind man." She rose and left the room never answering the question.

Every day he proclaimed his love for her. He complimented her and commented on her progress with the house. She rarely said a word in return. He rose and went to write to his family declining the invitation. If they did go as they were now, there would be questions about the marriage he didn't want to face. Did she regret marrying him? He'd thought they'd found something wonderful in spite of their difficult circumstances. Obviously, all the love was one-sided. Was he a fool? He didn't think she'd manipulated him.

No. Losing the baby changed everything between them. But how did he bridge the gap?

He wrote the letter and called for his horse. "I have to go check out some of the outlying homes as the weather looks to get bad."

"Cook has prepared items for you to give to the tenants in case they are in need."

"Very good." Phillip shrugged on his greatcoat and with the bags of food arranged over his horse he pulled himself on top and inspected the sky. The snow had already started to fall. He looked at his groom. "If I do not make it back tonight, assume I've sought shelter with one of the tenants."

"Perhaps you should not go, my lord," the young man said.

"No. It is my responsibility to see our tenants have what they need to survive. It's too early in the season for enough snow to keep me away. I should be fine." He nudged the horse into a trot and took off for the first home at the edge of the property.

Snow gave way to the rain making the ground slippery beneath his horse's hooves. He was miles from home when he came to the last tenant, the Brown family.

"Oh, my lord. Come in and warm yourself." Mrs. Brown took his coat and hat and motioned him to the fireplace. Their home was a two story that he'd seen received a new roof during the summer. Something he'd arranged before his fateful trip to London and finding a wife.

"How is Mrs. Westcombe?" Mrs. Brown asked as she poured him some tea.

"She is well, thank you."

"Mr. Brown will be in soon. He was checking on the cattle."

Phillip nodded. "I brought some items in this bag here for you from our cook. I wanted to make sure you had something in case the weather caught you off guard."

Mrs. Brown opened the bag. "Oh, this is lovely. Her jams are a treasure and the bread will go well with our dinner tonight. Will you be staying for our evening meal?"

From the window, Phillip could tell the sky had grown dark.

Mr. Brown entered, stomping his feet in the back hall.

"I doubt his lordship will be able to travel tonight, my dear." He came to warm his hands by the fire. "Your horse is in the barn, well cared for and fed. 'T'would be folly to attempt to ride home."

"Thank you for that. If you insist it is too dangerous to travel, then I will be forced to depend on your kind hospitality. Do you have space here or shall I join my steed in the barn?" Phillip grinned as he said the words.

Mr. Brown chuckled. "Serve you right to sleep in the barn. Utter foolishness to ride out on a day like this."

"Fool he may be but he did come bearing gifts," Mrs. Brown said. "And we have a comfortable room you may use. It won't be what you are used to but it is warm and dry."

Phillip grinned. "I'm no fool. I saved the best

home for last on my trip." He winked at Mrs. Brown, who blushed prettily.

"Oh, go on with you." She bustled out of the room.

"Will your pretty little wife worry about you?" Mr. Brown asked.

"I'm sure she'll be fine. I can travel home tomorrow after the sun comes out. She's busy working on the house she'll likely not even miss me."

"Ah, they always do, and heaven help ye if yer not where she thinks you ought to be. Trust a man whose got more years in the noose than you do."

"Don't listen to a word he says," called Mrs. Brown from the other room.

Mr. Brown chuckled. "See? You can never pull one over on them."

~*~

Beth paced by the fire. Phillip had failed to return from his tenant visits. Searching out the window she realized he would likely not be home tonight.

She chided herself for missing him when all she'd done was push him away for months in spite of his gentle reminder that he loved her. Her? She'd brought nothing but trouble to the man. He deserved better than a scarred woman with her past. She quit her pacing and went to her room.

She tossed and turned all night, finally rising early in the morning to pray. When she came downstairs she understood it would likely be mid-day before he'd arrive. The going could be treacherous on horseback.

She wandered through the house, unable to set herself to any task. Her hand rested on her stomach as she sat to search the bright white landscape for any sign of Phillip. Movement under her hand brought more fear and loss to the forefront. She was surely losing her mind. Why did she persist in thinking she was pregnant? She'd seen the perfect tiny body of their dead son.

~*~

Phillip slept well and enjoyed a hearty breakfast made merry by Mr. and Mrs. Brown and their two children almost full grown. The sun was shining bright. He'd be able to safely get home now.

"Thank you, I shall depart for home lest my wife has worried for me."

"Would you like help in the barn?" the son asked.

"It is good even for a lord to do some things for himself. I am capable of saddling my horse. Thank you for the offer." Phillip turned to his hosts. "I'm grateful for your hospitality."

"It was an honor to have you, my lord," Mr. Brown said as Mrs. Brown gave a curtsy.

Putting on his greatcoat and hat, Phillip strode to the barn and began to saddle his horse.

A young man he didn't know appeared. "Nasty day for travlin' m'lord. A letter came for you just now." He handed Phillip the paper.

"Thank you."

The young man left. Phillip sat on a stool and broke the seal on the letter and opened it.

Lord Westcombe,
You took what is mine and now you will pay. I have her, but will play fair and let you know she is currently on her way to Follett Hall. She came willingly. I want her for

*myself but will not hesitate to kill her should I be so inclined.
Her father is also not long for this earth if you do not arrive
quickly."*

    H. W.

Phillip hadn't sworn in months but now he kicked at the boards. He was at least an hour ride from home. He'd be doubling back to go to Ipswich. He could not afford the time to return. They, of course, would watch and attack when he'd left the house. How long had they bided their time, waiting for such an opportunity? He went back inside the tenant's home and wrote several missives to be dispatched as soon as possible. He left sufficient finances for the task.

"We won't fail you, my lord," Mrs. Brown assured him.

He hurried back to the stable where his horse waited impatiently. Mounting, he directed his steed toward Ipswich and Follett Hall, a portion of London he'd never been to previously. It was at least a two days' ride with the weather. He hoped he would arrive in time to spare Beth any harm.

~*~

The day wore on with no sign or word of Phillip and her worry grew. She cursed herself for the time she wasted in her grief, pushing him away. What if something happened to him? She would never again know the strength of those arms holding her, keeping her safe. She'd never again know the bliss of his kisses.

She went to her room to weep in regret for how her madness cut her off from the affections of a man who had been so faithful to her.

"I love you, Phillip. Please come back." She opened her Bible and sat in her room to read and pray. Darkness fell and she continued with her prayers for his safety. She begged God to forgive her for spurning her husband's love. *Give me another chance, Lord. I'll do anything to show him how much I love him.*

She awoke early the next morning in spite of her fatigue and dressed with care. Phillip would return today. She spent the morning pacing in the drawing room, watching out the window for any sign of his return. The snow continued to melt as the temperatures warmed. When he failed to arrive by mid-afternoon she went upstairs and wandered into Phillip's room, startling Fenway, his valet.

"Ma'am?"

"Would you mind if I spent time in here, Fenway?"

The valet bowed and left the room. She locked the door behind him for privacy and went to the bed. She picked up Phillip's pillow. Inhaling his scent on the pillow reminded her of him. She set it down, drew back the covers and crawled in to hold it tight as she rested. *Bring him home safe, Lord.*

By evening, once again she sat in her room, reading her Bible and praying. She turned in early, holding Phillip's pillow close. Maybe tomorrow…

~*~

The roads were slippery and the going slow. Phillip couldn't go far and stopped often to rest his horse and warm up. Was it possible for him to catch up to Beth? So far there had been no one at the coaching inns who had seen anyone matching his wife's description. Her captors were keeping her well-hidden or taking another route. Both seemed impossible given the conditions of the roads. He prayed they had not injured her. After several days of travel, he reached Ipswich and gained directions to Follett Hall.

"My lord, are you sure you want to go there?" the young stable hand asked.

"I received a message my wife is there and I need to get her."

"At least she's not at Wolton's."

"Why? Is that place close?"

"They be neighbors, but there's rumor of sacrifices there." He stopped to pause. "Wouldn't surprise me if Follett does that too. He's a creepy cove."

"Why do you suspect sacrifices?"

"Young girls go missing, ne'er to be seen again, 'cept for their bloody dresses." The last was said with a sinister whisper.

"Only young girls? Boys are not at risk?"

Phillip did not miss the shudder that rattled the boy. "Lots of strange happenin's out der. I'd stir clir if I were you."

"Thank you for your concern, young man. I must retrieve my wife."

"Might be the last thing you do m'lord. Lor' have mercy on ye."

Phillip mounted his horse in one quick movement and rode out of the yard.

Reaching the dilapidated gates to Follett Hall, Phillip experienced his own shudder of fear. The estate had been in disrepair for some time. The long path to the house presented difficulties for his horse with divots. Phillip dismounted to walk his horse and minimize any danger of injury to the animal. He stayed closer to the edge of the drive where the ground appeared more level. It was obvious no traffic had come down this road for days.

He arrived at a Tudor-style manse, which was a charitable term. The thatched roof was showing signs of wear and didn't appear as though it would provide shelter through the winter. Smoke arose from the chimney at the rear of the building, but there was no other indication of someone living there. He walked his mount to the empty stables. He wiped his horse down with straw and found some oats and water for the beast. Once that was taken care of he made his way to the front of the house.

The building was in disrepair, Phillip took a deep breath and knocked on the door. *Lord, please let Beth be safe.*

No one answered so he pounded harder. He heard no movement from within. He strode around to the back of the house, a chill settling into his bones even through his many-caped greatcoat. His toes were numb. Smoke was coming from the back of the building and he found a door, presumably to the kitchen. The scent of food cooking made his mouth water and his stomach grumble.

He knocked on that door.

It slowly opened and a wizened old man, bent over with age and a few white hairs on his head, greeted him with a growl. "Go away." The voice was soft, almost secretive. "No one is home."

The man tried to close the door but Phillip was quicker, stronger, and more determined. His boot halted the door and he pushed his way into the warm room, shutting the door behind him. "Is this Follett Hall, home to Lord Follett?" Phillip stomped his feet to get warmth to his toes.

"Who's askin'?"

"Pardon me, I'm Lord Phillip Westcombe, husband to Mrs. Elizabeth Westcombe."

The man squinted, tipped his head and shrugged.

"Formerly known as Lizzy Follett."

The man's eyes grew big. "We'z got trouble now."

Phillip peered at the man. "Where is my wife?"

"She's not here. Ain't been since the master took her to London to marry that evil Lord Wolton."

"What do you mean, 'she's not here?' Explain yourself."

"He already did, Lord Westcombe." Lord Follett appeared in the far entrance to the kitchen. "Lizzy is not here, which begs the question, why are you?"

"I received a note saying Beth was here."

"You lost my daughter?" Lord Follett frowned.

"She was home when a storm kept me away. I received a letter and posted after her immediately. I do not intend to lose my wife."

"Do you have the note?"

Phillip dug into his inner waistcoat pocket and produced the missive, handing it to his father-in-law.

Lord Follett appeared to shrink before his eyes. His face grew pale. Dropping his hand, the paper fell to the floor.

"Are you unwell?" Phillip stepped toward the older man.

"It must be a trap. Lizzy would never come here of her own free will. I'm afraid—"

"No need to fear, my friend." Another man emerged from the shadows, his voice booming against the walls.

Lord Follett began to shake.

"Lord Wolton, I presume?" Phillip asked.

"Yes, Lord Westcombe. How nice of you to visit us."

The hair rose on the back of Phillip's neck. He stepped toward the door. "It would seem you have a full house, Lord Follett. I apologize for inconveniencing you."

Before he could make it to the outer door, it opened behind him and three large men entered blocking the exit. They carried rope and knives.

Heart racing, Phillip clenched his fists. He was no match for those brutes. *Lord, help me.*

"I'm afraid we cannot allow you to leave, Lord Westcombe. Can we, Folly?"

Phillip's arms were yanked hard sending pain into his shoulders. Heavy ropes bound them together.

"I fear we're impinging on Lord Follett's hospitality," Phillip stated through gritted teeth.

"'Tis no imposition, is it Folly?"

Lord Follett grew paler and gripped his chest with his hand. He mouthed words but nothing came out.

Lord Wolton ignored his host and motioned to his men. "Take Lord Westcombe to a guest chamber and make him comfortable." He chuckled. "Lord Phillip, it was pure folly to come here but I'm glad you did." He put his arm around Lord Follett and escorted the man out of the room. "Come Folly, we have some things to discuss over a glass of whiskey."

~*~

Four days. There'd been no sign of Phillip. Grooms visited all the tenants and tracked his movement but there was no sign of him. He'd left three days hence, having posted letters but none reached her and the young man couldn't remember who they were made out to as he couldn't cipher Phillip's penmanship. Beth sent letters to Lord Remington, Lord Harrow and Sir Tidley but realized any response could take time.

She chewed her nails to the nubs and wept all the time. She regretted the distance she'd placed between Phillip and herself. *Lord, just bring him home safe. Don't let any harm befall him. Please?*

When the butler came in with a letter she hoped it was finally from Phillip.

It was not. The spikey narrow handwriting was unfamiliar to her. A chill ran through her as she held the envelope. She broke the seal and took a deep breath before opening the page.

Mrs. Westcombe,

I regret to inform you that your husband traveled to Follett Hall to seek vengeance against your father. If you hope to save either of them it would behoove you to return to your childhood home post haste.

H.W.

Elizabeth dropped the letter. What was going on? She was certain her father was at Follett Hall, but Phillip had forgiven her father and no longer had a desire for revenge. She believed that with all her heart. Her husband was a man of his word and took his faith in Christ seriously. The initials, though. The W could be for Wolton but she wasn't sure she remembered his first name.

It took her three-quarters of an hour to locate Debrett's book on the peerage. It listed the families of the *beau monde* and their names and connections. Lord Harold Wolton.

He'd struck. She straightened her spine in determination. Lord Wolton may have stolen her childhood, her innocence, and her pet. She refused to let him take Phillip from her as well.

She called for Elsa and Fenway and explained their master was in trouble and to pack for a journey. They would leave in the morning. She told Fenway to pack medicinal supplies as well. She had no idea what they might do to him before they arrived. He would likely need assistance and care.

Beth arranged for the carriage and footmen for the journey. She sat at Phillip's desk and penned notes to post to Marcus, Theodore, and Michael. She left identical ones on the desk in case they arrived here before receiving her letters. She hoped they would not be far behind her.

Beth left for her room and fell to her knees in prayer for her husband's safety. She didn't fear for her father. Wolton only ever really wanted her. She would trade herself for Phillip's safety if need be. Her husband had suffered enough on her behalf.

The next morning, armed with a small pearl handled pistol in her reticule, a gun in the coach, and a stiletto knife strapped to her thigh, they departed Stanton Hall to travel northeast to Ipswich. Thankfully the snow had melted. Pushing hard they might make the journey in two days.

Hold on, Phillip. I'm on my way.

19

Phillip tripped as he was shoved down stone steps to a lower level of the house. Damp, dank, mildew assaulted his senses, causing him to sneeze. The temperature dropped as they traveled away from the fireplace in the kitchen. At least they'd left his greatcoat on him. The men lit a torch and one went in front of him. Could he kick the man down? He decided that with his hands tied and the darkness that ensued, his ability to battle the other two men was slim. He'd bide his time.

The corridor turned to the left, away from the main house, and they descended even more stairs. The temperature grew cooler, but not as cold as it had been outside.

The men stopped at a door, opened it with a key and shoved him inside.

He fell to the hard stone floor. "Enjoy your stay at Follett Hall." The men laughed as the door slammed shut and the key turned. They left with the torch. His shoulders ached as he sat on the floor in the darkness. Fear taunted him in the silence that followed. *Lord, please protect Beth. And if You think of it—save me.*

~*~

Beth fidgeted as the carriage barreled down the road. Travel was slow and the bricks under their feet didn't keep them warm for long. She chafed at the stops they were forced to make to change horses and warm up. The poor coach driver struggled the most. Beth drank hot tea to warm up, burning her tongue in the desire to return to traveling. Later in the day, they had stopped again.

"I'll arrange for rooms," Fenway said.

"The moon is out, we can travel further," Beth offered.

"Ma'am. You need your rest. Lord Westcombe might need you and you must be well rested for whatever tomorrow holds," Elsa pleaded.

Beth gave in. With a simple meal brought to her room, she prepared for bed. Once Elsa had left to her own quarters, Beth knelt by the bed, her large stomach protruding. She thought she saw it move. Impossible. She gulped. *Lord, save me from this insanity long enough to rescue Phillip. He doesn't deserve a wife destined for Bedlem. Spare him that humiliation. I can't do this without You. Watch over him. Keep him safe. You blessed me in so many ways I don't deserve and he shouldn't suffer for that. We love You. Please rescue him.*

The next morning, they were on the road early. They were getting closer to Ipswich. They stopped at another inn to warm up, change horses, and give the driver a chance to recover from the elements. Walking into the public room three men stood.

"Mrs. Westcombe? What brings you here?" Sir Tidley asked.

"Perhaps this conversation should be had in private?" Lord Harrow said and went to speak to the innkeeper.

"Mrs. Westcombe, let me introduce you to Mr. Neville. He's a Bow Street Runner we've used in the past to help us," Sir Tidley said.

"It is a pleasure to make your acquaintance, Mrs. Westcombe." Mr. Neville nodded to her. Soon they were ushered into a private parlour and food brought in.

Beth sat and the men followed suit.

The door closed and Sir Tidley asked his question again. "Beth, why are you here? Our understanding is you were at Follett Hall and Phillip had gone to rescue you."

She sighed. "I take it none of you got my missive asking for assistance in rescuing Phillip?"

"We did not. We received Phillip's request to help save you," Theo stated.

"Sounds like Wolton finally decided to strike and tricked both of you to coming there." Michael cleared his throat. "Marcus was unable to join us. Josie's due to have her baby any day and he needs to be by her side."

Beth fought off the sting of disappointment while placing a hand on her own swelling stomach. The men graciously avoided commenting. Something moved under her hand. Tears threatened and she sucked in a breath. Surely, she was going mad. *Be brave. Phillip needs me. He will be better off without me given the direction I'm headed.* She straightened up, resolve taking over. "We need a plan to save Phillip. We talked months ago about using me as a lure to draw out Lord Wolton, but Follett Hall is a difficult place to wage a rescue."

"You are well acquainted with the property, ma'am?" Neville asked.

"I am. Perhaps we can map out the house and the dungeons. I suspect Phillip is being kept in the lower dungeon." She paused and placed a hand over her eyes, sudden grief at what Phillip might be experiencing at the hands of Lord Wolton threatening to overwhelm her.

"What kind of danger is he in, Beth?" Michael inquired gently.

"He is likely bound, held in a dark room. The worst would be if he is being tortured." Tears escaped. Theodore offered her a handkerchief but she waved him off and reached for her own, the one Phillip had given her so many months ago, freshly laundered and pressed. "Ask the innkeeper for paper and ink and I'll draw a map. Wolton is expecting me to arrive and we would not want to disappoint him. However, he is not expecting the three of you so we need a plan." She expected the men to argue her involvement but none did.

They fetched the articles requested.

She proceeded to draw her maps and instruct them on what to expect at various parts of the property. When she was finished, she slumped. Fatigue weighed her down and her back ached.

Sir Tidley came to her rescue. "We all need to rest. We won't manage anything else today. I'll arrange for rooms for the night here. We're only a few hours out of Ipswich, we can execute our plan tomorrow."

Beth nodded and allowed them to care for her. Theo escorted her to her room where Elsa awaited. Once she was ready and her maid left she collapsed into bed. *Thank you, Lord for providing friends to help. Grant us success tomorrow and keep Phillip in Your care until then.* Peace flowed over her. For the first time in days, she slept.

~*~

Michael paced the room, periodically looking at the map Beth had drawn for them.

"I'm not comfortable putting Mrs. Westcombe into the middle of this," Mr. Neville said.

"We thought she'd lost the baby, but she's obviously large with child. We need to be even more careful. We cannot fail Phillip by putting her in any danger," Michael stated.

"If Wolton is as evil as she claims, I doubt there is any way to guarantee the safety of anyone in this venture." Theodore sipped some wine. "Even if she were not with child, Phillip would be devastated if anything happened to her. She has become everything to him."

"With the exception of God," Michael said.

"God?" Mr. Neville asked.

"Both he and Elizabeth have a relationship with Jesus Christ. I don't understand it myself but Marcus and Josie have that too. They had talked that this battle was spiritual, not just physical. There are satanic forces at work and the four of them stated this battle is not only against, how did they put it? Not against flesh and blood but against spiritual forces in the heavens." Michael sighed.

The words hung for a moment before Mr. Neville spoke. "I have worked the dives in London long enough to know that what they are saying is true. I'm not sure about who Jesus is, but to be honest, what lies ahead terrifies me more than the darkest stews of Seven Dials. Maybe we should be praying ourselves."

"Are you a believer as well, Mr. Neville?" asked Theodore.

"I've never considered myself one, but there are

times, like this, when I'm forced to reconsider my position in light of greater truths." Mr. Neville rose. "I'm headed to my room. I have some business to do with God before we step into this rescue tomorrow. I will see you in the morning. Hopefully, we will all have a clearer idea of how to proceed and keep Mrs. Westcombe safe." With that, the Bow Street Runner departed, leaving the two friends alone.

Michael lifted a glass of wine to his lips and sipped. "So, Theo. What do you think of all this spiritual talk?" The talk made him uneasy. He didn't doubt there was evil, just that God could help them through it. Or more importantly, would help him.

"My family always attended church. I support a parish. I believe in God. But what Marcus and Phillip have is more—personal than that. They are as devoted to Jesus as they are to their wives, or their friends. Perhaps even more so."

Michael sighed. "Marcus has talked of this many times, about Jesus and his love for Him. He's never pushed his faith on us which I've always appreciated. But now, Phillip and Beth? Is it contagious?"

"Consider this, Michael. We weren't forced to accept Josie or Beth as friends. I love them as sisters because of my affection for Marcus and Phillip. I would do anything to ensure their safety. Relationships, the important ones you'd risk everything for, can't be forced on someone—they grow in the heart."

"Is your heart growing toward a relationship with Jesus?"

Theo shrugged. "The more I understand about God, the real person of Jesus, and not the cold impersonal version of God I learned in my youth, the more I desire to know. I'm not ready to commit myself to it like they have."

"I'm not sure Jesus would have me, Theo. Relationships go both ways, don't they?"

"It takes time to get close to someone. Perhaps it's the same with God?"

"Possibly."

"I'm for bed. Maybe I'll take a look at the Bible Marcus gave me years ago. For some reason, I always seem to carry it with me when I travel."

Michael rose, setting his glass on the table. "I have a small one as well." He patted his pocket. "Interesting that we both brought them to a spiritual battle in spite of our doubts. I don't understand all of that."

"Perhaps understanding is not as necessary as trusting God."

"You could be right." Michael followed his friend out of the room, questions tumbling through his mind even as he tried to sleep. *God? If You really do care, please protect Phillip and Beth.*

~*~

Phillip rolled to his other side as his arm grew numb underneath him. There was no comfortable position to be had. Water dripped and rats scurried somewhere. He recalled Beth talking about being tied up and put in a closet for days before being molested by Wolton and others. Fury erupted within to give him the will to survive. He'd forgiven Lord Follett for his negligence as a father, but Wolton was evil personified.

He struggled to his feet, walked to the door and around the room. He was trying to conserve strength but he needed to move to keep from being stiff. He didn't want to be unable to fight if the need came for it. The stone walls were damp. The room was huge and a large table sat in the middle. He found a chair. His foot pulled it out from the table enough that he could sit down on it backward. He was able to lean forward and rest his head. He kept trying to work his arms free but the rope dug into his skin, rubbing his wrists raw. Finally, he slept, dreaming of better days with Beth. He prayed even as he slept that she would not be lured to her death as he obviously had been.

~*~

Beth woke with a start. Her hand went to her abdomen and the swelling there. Heaviness overtook her body and soul. *Lord, please remove the madness that has overtaken me.* She rose and paced by the fireplace. She stopped to pick up her Bible, hoping God would find some comfort for her as she faced this day.

Thou will keep him in perfect peace, whose mind is stayed on Thee: because he trusteth in Thee.

Peace, yes. Peace was what she needed as she headed into this evil. She prayed for peace and success in rescuing Phillip from certain death. She wept over the scripture in prayer as she prayed it back to God.

Elsa soon came to assist her with her gown.

Today Beth chose a serviceable green wool gown. It was warm and she instinctively realized she might need a dark color to survive this day. She was joined in the breakfast parlour by Theo, Michael, and Mr. Nigel Neville. After the food was brought in by the waitress, they heard a knock.

Fenway entered. "Pardon me."

"What is it, Fenway?" Beth asked.

"I would like to join you today in rescuing Lord Westcombe."

"Your devotion to your master does you credit, Fenway. Neither he, nor I, expect you to make such a sacrifice. I need you at the Red Rooster in Ipswich, awaiting his return. We don't know if he's been injured and he may need your care and assistance then. "

Fenway frowned and shuffled his feet.

Mr. Neville chimed in. "It would serve us better to have you at the inn. I have requested several men from London to join us and they may arrive while we are gone. You can help them understand the layout of the property and our plans so they can ascertain how best to assist us. Won't you sit with us as we discuss it?"

Fenway joined them and Beth went over the layout of the house, its entrances and potential avenues of escape. As a group, they strategized their plan.

"Elizabeth, I am not comfortable with your part of this," Michael protested.

"I understand. This entire problem is because of me. Phillip would not be where he is today if he hadn't helped me escape marriage to Wolton. I will not sit by in comfort without doing something to free him."

"But if something were to happen to you..." Theo said.

Beth lifted sad eyes to Theo and Michael. "He has the best of friends and family. He deserves the opportunity to enjoy them for a long time to come. I will do anything in my power to ensure that happens."

Michael's eyes grew wide, he opened his mouth, shook his head, and said nothing. Closing his jaw, he dropped his gaze and nodded.

"But—" Theo was elbowed by Michael.

"We should pray before we depart," Beth said.

The men bowed their heads and prayed. "Lord, only with Your help can we have victory today. Protect Phillip and his friends as we seek to rescue him. Give us favor and success. Defeat our enemies, Lord, and bring this evil to an end."

Michael assisted her into the carriage. "Have a care, Beth. We all love you as well as Phillip. Please do not take any foolish chances today."

Beth squeezed his hand. "Phillip is blessed in his friends. Thank you for your help, Michael. God bless."

The door shut, the men mounted up, and soon they were off to Ipswich. They arrived at the Red Rooster a few hours later and discovered Phillip had been there days earlier. Luggage was deposited and rooms paid for.

Lord Harrow, Sir Tidley and Mr. Neville departed on horseback to circle around the property and await Elizabeth's arrival.

Storm clouds hung in the distance. This was it. She would do whatever it took to save Phillip. She bit back the tears. Her husband needed her. He'd traveled all this way for her. She had much to repent of. If her debt was paid with her life it was only as it should be. She'd left a note with Elsa to deliver to Phillip should she not return alive. She very much doubted she would. She'd been very clear with the men that Phillip was to be saved at all costs and to not come for her until that was accomplished.

Entering the lane to the house was a strange experience. This had been her home, but she'd rarely left it or seen it from this perspective. The fields were filled with weeds and the pitted road jostled her and the carriage without mercy. The dilapidated house appeared to be uninhabited but for a small wisp of smoke rising from the kitchen chimney. She left this home in the spring hoping to never return. She praised and thanked God for rescuing her and bringing Phillip into her life. *Save him, Lord. Take me if You must. Give me courage to face Wolton.*

The carriage pulled up in front of the house. She doubted any staff was available to answer the door. The footman helped her down and she straightened her spine, inhaling deeply before taking the steps. She didn't need to be afraid, but her pulse raced. She wasn't returning as a victim but as a child of the King of kings. She'd never needed to put her faith to the test like this. *Lord, glory and honor be Yours today. Grant me strength.*

The roof looked rotted and likely to collapse. Everything was wet. She was grateful for her muff to help warm her. She knocked on the door.

The worn wood swung open and there stood her father. Filthy and unkempt. His beard carried mementos of his last meals, most likely alcohol. They stared at each other.

"Lizzy. Leave. You shouldn't be here." He tried to shut the door on her.

She stopped him and stepped into the hall. "I've come for my husband. I assume you've seen him."

His eyes grew wide and his shoulders slumped further. He frowned and shook his head. "Just leave, Lizzy. There's naught you can do."

"Father, you did not perpetrate this evil. Trust me and grant assistance. More than that, trust God."

"No. It is too late for God, Lizzy. Please. I could not save you when you were younger, but I might save you now. Please. Leave."

"I refuse to leave without my husband. He is

here."

"You are well informed, Mrs. Westcombe." Lord Wolton emerged from the far end of the corridor. "You made good time in your arrival in spite of the weather and the state of the roads. You wisely chose to come unattended." Lord Wolton walked toward her, coming around to face her.

Standing before her, face red and bloated, eyes glassy, she repressed the shudder of fear that threatened to ripple through her.

His hand reached up to grasp her jaw and hold her firm. "Finally. I will have what I was promised months ago. You. Will. Be. Mine."

His breath almost caused her to lose her last meal. The thought of vomiting on this villain gave her perverse delight. He tried to pull her to himself for a kiss but she managed to resist him and tug free from his grasp.

He missed her lips and kissed her ear instead.

Elizabeth steeled herself. She would not recoil at his touch although her body argued the matter. Her ability to manage this man could mean the difference between life or death for Phillip.

"I believe the correct etiquette would be to show me to the drawing room. Preferably with a fire. I am, after all, a visitor here and it is quite cold outside. Once I am fortified with a cup of tea, perhaps you and I can arrive at some sort of understanding."

Lord Wolton dropped his hand and took a step back. "Folly, go fetch some tea while I entertain your lovely daughter."

Lord Follett didn't move.

"Father. You may go. I truly do wish for a bracing cup of tea." She swept past both men, walked down the hallway to the drawing room, entered, and awaited Lord Wolton, who wasted no time in joining her.

The door shut behind him and the key scraped in the lock. That didn't surprise her. She turned to Wolton. *Lord, lead me. Give me the right words.* She needed to buy time for the men to free Phillip. The longer she kept Wolton busy, the better the chances that Phillip might come out of this alive.

She turned to face her foe. "Lord Wolton, would you please tell me what you've done with my husband?"

~*~

"Concerned for him, are you?" he sneered. He walked around the furniture in the room, keeping an eye on her. Arriving at the window, he drew back the moth-eaten drapes to peek outside. No movement. She'd come alone but that didn't mean others weren't around. He patted his pocket where the bloodied fabric from her clothing resided. The material had been his comfort in the wait. Now his prey was here, in the flesh.

And a lot more flesh from the swell at her waist. A bonus. Destroy the lord, master the woman, and crush the child. His day had grown incredibly brighter. He grinned.

Tossing her muff on the chair, Lizzy went to the fireplace to put some kindling in and reached for a flint to start the flame. As it raged to life, she held out her gloved hands to the blaze.

She appeared unaffected by him but he knew her better. She was terrified. She always had been. There was nothing more exciting than watching her shiver in fear before him.

"My husband?"

"He lives."

"Your plans for him?"

He admired her cool reserve in facing him as she did. She'd matured. It would be all the more enjoyable to break her.

"I intend to slowly torture him, make him watch you and I consummate our marriage, before he dies a miserable death. He will beg to die before I finish him off."

"Has he been fed? Given water?"

"No. Why?"

"It would not serve you well to have him passing out from hunger or thirst and missing out on the fun you've planned for yourself."

Wolton frowned. "He is strong enough to survive. He will be so enraged he'll be unable to take his eyes off us." He licked his lips in anticipation of the feast he'd planned.

"Tell me more of your plans." Beth seated herself and motioned for him to do likewise.

Ah, let the torture begin. He was a master of the mental part of this game. He'd have her a quivering mess by the time he started his physical assault. There was no rush now that she was here. He'd savor every moment. Every flash of fear in her eyes. Every shudder that overtook her lovely body. His. She was all his. He could taste the victory already.

20

Outside along the banks of the river flowing a mile past the property, three shadowy figures searched under the darkening afternoon sky for a cave, or door or some kind of entrance that would lead them into the lower dungeons Beth mapped out for them.

"I found it," hissed Michael, motioning for the men to follow him. They entered the darkness and lit torches stored close to the entrance, obviously used by others in the recent past. They searched the large area and found adjoining rooms filled with boxes containing guns, explosives, and ammunition, originally destined for British troops, but nowhere near the ports they were usually shipped from. "I think we can deduce how Wolton plans to bring down Prinny," Neville stated.

"Treason for sure, but how do we prove it is Wolton and not Follett?" asked Michael.

Neville shook his head. "We'll need to collect more evidence if possible." He stepped into the entryway Beth indicated on her map and started to maneuver through the tunnels. At times, they were almost crawling their way uphill toward Follett Hall. Eventually, they entered a stone tunnel with steps heading up to a door.

At the top, Michael tried the door. Unlocked, he opened it slowly. Once inside, three tunnels were evident. Beth described how they all came back around to the main stairway leading up to the house. Other doors led to other tunnels with exits at various places around the property allowing for covert entrances and exits. At the center of all the tunnels and smaller rooms was a large room where, Elizabeth was certain, Phillip would be held. The men headed for that space.

They traveled slower than they wanted as the tunnels were narrow and the stone echoed any noise. They didn't want to alert any guards. There were no lights as they approached the door. It was heavy wood and locked.

Neville gave Theodore his torch and bent down with a kit he carried.

"You pick locks?" Michael asked.

"Sometimes you need a good understanding and training in criminal arts to defeat them," Neville answered with a whisper.

The lock clicked and they opened the door.

Michael took the lead and went in alone while the other two waited outside to keep watch and await his call. He made his way slowly around the large room. He could not see the entire space from one spot as the torch didn't illuminate that wide of an area. A table took up the center of the room, made of sturdy wood, rough and stained with dark spots he assumed was blood. He moved around the table and found Phillip unconscious on the floor, with a chair tipped over next to him. Michael knelt down. He sighed in relief when he found a pulse. The man was freezing cold. "Hold on, buddy. We'll get you out of here."

He went to the other door to listen but there was no sound. No one was there. Back at the first door, he motioned for the men to enter.

Theo moved to where Michael pointed, knelt by

Phillip's side, and began to work at the rope with a knife.

Michael patted his friend's face. "Come on, Phillip. Wake up. We need to rescue your wife." He looked to Theo as the bonds broke free. "We'll have to take him out whence we came. I hope Beth buys us enough time."

Phillip moaned.

"Shhhh, Phillip, we'll get you out of here."

"Theo?" Phillip asked groggily.

"Michael's got you too. Just a little further and we'll take you to safety."

"Beth? Where's Beth?"

"Shhhh, we'll tell you all we can as soon as we're safe." Michael grunted as they navigated the narrow tunnels. They came to a larger space and sat Phillip down next to a box of ammunition.

"Do we leave him here?" Neville asked.

"Theo, why don't you take him back to the Red Rooster where Fenway can care for him."

"He's passed out again. I'll have to drape him across my saddle."

"Whatever it takes. Just get him to safety."

Freezing rain had begun to fall. The men worked to help Theo put Phillip on the horse and they departed for town.

Seeking shelter back in the cave, Michael frowned. "I wonder if we shouldn't take advantage of this wealth of ammunition."

"What do you have in mind, Tidley?"

"If we set an explosion on this side of the property it might be enough of a distraction to help us get up to the house to free her."

"Great idea. We need to give ourselves enough

time to make it through the dirt tunnels. We'll be blocking that exit."

"I'll set a long enough wick that should give us plenty of time." Michael started collecting supplies. The two men worked together to pack the explosives around the entrance to the room and placed a sign outside as a warning in case anyone else tried to enter.

"I'm ready, are you?" Michael asked.

"As ready as ever." Nigel nodded.

A torch was set to the wick. They watched it start to burn and hurried back through the tunnel to the room where they'd found Phillip.

~*~

Wolton was tired of pleasantries. He itched to get his hands on Lizzy. It was time to take control. He'd waited long enough. "I think we should visit your husband."

"I would like that."

She rose with grace which irritated him. She acted as if this was nothing more than a social visit. He needed to establish control. He grabbed her arm roughly and made his way to the door. Once unlocked, they discovered Lord Follett pacing the hallway.

"I suggest you keep yourself occupied, Folly. Your daughter and I have some unfinished business to attend to."

Beth was close to her father but Wolton heard her words to the broken-down man.

"God forgives everything."

Wolton growled and jerked her toward the rear of the house. No one and nothing would stop him now.

~*~

Awareness dawned as sharp pain exploded down his shoulders and back. The rhythm of a horse jolted him as icy needles fell from the sky. He closed his eyes as the landscape moved from his strange position draped across the horse.

"Phillip?" Theo's concerned voice asked. A tight grip was held on his trousers lest he slip.

"Hmmm."

"Hang on, we'll get you somewhere warm soon." The horse pulled up. "Whoa," Theo whispered. "We've got trouble."

"What have we here?" The booming voice sounded familiar. A hand grabbed his hair and pulled his neck back and Phillip was assaulted by the stench of the man's breath.

A voice spoke. "I suggest you dismount. No quick moves or you'll both die."

"Sorry, Phillip. I tried," Theo whispered as he dismounted.

Another voice came close. Theo was by Phillip as if he could protect him even now.

"What have we here? Someone managed to free our prisoner. Wonder what the Master will think of that?"

"He might have our heads if he finds the bloke gone," the first voice said.

"We'd better get him back inside."

The horse began to move and Theo kept to Phillip's side, walking next to the horse with a hand on his back to keep him from sliding off. They slowly made their way through the woods, taking a path directly to the stables and the kitchen garden.

"Get him off of there," a man bellowed.

"Sorry, I'm afraid this is going to hurt," Theo apologized as he dragged Phillip off the horse and brought him to the damp ground.

Phillip shivered.

One of the men motioned for Theo to help Phillip up. Theo struggled and Phillip worked hard to get his feet to support him. He leaned heavily against his friend and closed his eyes. The men didn't realize Phillip was awake. Theo was shoved from behind, almost dropping Phillip. "Drag him there if you have to."

"A little help would be nice," Theo whispered.

Phillip tried to assist but weakness and pain limited him. His mind told him he could do far more than his body was able to agree to. Frustrating. How would he rescue his wife if he couldn't even stand on his own, much less fight?

They headed through the kitchen and to the door to the lower levels. "*Déjà vu*," murmured Phillip as he tried to help Theo on the stairs. It was a slow and clumsy process.

Coming to the first landing the large man saw light ahead of him. "You've been caught out. The Master is ahead of us and he's got a lady with him."

One of the men chuckled. "We'll see some fun now. Do ya think he'll let us have what we were denied when we attacked her in the woods?"

"Don't be a fool. He wants her to himself and the Master doesn't share."

"Neither do I," Phillip muttered to Theo. Strength surged along with the hope he could help in spite of the weakness, pain, and bone-deep cold. He shivered. God would be with them but he prayed Theo had brought others to help. Theo had mentioned Michael.

Where was Sir Tidley?

They began to catch up to Lord Wolton and Beth.

She turned and caught his eye. He gave her a wink.

Beth shrugged. "Why Lord Wolton, there is my husband now. He doesn't look in good enough shape to enjoy all you've planned for us. I suggest you send some of your men back to the kitchen for food and water. It would not serve your purpose to have him unconscious or dead before you've finished your plans for me."

Lord Wolton growled.

Phillip kept his head down and acted limp. It wasn't much of an act. He leaned heavily against Theo who struggled to hold on to him.

"Fine," Wolton bellowed. "You two in the back. Fetch some water and food. We'll manage down here until you return."

The men walked back up the stairs muttering to themselves.

Phillip grimaced in pain. Beth had been wise to send away two of their captors. It gave them a greater chance of survival. He'd married a savvy woman.

Apparently not smart enough to have stayed away, though. She shouldn't be the one rescuing him.

"I wonder how you managed to escape, Lord Westcombe? But now you and your friend will have to die." He motioned them all into the large room.

Theo stood in the doorway holding Phillip up as Lord Wolton moved around lighting the torches placed in the walls. The space filled with light although shadows remained. Benches surrounded the large table at the center of the room. A few chairs, including one tipped over, where Phillip assumed he'd been when he was rescued.

Lord Wolton motioned to Theo. "Put Lord Westcombe in this chair and sit next to him here," motioning to another chair. "Keep him from falling off. I don't want him to miss the show."

Wolton came to stand in front of Phillip, who continued to act limp. The man grabbed Phillip's jaw and tilted his head back. Philip blinked and closed his eyes again. The stench from the man was enough to cause him to empty his grumbling stomach.

"Ah, so you are awake. Barely." Wolton stood and walked over to Beth. "Come, Lizzy. Now it's time for you and I to get reacquainted."

"Before we begin, I'm curious about a few things. Would you indulge my curiosity before my husband is fully revived since we need to wait for the food and water before we start?" Beth asked.

"What is it you desire to know? As you will all die anyway, I have no problem answering your questions."

Careful, Beth. This man is dangerous. What did she think she was about? Phillip prayed for God's help. He failed to envision any scenario where they emerged from this alive.

~*~

Beth freed her arm from Wolton's grasp. She walked around the table, lightly touching it and fighting back the fingers of terror that threatened to overtake her. Memories of events in this room reared up in full horror as she spied the blood stains seeped into the wood. "Why are you so intent on having me? I never understood the reasoning. Why wouldn't any woman do?"

"You are beautiful. Any man would desire to have you in his bed. I've tasted your charms in the past and enjoyed your screams for mercy." He laughed, a deep dark sound that erupted into coughing. When he finished he leered at her. "I serve Napoleon, and dark forces, whose worship you've borne witness to. It should not come as a shock to you that a sacrifice will enhance my plans to overthrow the British government. I need the blessing of the Evil One. It is the price of power. Someone must pay it and it is to be you."

"The Black Diamond?"

"He serves a higher master as well."

"I thought virgins were necessary. I most certainly do not fit that criterion." She motioned to Theo and Phillip. "And why must they die? They know little to nothing. Their deaths do not benefit you." Her heart ached. She longed to go to Phillip and assure him of her love and apologize for all that had happened between them. She needed to play this out in an attempt to win his life, and Lord Harrow's. No one else should suffer for her past, other than her.

"They are not necessary except to keep me from being exposed as a traitor. They possess too much information. I'm aware of the investigation. My goal is to finish this tonight. A ship will come and collect the ammunition, guns, and explosives waiting by the shoreline, and I will depart for France to await my return in victory when the Little Emperor wins the war."

"You could leave them here until after you've gone. If what you say is correct, once you are off the shores of Britannia you would escape charges of treason. When you return in victory you might be a hero. There is no need to take any life other than my own to accomplish your purposes." Beth stepped up on the bench and unbuttoned her cloak revealing her plump figure. She placed the cloak carefully on the table and sat down on the edge.

Wolton drooled. "So, you are with child after all. A double sacrifice will greatly please the Dark Lord."

"I must disappoint you, my lord. I lost the baby two months past. I have not regained my figure."

Wolton walked over and placed a hand on her swollen stomach.

Even she felt the kick where he pressed.

"You lie. There is most certainly a babe here. Would you like me to prove it to you?" He dragged a long sharp knife out of his belt and aimed it at her middle.

~*~

Phillip gasped aloud. Horror filled him at the scene playing out before him. She was trying to give them time, but for what? He wished his arms would work. Theo continued to support him.

Wolton turned. He placed the knife in its sheath and walked over to Phillip. He pulled Phillip's hair, jerking his head back again.

Phillip grimaced at the rancid breath.

"You are not as weak as you pretend, pretty boy. Shall I show you how to treat a woman? Would you enjoy watching her suffer, squirm, and scream as your last images of life on this planet?"

A vibration rocked the room. The torches shook on the wall and dirt fell from the ceiling. A roar grew louder coming from the door opposite where Phillip sat.

Wolton motioned for his man to go find out what happened.

The big guy strode to the door and opened it but closed it quickly as the odor of gunpowder and smoke poured into the room.

Beth coughed.

Wolton yelled, "Go out the door, you fool!"

The big man walked over to Lord Wolton, grabbed him by his cravat and hauled him off his feet. "You don't pay me enough for this. Do your own dirty work. I'm done." He took a torch and stalked out the door leading up to the house, slamming it behind him.

It was all the distraction Theodore needed. He jumped up and landed a facer on Wolton, who stumbled back against the table. On the opposite side of the table, the bench moved out and Michael and Mr. Neville appeared aiming guns at Lord Wolton.

Phillip fell off the chair and closed his eyes in relief. Everything hurt and tears leaked from his eyes.

Wolton sputtered. "No. You cannot do this. I will be famous and powerful. I'll ruin you! You cannot deny me my destiny."

"Your shipment of arms vanished, Lord Wolton, as well as your access point to your rendezvous. You may as well surrender with grace. I have enough testimony to see you locked in the tower." Neville walked around the table aiming a gun at Wolton's chest.

Wolton struggled but Michael held the creep's plump arms behind him and began tying them.

Phillip tried to sit.

Beth collected her cloak, placed it over her shoulders, and was soon by Phillip's side. She enveloped him in her arms and held him fast. He brought his own around her. She helped him rise. He braced himself against the table and leaned in for a kiss. *How long had it been?*

The door flew open before their lips could meet. The three hirelings who had left before tumbled into the room, falling over each other as the door shut behind them. "We're doomed! The house is ablaze above us!"

Beth turned. "My father?"

"Folly can rot in hell for all I care," Wolton spouted. He yelped as Michael jerked his arm up and back.

Phillip looked at Beth. "Are we trapped here? With the one exit closed by explosives and the house on fire at the top of the stairs?"

She shook her head. "There is another tunnel. It's old and not sturdy. It could have been damaged by the explosion."

"It might be our only option," Theo suggested.

"We'll need to hurry." She walked over to a moldy tapestry and unhooked it from the wall, letting it drop to the floor. Behind it was a smaller door. Beth grabbed Phillip's hand and in her other took a torch. "Can you manage?" she asked him.

"Might need some help. Theo?"

Lord Harrow was by his side and grinned at Beth. "Ladies first."

She opened the door and pushed the tapestry away from the bottom of it. A gust of dank, damp air entered the room causing the torches to flicker. She stepped into the tunnel.

"Wait! You cannot leave. You are my prisoner!" Wolton cried.

Phillip turned to see the big thug haul off and punch the aging lord. His nose began squirting blood.

"You have two choices, Wolton. Come with us and face charges of treason. Or stay here, tied to this table, as your own sacrifice." Neville motioned to the rope on the floor.

"Tunnel," said Wolton.

"Who wants to do the honors?" Michael asked.

The big guy grinned and came forward. "It would be my pleasure." He roughly grabbed Wolton's arm and the older man grimaced in pain due to his bonds.

Beth stepped into the tunnel followed by Theo, Phillip, Michael, and Neville. Bringing up the rear was Wolton and his three minions. Several grabbed torches to help light their way in the darkness.

21

Elizabeth stumbled and tripped over the uneven surfaces. She gasped for air as fear closed in around her within the confined space.

Theodore struggled behind her in assisting Phillip. They couldn't walk side by side in the narrow tunnel and the ceiling grew lower.

Another explosion rocked the earth and a gust of wind came down the tunnel snuffing out her torch.

She froze. Her hand reached out to the dirt wall on either side of her. *Keep walking. I can do this. Lord help me!* She ran into a wall and her hands found the rough rungs of a ladder. "I've reached the end of the tunnel. Wait until I get the surface door open." She climbed to the top. Hard to manage with her big stomach getting in the way and her long skirts. She reached the top, hitting it with her head first. "Ouch."

"Beth?" Phillip's concerned voice traveled up to her.

"I found the door."

She pushed and longed to scream against the darkness. Her shoulder became bruised from the effort but panic at the dark gave her the strength to continue until it budged. Her hands were bloodied as she shoved it open. "I'm out." She pulled herself into the small hunting lodge and struggled to her feet. She found a flint and lit a lamp to shine into the hole. She turned to kneel and help Phillip as Theo pushed him from behind. As Phillip collapsed on the floor she set the lamp aside and pulled him free, holding him close.

Theodore emerged followed by Michael and Mr. Neville.

Another explosion rocked the earth beneath them and dust started to filter up through the door.

"Wolton?" Neville shouted down into the tunnel.

No one answered.

"We need to get to the house!" Beth pulled to her feet and struggled to help Phillip stand with Michael's help. She ran to the door of the lodge and opened it up to a black night. A shimmer of ice rested on top of a thin layer of snow. Flames could be seen a mile away.

"Beth, even if we had the fastest horses, we'd never get there in time. I cannot travel on foot." Phillip wrapped an arm around her as he leaned against the doorjamb.

Michael stood on the other side. "I'll go to where we left our horses and bring them here. I'm sorry, Beth. Phillip is right. We cannot make it in time."

Beth turned into Phillip's chest and let all the fear of the day leak into his shirt exposed through his open coat. A light kiss on her hair as he squeezed her close told her he understood.

Michael and Theo left to get the horses while Neville headed toward the house on foot.

Phillip found a chair and sat, pulling Beth to his lap.

She put a hand on either side of his face. "Are you well?"

"Weak, hungry and thirsty, but otherwise unharmed."

She pulled his hand away to check his wrist. "And a liar."

"He planned far worse for you. Thank you for

coming for me."

"How could I not? I've been a horrible wife and you deserved none of this. It's all my fault."

"You are not responsible for your father or Wolton's choices, darling."

"I pushed you away. You've been faithfully telling me of your love, and I've been too selfish to even consider how losing our child hurt you."

Phillip's hand rested on her stomach. It moved. "Are you sure there isn't a baby in there?"

"How could there be? We lost our son. I keep feeling it, and feared I was mad. I was hiding myself from you because I was afraid you'd learn the truth."

"That I really am going to be a father?"

"That your wife had lost her mind and was destined for the Bedlam."

"Never. Although offering yourself to Wolton like that I began to wonder."

"Will you forgive me for pushing you away?"

Phillip nodded. "I love you, Beth. That hasn't changed. I understood you were in pain. I hoped in time you would return to me. It sure got lonely in my bed at night."

"I missed you too."

"We were interrupted earlier."

"We were?" Beth grinned.

"I love you, Beth." He reached up and pulled her head down to his own. Their lips met and she relaxed into the affection he offered her.

Thank you, Lord, for saving us.

Hoofbeats alerted them to company.

~*~

Arriving at the house, there was not much to be done. The structure had been overcome by the flames. Wooden beams had fallen from the upper floors and the thatched roof had burnt to ashes. Phillip held Beth back. "We can't go in now. It's not safe."

Michael had made tentative steps into the structure calling for Lord Follett but received no answer.

Neville returned to the hunting cabin to check on the collapsed tunnel. He couldn't access it. His prisoner must have died in the collapse.

"Let's head to the Red Rooster to rest. We can return in the morning. Perhaps we'll find something then."

"It'd be too late," Beth protested.

"Honey, if he was in there, it's already too late for him." Phillip tried to assure her.

Theo brought the carriage for them. Phillip collapsed into the interior as his wife followed. The rest of the men would return on horseback.

"I'm sorry, Beth."

She hugged herself. "You have nothing to apologize for."

Arriving at the Inn, Phillip was assisted from the carriage by his valet. He was taken to his room, bathed, fed and given plenty to drink. Fenway helped him to bed and he lacked the strength to fight. "Beth will be here soon."

"She needs her own rest."

"Try to keep her away." Phillip winked.

His valet blushed.

Noise from outside the door drew Fenway to answer.

Beth stumbled in.

"Ma'am. His lordship is resting," Fenway said.

"I tried to stop her," Elsa protested from the hallway.

Beth pushed past them both to Phillip. She sat on the bed.

"I told Fenway you wouldn't stay away." Phillip grinned, looking past her to the servants in the doorway. "You can both leave."

The servants left them alone.

Phillip moved over to make room for his wife under the covers. Finally, after so long a struggle, every appetite was satisfied.

~*~

The next morning, Beth took the steps to her childhood home. The odor of burnt wood lingered in the air and soot covered everything. Her hands grew black with the few things she touched. She found the study. Her dad's favorite spot. Phillip was behind her. The remains of her father were there. The safe above his body was shut but not locked. Phillip opened it and drew out a metal box. Inside was a book and a letter addressed to Lizzy.

"Do you mind if I open this?" Phillip asked about the bound volume.

"No." She held the letter in her hands.

Phillip opened the journal. "Mr. Neville?"

The Bow Street Runner entered "Yes?"

"You might want to see this. He recorded the names of those involved in the smuggling and treason."

"The Black Diamond?"

"Not even Follett knew who it was."

Nigel lifted the book. "Mrs. Westcombe, may I take this to the authorities in London?"

"You may. Thank you for all you've done to help."

"I'm sorry for your loss, ma'am."

Phillip wrapped an arm around his wife and led her from the house.

They remained in town to see to Lord Follett's burial. The ceremony was simple and Michael and Theo stayed with them.

They parted ways after that, the two men returning to London and Phillip accompanying his wife back to Stanton Hall.

~*~

They arrived at the hall to find a letter from Lord Remington awaiting them. Phillip broke the seal. "Beth?"

"Hmmm?" She came to stand by his side.

"Marcus and Josie have a daughter."

Beth nodded and turned away.

"Beth." He pulled her back and held her close. "I want to call for the doctor. I don't think you're going mad."

"It's wishful thinking."

"And that's a bad thing?" Phillip grinned. "What if somehow you are still pregnant?"

"You can summon the doctor." Beth walked away.

Phillip sighed. His wife was once again returning his affection but grief over her father was a new obstacle to break through. The unknown question with her health was also a concern. He was cautiously optimistic that his introduction to fatherhood was on the horizon.

~*~

Beth settled into her room. Once Elsa had unpacked, Beth was alone. She went over all that had happened as she held her father's unopened letter in her hand. The fireplace was burning brightly but she shivered against the cold and the depth of evil they'd faced in the dungeon. If it hadn't been for Phillip's comfort during the night she'd have succumbed to horrid nightmares. It was as if he sensed them coming and would hold her close and whisper words of love to her in his sleep keeping the evil at bay.

She broke the seal to the letter.

Dear Lizzy,

If you are reading this, I am most likely dead. I had nothing left to lose and could think of no other way I might possibly help you than to burn the house down and hopefully create a diversion. If you are alive, perhaps that means I've done one thing right in my life.

Do not mourn for me. I've made peace with God. I'm unsure whether the Jesus you believe in has truly forgiven me, but I deserve nothing more than to spend eternity with the gods I've served. I pray by the mercy and forgiveness you and your husband have shown me, that God will extend the same to this old, repentant heart.

In spite of all my sins against you, I loved you. I wish I could have done better by you. When your mother was taken from me, something inside me died. Yes. She was a victim of Wolton as well, but never fear, you are truly my daughter. Of that, I have no doubt.

I am grateful you have your faith and Lord Westcombe. I pray together you will forge a new path, escaping the evil perpetrated here. Another good reason for the property to be destroyed. Even if you conquer Wolton this time, remember there is a spiritual enemy that will continue to seek to destroy you. I'd prevent that if I were able, but spiritual battles are beyond my ken.

May God richly bless you, daughter. Do not grieve for me. Instead, rejoice in the love and new life God has brought to you.

Sincerely,
Felix Follett

Elizabeth folded the letter and placed it in the front of her Bible. Her father had accepted Christ, sacrificed his last moments of his life sharing his love with her, and had died to save her and Phillip. She was now an orphan. With her new life with Phillip and her friends, she didn't feel the loss of family as much as she thought she would.

Her hand came to rest on her stomach. Wolton swore there was a baby. Her heart longed for that to be true.

Phillip entered the room. She rose to go to him, grateful that this man had saved her in more ways than he realized. *Thank you, Lord.*

~*~

The doctor arrived the next day.

"Mrs. Westcombe, it is a pleasure to meet you." He began his exam silently nodding. When he finished he sat down with Beth and Phillip. "I want to assure you, my lord. Your wife is in excellent health. She is not losing her mind. You, dear Mrs. Westcombe, are definitely pregnant. I would guess you to have a month left in your pregnancy. I anticipate an uncomplicated birth."

"But I lost the baby. I saw his body. I remember the cramping. The blood," Beth protested.

"My guess is you had twins. I do not deny the loss you experienced. In my professional opinion, in spite of that loss, God has granted you one child to raise, instead of two. "

Hope welled up inside Beth. She wiped away a tear. "I'm not losing my mind? I'm going to be a mother?"

The doctor nodded. "Rest. Your recent grief and sorrow over the loss of your father is natural but should not harm the baby. Congratulations."

Phillip squeezed her hand and smiled. "Thank you, doctor."

The man rose and left.

Phillip turned to Beth. "I'm a father."

"I am a most blessed mother. We're really having a baby."

"Best Christmas gift ever," Phillip stated.

"It is Christmas in a few days, isn't it?"

Phillip nodded. "We've been busy."

"Is it too late to decorate and celebrate?"

"I think we can celebrate first—and decorate later." He winked at her.

Beth grabbed his cravat and pulled him close. "I like the way you think." She kissed him and savored the sensations it brought. Merry Christmas indeed.

22

Late January 1811

Phillip heard his son's wails. "I'll get him." He struggled out of bed and crossed over to the bassinette where his son loudly complained. He picked up the little boy. "Edward Marcus Westcombe, I hope I can teach you better manners than that. It's not polite to cry for your supper." He placed a kiss on his son's pale, downy locks.

"Don't tease him, Phillip. Bring him here."

"Shouldn't I change him first?"

"And let him wake the entire house?"

Phillip brought his son to the bed and sat by his wife's side as she nursed him. "Have I told you how much I love you?" he asked.

"Quite often."

He leaned over to kiss her. "Hmm."

She smiled at him. "I was thinking…"

"At this time of night?"

"I know you missed being with your family over the holidays. There is not much to be done on the estate right now. The weather has been fair and Edward and I are doing well. I thought perhaps we could go to town for a few months."

"London?"

She nodded. "I need a new wardrobe, as does our little man here. And I never did decorate the house. This would be the ideal season to undertake some of those tasks. And I know you miss seeing your friends. I would never want to keep you from them."

"When are Josie and Marcus coming?"

"I'm not sure Josie will come to town with Isabella this spring. The baby has had terrible coughs. Marcus likely will arrive for Parliament."

"Yes, my love."

"Really?"

"My mother and father will dote over the baby. Perhaps we'll be ready to go out in society again when the season starts."

"Not too much."

"Only for a few select events."

"Wonderful. By the time we get there Edward should be sleeping longer."

"Good."

"Yes. We'll have more time for ourselves then."

Phillip grinned. "I like the sound of that."

"Do you miss your nice, orderly life?"

"Orderly is overrated. I wouldn't trade what I have now with you for anything."

"I'm grateful God led me to you, Phillip."

"He knew what I needed before I even did." Phillip lifted the soothed infant back into his arms and changed the nappy. He swaddled the little man up and held him to his shoulder.

"You need to let him sleep in his bassinette."

"But he is so soft and snuggly."

"So is your wife." She wiggled her eyebrows.

"I get your point." He gently placed the infant in his bed and caressed the child's cheek. With a sigh of contentment, he turned back to his wife and crawled in next to her. She was right, she was soft in all the right places. "I love you, Beth."

She wrapped her arms around him and he drew

her close.

Her kiss told him everything he needed to know. *Thank You, Lord.*

Acknowledgements

It would be impossible to thank everyone who has helped me on my journey, so I apologize in advance for those I will miss. It doesn't mean you are any less valuable and thankfully, God keeps better track of those things than I do and His "well done, good and faithful servant" has more merit than any thanks written here.

So here it goes. Special thanks to:

Elizabeth Herman–you amaze me. Thanks for all the ways you've invested in me.

Doris Pollard Wichern–another early reader and one of my most faithful cheerleaders in this writing adventure. I'm sad you weren't able to live to see this an so many other books you read rough drafts for, published. I miss you.

Lisa Lickel–thanks for being such a wonderful mentor, friend, and shoulder to cry on when the publishing process throws me those curve balls. I don't think I would have ever taken that first step in this journey to publication without your gentle push.

David Mundt and Ken Nabi–for unwavering support and believing in me and the calling God has on my life.

Sally Shupe–my faithful editor. Thank you for finding all those silly errors!

Nicola Martinez–my beloved Editor-in-Chief who continually supports my writing while allowing me the joy of helping others on their journey to publication. I'm grateful for our partnership and friendship.

Biography

Susan M. Baganz chases after three Hobbits, and is a native of Wisconsin. She is an Editor with Pelican Book Group, specializing in bringing great romance novels and novellas to publication. Susan writes adventurous historical and contemporary romances with a biblical world-view.

This book is the second full-length novel in the Black Diamond Christian Gothic Regency series. *The Baron's Blunder*, Henrietta's story, is a novella and prequel, which is part of the *Love Is...*series by Prism Book Group. The first stand-alone novel is *The Virtuous Viscount*. Future novels are: *Sir Michael's Mayhem*, *Lord Harrow's Heart* and *The Captain's Conquest*.

Susan speaks, teaches, and encourages others to follow God in being all He has created them to be. With her seminary degree in counseling psychology, a background in the field of mental health, and years serving in church ministry, she understands the complexities and pain of life as well as its craziness. She serves behind-the-scenes in various capacities at her church and is a member of American Christian Fiction Writers (ACFW), and serves on the board of the southeast chapter. Her favorite pastimes are lazy...snuggling with her dog while reading a good book or sitting with a friend chatting over a cup of spiced chai latte.

You can learn more by following her blog www.susanbaganz.com, Twitter feed @susanbaganz or fan page, www.facebook.com/susanmbaganz

Thank you

We appreciate you reading this Prism title. For other
Christian fiction and clean-and-wholesome stories,
please visit our on-line bookstore at
www.prismbookgroup.com.

For questions or more information, contact us at
customer@pelicanbookgroup.com.

Prism is an imprint of
Pelican Book Group
www.PelicanBookGroup.com

Connect with Us
www.facebook.com/Pelicanbookgroup
www.twitter.com/pelicanbookgrp

To receive news and specials, subscribe to our bulletin
http://pelink.us/bulletin

May God's glory shine through
this inspirational work of fiction.

AMDG

You Can Help!

At Pelican Book Group it is our mission to entertain readers with fiction that uplifts the Gospel. It is our privilege to spend time with you awhile as you read our stories.

We believe you can help us to bring Christ into the lives of people across the globe. And you don't have to open your wallet or even leave your house!

Here are 3 simple things you can do to help us bring illuminating fiction™ to people everywhere.

1) If you enjoyed this book, write a positive review. Post it at online retailers and websites where readers gather. And share your review with us at reviews@pelicanbookgroup.com (this does give us permission to reprint your review in whole or in part.)

2) If you enjoyed this book, recommend it to a friend in person, at a book club or on social media.

3) If you have suggestions on how we can improve or expand our selection, let us know. We value your opinion. Use the contact form on our web site or e-mail us at customer@pelicanbookgroup.com

God Can Help!

Are you in need? The Almighty can do great things for you. Holy is His Name! He has mercy in every generation. He can lift up the lowly and accomplish all things. Reach out today.

Do not fear: I am with you; do not be anxious: I am your God. I will strengthen you, I will help you, I will uphold you with my victorious right hand.

~Isaiah 41:10 (NAB)

We pray daily, and we especially pray for everyone connected to Pelican Book Group—that includes you! If you have a specific need, we welcome the opportunity to pray for you. Share your needs or praise reports at http://pelink.us/pray4us

Free Book Offer

We're looking for booklovers like you to partner with us! Join our team of influencers today and periodically receive free eBooks and exclusive offers.

For more information
Visit http://pelicanbookgroup.com/booklovers